12/09

The
Charleston
Vampire

The Charleston Vampire

His Journey to the New World

Steve Brown

Chick Springs Publishing
Taylors, South Carolina

First published in the USA in 2009 by
Chick Springs Publishing
PO Box 1130, Taylors, SC 29687
E-mail: ChickSprgs@aol.com
Web site: www.chicksprings.com

Library of Congress Control Number: 2009907830
Library of Congress Data Available

ISBN: 0-9712521-9-X
           978-0-9712521-9-6

10   9   8   7   6   5   4   3   2   1

Author's Note

This is a work of fiction. Names, characters, places, and incidents are products of the author's imagination or are used fictitiously. Any resemblance to actual events, specific locales, organizations, or persons, living or dead, is entirely coincidental and beyond the intent of either the author or the publisher.

Acknowledgments

For their assistance in preparing this story, I would like to thank Phil Bunch, Mark Brown, Sonya Caldwell, Sally Heineman, Caroline Hummer, Missy Johnson, Kate Lehman, Jennifer McCurry, Kimberly Medgyesy, Mary Jo Moore, Ann Patterson, Allison Pennington, Stacey Randall, Chris Roerden, Susan Snowden, Deanna Sowards, Robin Smith, Helen Turnage, Dwight Watt, and, of course, Mary Ella.

For Jane Austen

Cast of Characters

Crew of the *Mary Stewart:*
James Stuart, captain
Martin Chase, first mate
Kyrla Stuart, helmsman
Alexander, quartermaster
Billy, cabin boy

Passengers:
John Belle, upcountry woodsman
Phillippe Belle, heir to Cooper Hill
Susanna Chase, indentured servant
Edmund Ladd, major, British Army
Katherine Ladd, his wife

The Vampire Family:
Lucius, leader
Donato, his assistant
Gabriel, singer
Portia, his sister
Oren, manservant

The Bentley Family:
Mr. Bentley
Mrs. Bentley
Alicia
Marion
Katie
Lindy

The loss of virtue in a female is irretrievable; that one false step involves her in endless ruin.

—Jane Austen
Pride and Prejudice

The Three Laws of Vampirism

1. Vampires must be invited into wherever they wish to go, whether that be a house, an organization, or a country.

2. Vampires are usually slain by thrusting a wooden stake through their heart, though sunlight and religious artifacts can also be deadly to vampires.

3. Vampires are well-known for their shape-shifting ability, changing into bats, wolves, or fog of the night.

Prologue

The following evening he came at me again, and I knew I wouldn't be able to kick my way out of his clutches—not a second time. For that reason, I went to bed with a knife used to fillet fish. He wasn't expecting the knife, nor did he much like it.

One

The knock at the door startled her.

Agnes sat up at her end of the bench and involuntarily tightened her grip on the needle she was using to sew her husband's cheek together. William yelped as the thread went taut and pulled him toward her.

"Who could it be?" Agnes looked toward the door.

Her husband gripped the hand holding the needle and drew it back to him. "Finish your work, woman."

His wife worked by the light of a candle placed at the edge of a table where the two of them, and the girl, had taken their meals. William sat at the head of the table in the only chair. Their house of stone with a thatched roof included a loft filled with hay where the girl had slept, along with a ground-floor fireplace, the table and benches, and a low bed—more of a pallet—where the husband and wife slept. That is, until last night, when the girl's presence became too powerful a lure and drew William Withering up the ladder and into the loft.

The next rap was not from a knuckle but of a cane striking their door. "Open up, Withering! This is the magistrate."

Agnes dropped the needle, stood up, and wiped her hands on her apron, leaving the bloody thread and needle trailing across her husband's cheek and shirt.

"You don't have to answer," whispered her husband. "They don't know anyone's in here."

"It's the magistrate, William, and I'd like to know just what sort of trouble we're in."

"We're not in any trouble."

His wife snorted. "Magistrates always mean trouble."

"Then let him seek us in the fields," said her husband, rising from his chair. "We can always slip out through the coal chute."

"Any clever magistrate would have a man out back, too."

"Open this door immediately or I shall be forced to break it down!"

That got Agnes moving. Plenty of their neighbors coveted their fine home, which, within seconds, might be cursed with a door that would never again close snugly on long winter nights.

"Coming!" shouted the woman. "Coming!"

Her husband snatched a bloody cloth from the table and pressed it to his half-repaired cheek. From under the cloth, he cursed her.

Gripping the door latch, she turned to him. In a soft but firm voice she said, "Watch your tongue, William. Remember who disposed of your handiwork."

William removed the cloth from his cheek. "Then she's dead, is she?"

"You know I don't do things in half-measures."

Before throwing the latch and pulling back the heavy wooden door, she shook the apron tied around her waist. The apron pocket jingled with coin.

"Shillings?"

"Crowns," she said with a smile.

"Crowns? Oh, my . . ."

"Don't look so happy, William. You've just lost a stepdaughter." And she swung open the door.

In the growing dusk of the evening, she saw a tall, skinny man dressed all in black, from his boots to his tricorn hat, with the exception of his heavily starched white shirt. Both hands gripped a handsome wooden cane. He leaned on it and peered down at Agnes as if viewing her from a perch.

Behind the skinny man stood a different sort of fellow: shorter, more muscular, and also much younger, with sunburned skin. He wore work clothes and boots, and had longish brown hair. He did not appear to be a farmer, nor did he smell like one. The Witherings' chickens and hogs had begun to gather around him, sniffing out these new odors.

Behind the rock wall stood a barouche, and in the carriage box sat a boy holding the reins. Up and down the lane, Agnes noticed the curious strolling in the direction of their house, several carrying farm implements, one leading a mule, women wiping their hands on aprons. On the far side of the road, beyond the ridge, the sun sank into the Irish Sea.

The elderly magistrate tipped his hat. "Good evening, Agnes." One hand still on his cane, he gestured to the sunburnt man behind him. "This young man is James

Stuart, a sea captain from our American colonies."

James Stuart? Where did she know that name?

The thought almost distracted her from performing a curtsy. "To what do we owe this honor, Magistrate?"

"I've come to see the girl."

"The girl?" Agnes glanced into the interior of the house.

The sea captain edged forward, the magistrate peered into the semidarkness of the home.

"I placed the child in your custody, believing you would have someone to care for you and William in your declining years. A fair trade, I thought, food and lodging for the girl, and this house a future dowry for the girl's husband, you and William being childless."

"Yes, yes, my lord, and we certainly appreciate all you have done. Why I can remember times—"

"Agnes, I did not come to reminisce but to see the girl."

"She's not here." Agnes put a hand in her apron pocket so the coins would make no noise.

"And where shall we find her?" The skinny man looked left and right, then glanced down the road where it disappeared over the ridge. "Is she drawing water, feeding livestock, what?"

The magistrate's gaze fell on the sea captain. Hogs rooted around the sailor's boots and chickens pecked at the ground. With a sideways kick, the young man sent a chicken flapping and squawking. The pigs squealed and scattered. After that, he was no longer bothered by the Witherings' livestock.

"The girl's my responsibility, Agnes. I'm the one who put her in your charge."

"Then," said the woman, straightening her shoulders, "I'm sorry to inform you, sir, but the girl left last night and she's not returned."

"Left? What do you mean left? You allowed a young woman to wander the countryside unescorted?"

"Oh, no, sir. She run away."

"Ran away?"

Before Agnes could respond, the sea captain shouldered his way past them and entered the house. Moments later came a yelp from inside, followed by William Withering tumbling through the doorway where he landed on his hands and knees at the feet of the magistrate.

When William looked up, it wasn't into the eyes of the magistrate but also a good number of neighbors peering at him from the far side of the rock wall. William's cloth had fallen to the ground, and he hastily picked it up and pressed the soiled material against his cheek. Still, he wasn't quick enough to stanch the flow of blood. The needle, unfinished with its bloody work, hung by its thread from his cheek.

The magistrate bent down for a closer look. "William, it appears you've been injured. Now, how did that come about?"

William twisted away from the skinny man, only to slam into a knee of James Stuart as the sea captain exited the house. With another yelp William, once again, snatched the soiled cloth from the ground and slapped it to his face. The chickens and hogs returned and began to examine their master in this odd position. On the far side of the wall, his neighbors began chattering.

Stuart opened his hand and extended it to the

magistrate. In the palm lay a necklace with a gold cross. "I found this on the floor. The girl wouldn't have left it behind. Not only would it fetch a good price, but she would've believed the cross would afford her some measure of protection."

"That, sir," said Agnes, "is a family heirloom and never belonged to the girl."

But when Agnes reached for it, Stuart's hand closed around the cross and chain. "Are there any more Witherings in this family?" he asked the magistrate.

"No. That is why I placed the girl here. The girl is a distant relative of Agnes."

Stuart stepped to the corner of the house and shouted "Alexander!" then returned to the doorway. "Where's the girl?" he asked.

Instead of answering, Agnes turned to her neighbors on the far side of the rock wall. "Wouldn't say her prayers—no, no, not that girl, and when William chastised her, well, you can see what she's done." She gestured to her husband's face and lowered her voice to the magistrate. "A closet Catholic, if you ask me."

"Where's the girl, William?" asked the magistrate of the man on his hands and knees.

William whimpered and shook his head. From the rear of the house, a large black man missing an arm appeared around the corner, crossed the yard, and returned to the horse and carriage.

The sea captain gripped the farmer's arm and jerked him to his feet. "On your feet, landsman!" Stuart threw him against the house.

Chickens flew, hogs ran, and William cried out in pain, especially when Stuart placed his forearm across the man's neck. Again, the bloody cloth fell to the ground, and blood seeped from the man's cheek. The crowd on the far side of the wall grew quiet.

Stuart pulled out a knife and held the blade at eye level. William twisted away, and the tip of Stuart's blade followed his cheek, drawing a line of blood across the unmarked one. On the other side of the wall, women gasped and crossed themselves.

Stuart leaned into Withering. "Now, William, since cuts on the cheek don't appear to cow you, I'm going to take out an eye. Would you care to tell me which eye you'd like to keep?" Stuart tilted the blade between the man's eyes.

"No, no!" screamed William, jerking back.

"Then where's the girl?"

William moaned, his legs weakened, and he wet himself.

"Leave him be," said Agnes.

The other two men looked at her.

"Woman," said Stuart, "if you know something, spit it out!"

Agnes looked away, in the direction of the ridge. Below that ridge sat the city of Liverpool.

That drew the sea captain's attention, as many a glance or look on a ship could mean impending disaster.

"If the girl's been harmed," said Stuart, releasing the woman's husband and returning the knife to its sheath, "I'll be at sea when you and your husband are found murdered in your beds. And you can be sure there's more than one sailor in Liverpool who'd gladly ingratiate themselves to the captain of the *Mary Stewart*, and just such an act would do the trick." Stuart flashed a wicked smiled. "Or you can tell me where the girl is?"

"Captain Stuart, you cannot threaten this woman," said the magistrate.

"Agnes," asked Stuart in a low voice, "where's the girl?"

When Agnes did not answer, Stuart grabbed her arm and pulled her toward the gate and the open carriage.

"Then prepare to take your first sea voyage, madam. That girl was indentured to my ship as a scullery maid, and I have found my substitute." Hurrying Agnes toward the gate, Stuart called to the boy in the carriage box, "Billy, have the ship make ready to sail."

"Aye, aye, Captain!" The boy snatched up his flags and leaped to the far side of the road.

"Please, God, no!" shouted Agnes. "You cannot do this to me."

The magistrate followed them. "Captain Stuart—"

"And have the cannons ready, Billy, in the event anyone should object to our sailing."

"Aye, aye," shouted the boy at the top of the ridge.

Stuart pulled back the gate and shoved the woman through. The one-armed African opened the half door of the barouche, but Agnes refused to climb in. She had finally realized who this sea captain was.

"Oh, help me," she pleaded with her neighbors. "Please help me! I've fallen into the hands of James Stuart."

The magistrate caught up with them as Stuart scooped up the woman and lifted her into the carriage.

"Captain Stuart, unhand that woman!"

Encouraged by the magistrate's words, Agnes gripped the sides of the carriage and pleaded again for assistance. Instead, her neighbors backed off. Most everyone knew that James Stuart had killed the notorious pirate Blackbeard.

Behind them, William, bloody needle hanging from his face, crawled to the gate. Tears and blood ran down both cheeks.

"Help us! Oh, please help us! My wife is being kidnapped."

"Actually," said Stuart, whispering into the woman's ear, "being pressed into service like any good Englishman."

"Agnes," said the magistrate, "you must tell Captain Stuart what he wishes to know."

"No, no," said the woman, gripping the sides of the carriage and refusing to sit down, "you must save me from this monster."

"Agnes, if we are to discuss monsters, then we shall have to discuss what has happened to poor William's cheek."

"My lord, please, the girl turned on us—"

"Agnes, do not condemn your soul to eternal damnation."

"But it's just as I have said—oh, I swear it's so!"

Seeing the risk of eternal damnation made no impression on the woman, the magistrate played his trump card. "Speak the truth, Agnes, or I shall order Mrs. Givens to finish sewing up William's cheek."

Agnes's eyes widened and her grip loosened on the carriage. "But you can't do that. Mrs. Givens suffers from the arthritis."

"Then tell us where we may find the girl."

Two

"No, no, no!" screamed the woman from the forward facing seat in the barouche. "I've told you what you wish to know, but you mustn't take me there. What will people think?"

"And what will people think of the girl?" asked the magistrate, pulling the woman down beside him on the forward-facing seat. When Agnes tried to rise, the magistrate gripped her arm, saving her from a deadly tumble into the road.

The sea captain had left the door open when he joined the one-armed black man in the open carriage box, and taking the reins, he had wheeled the carriage around, causing the open door to flop back and forth. The carriage paused only long enough for Billy to race from the ridge and leap inside.

The boy slammed shut the low door and took the seat facing the magistrate and the farmer's wife. Hugging his flags against his chest with one hand, he gripped the side of the barouche with the other. Agnes's husband was left outside the gate, shoulders slumped, finally dropping to his knees and wailing for his wife.

Agnes called out to her husband but stopped when Stuart shouted, "Silence, woman, or I'll sell you to the bordello, too!" Of the boy, he asked, "Did you signal the location to the ship?"

"Aye, aye, sir, and the woodsman shall be there."

Stuart glanced at the road, then looked hard at the boy. "No more, no less."

"Aye, aye, Captain. No more, no less."

"Very well. We don't need a riot on our hands."

The African beside him nodded. A young girl in danger drew the attention of all sorts of characters, many emerging from the darker corners of the world.

A little over a mile from the house, the carriage took a switchback and raced down the hill to the cobblestone streets of Liverpool. Here, the magistrate leaned forward to shout directions to the carriage box.

"I know the place," answered Stuart. "I have dragged more than one crew member out of there."

And the sea captain bore down with the whip on the flank of the horse while the one-armed African bellowed warnings to those on the street.

Behind them, Agnes gripped the magistrate's jacket. "Oh, kind sir, but you cannot take me to such a place. What of my reputation?"

The skinny man turned an icy smile on her. "I'm sorry, madam, but I thought you were familiar with the place."

"Only to deliver the girl." Eyes downcast, she murmured, "Really, that's all I did."

The magistrate looked down the street, and from the opposite seat, Billy clutched his signal flags.

"But, sir, she's an ordinary scullery maid, no one of any consequence."

The skinny man returned his attention to the woman. "It does not seem to be some small matter to Captain Stuart, and if the girl's been shamed, he'll request you and your husband spend some time in the stocks."

A thought crossed the magistrate's mind and he grabbed the apron and ripped it from the woman's waist. Turning his back on her, he thrust his hand in the pocket and came out with the coins.

Agnes tried to reach around the man. "Sir, those are mine!"

The magistrate glanced at the coins. "This many?" He glanced at the woman. "Sold her as a virgin, did you?"

He pocketed the money and righted himself in the seat. "If I thought you'd deposit them in the poor box, I'd return them, but I imagine that chore shall also fall to me."

Passing the exchange building, Stuart ran a buggy off the street and into the public market underneath. Men screamed and cursed, then doffed their hats and apologized to their ladies for using such language. Still, fists were shaken in the direction of the carriage as it continued toward the harbor.

Stuart shook his head. "I'll never be able to operate one of these contraptions like a landsman."

"Then learn fast, Captain," said the African as the orange ball disappeared into the Irish Sea. "When the sun goes down, that girl's life will change forever."

Originally a few fishermen's huts scattered around a harbor where the occasional ship tied up, Liverpool had grown into a town with houses of brick and stone. Built at the mouth of the River Mersey on the Irish Sea, Liverpool made its money trading with the colonies, especially tobacco from the colony of Virginia. And along the cobblestone streets, many of its residents, fashionably dressed, enjoyed strolls toward the harbor to watch the sun go down. Lining the harbor were the usual warehouses and bordellos, and in front of one of the older houses, its windows shuttered and needing a good whitewashing, sailors stumbled in and out, some buttoning their flies, a few pulling on jackets.

Stuart jerked tight the reins, and the barouche came to such a quick halt that the horse reared up and the wheels slid forward, forcing the horse to stumble before the carriage skidded to a stop. He handed the reins to the African and leaped to the street. From under the seat he drew a long, wide, thick-bladed weapon.

"I shall handle this," announced the magistrate.

Stuart reluctantly put away the broadsword, and the magistrate climbed down, leaving the farmer's wife behind. As if it mattered, Agnes reached over and pulled shut the half door of the open carriage.

Sailors had been given liberty, but they didn't venture far, knowing the reputation of the Liverpool police. Most of them hung around the wharf and gripped mugs of ale purchased from an open-sided building where two barmaids behind a shelf could hardly keep up with the demand.

Stuart made way for the magistrate, and several sailors cursed him, especially those waiting for their

chance to enter the shuttered house. These, too, Stuart
shoved out of his way and hurried up the stairs. At the
door, he met a huge, bald man with muscular arms
folded across his chest, and those rather large arms
were covered with tattoos. Stuart tried to slip around
him, but the baldheaded man grabbed the sea captain's
arm and threw him across the porch where he stumbled
back down the steps.

"You'll wait your turn like everyone else!" He followed
Stuart to the edge of the porch.

From the foot of the steps, the magistrate announced
that he had business with the matron.

"I'll bet you do!" shouted a sailor, and the integrity of
the line broke down, sailors surrounding the two men,
mugs sloshing ale to the ground.

Pointing at Agnes in the carriage, a sailor shouted,
"Why does he need a turn? He has his own woman!"

This caused Agnes to slide to the far side of her seat
and Alexander to summon the boy. Billy put down his
flags, climbed forward, and took the reins from the one-
armed man, who pulled the broadsword from under
the seat, climbed down from the barouche, and forced
his way though the crowd.

The magistrate glanced at the carriage. "But—but
you don't understand. I've come for the girl—"

Sailors laughed, and some shouted, pointing at a
sign near the door. "So have we!"

Posted on a hastily written sign was notice of a new
virgin in residence, and everyone knew virgins could
cure venereal disease, though most had not come for
that reason. And because sailors rarely demonstrate
respect for shore-side governments, mugs of ale were

poured on the skinny man, starting with his tricorn hat.

The magistrate stepped back and tried to brush off the sticky liquid. "But—but you don't know who I am."

More ale flew. This was followed by a good number of insults, but not as many as before, as many of the sailors, seeing their mugs empty, returned to the small building to have them refilled at the shelf.

"I know your kind quite well," said the baldheaded man from the edge of the porch. "More than one of you self-important fellows tries to use his influence to move ahead in line." The baldheaded man looked out over the swelling crowd. "But we're all equal here, aren't we, mates?"

A riotous cheer was followed by a sailor returning with two mugs. "And only have one thing on our minds!"

The crowd rocked with laughter, and the sailor toasted his mates with one mug and drained the other.

Stuart felt his broadsword pressed against his leg.

"Sun's down, Captain," said Alexander.

Stuart glanced toward the harbor and realized the only light came from lamps on the front porch of the bordello. He took the sword as Alexander announced in a loud voice just who he was.

"Pirate hunters don't impress me," said the baldheaded man.

The bouncer appeared oblivious to sailors sneaking in behind him, probably because they were snagged by another pair of muscular men that hustled those sailors out of the building and threw them off the porch.

Alexander noticed his announcement had no affect on the crowd. "That's odd, Captain. Usually your reputation precedes you."

"The younger generation has no respect for its elders."

Stuart brought up the broadsword, and when he did, those in the immediate area backed away. To the baldheaded man, he shouted, "Then maybe this beauty will impress you." Nodding to the sword held upright with both hands, he added, "Still has a bit of Blackbeard's blood on it, but there's room for plenty more."

The other two bouncers drew their knives, joined the first one at the edge of the porch, and moved down the steps. The secret of taking a man armed with a broadsword was to get in close and get in fast.

Before they could, an arrow thudded into a post behind them. Any Englishman worth his salt recognized that sound, and the crowd gaped at the vibrating arrow. As children, they had been told tales of great battles won by the English longbow.

Another arrow sailed out of the darkness, shattering one of the lamps by the door. Whale oil ran down the wall onto the porch. It was quickly followed by a trail of fire. Patrons leaving the bordello were immediately covered with flames and fell back into the house, taking the fire with them.

Three

Susanna was climbing out the window when the madam returned to the boudoir, its centerpiece a canopy bed with ruffles, its mattress made of straw. The only light came from a candle on a night table on the far side of the bed, and the madam had difficulty understanding exactly what she was seeing.

The girl who had been brought to her at the crack of dawn, and who had been terribly hard to subdue, even bathe, had one foot on a chair, the other on the windowsill, both hands on the jamb. The shutters of the second-story window had been thrown back.

The girl had been fitted in the prettiest dress from the house's closet, and the madam didn't care to see the dress soiled when the girl plunged to her death in the alleyway below.

"You!" shouted the madam. "Come back here!"

The shout from the madam startled Susanna and caused an older girl behind the privacy screen to stop doing her business and to peer over the top. Susanna jerked her trailing foot from the chair to the windowsill and gripped both sides of the jamb. There, she faltered, not from the madam's shout but from the sight of a young man extending his hand.

"Jump to me, young miss! I'll catch you."

The young man was handsome enough with dark hair and dark eyes. Even his clothing was dark, but Susanna couldn't make out his boots. From where she crouched on the windowsill, the young man's feet seemed to disappear into the darkness below. A stink rose from the alley. Pigs could be heard rooting around in the garbage, and in the breeze off the harbor, the young man's split-tail coat whipped around in the air behind him. Strands of black hair fluttered across a forehead appearing unnaturally pale. His lips were ruby red.

"I've not been invited inside," he added, "so you must jump to me."

That seemed a rather perverse set of manners, and before Susanna could make up her mind, the madam grabbed her arm and pulled her from the window. Susanna cried out when she hit the bare wooden floor. Still, after years of resisting the advances of so many "young gentlemen," it was only moments before she was rolling away from the madam, who bent down to grab her.

From behind the privacy screen, the older girl appeared, settling her dress around her hips. Having suffered the wrath of the madam before, the older girl quickly assisted in Susanna's recapture by grabbing her wrist. And almost as quickly, she felt Susanna's arm jerked away.

"Leave me be!"

What Susanna had done was twist her wrist back against the older girl's thumb and forefinger, breaking the hold at the weakest point.

The madam had been trailed through the door by a bearded man who had paid for his evening with the virgin. The well-dressed customer held a tricorn hat, and his stomach preceded him across the room. He tossed his hat on the bed and hustled the madam and the other girl from the room.

"Go now! I can handle this!" Closing the door behind them, he turned the key in the lock and faced Susanna. Rubbing his hands together, he advanced across the room. "I always like a girl with a bit of fire."

"Stay away from the girl!"

The customer looked at the open window. "And what are you doing there?" he demanded of the young man.

"I've come for the girl."

"Well, you shall have to wait your turn, and if that doesn't suit you, I'll kick your ladder away and you can listen to your girlfriend lose her virtue while you lie with the pigs in the alley."

Returning his attention to Susanna, the fat man removed his coat and tossed it on the bed. "Now, young lady, let's you and me tend to the business at hand."

Susanna looked around for a weapon but saw her usual weapons of porcelain bowl and pitcher on the far side of the room, the candlestick holder on the nightstand on the other side of the bed.

The fat man saw the look and waved a finger. "Now, now, young lady. No reason to put off the inevitable."

"Sir, the inevitable remains to be seen." And Susanna grabbed the edge of the privacy screen, dumped it over, and picked up the chamber pot.

As the pot came up, the man backed away. "Now, now, Miss, let's be careful with that."

The girl stalked *him* across the room—where he found the locked door to his disadvantage. Before he could turn the key in the lock, the porcelain pot shattered against the wall, spraying him with much of its contents.

"Oops!" Susanna tried to hide her smile behind her hand. "Seems like I missed, sir."

The customer felt the dampness seeping into his shirt and the back of his head. The girl had intentionally thrown the pot against the wall. In a rage, he faced her, only to find the girl had leapt onto the bed and was reaching for the candlestick on the other side of the bed.

"Stay away from the girl!" shouted the young man once again.

Now there appeared to be two young men at the window, but neither came to Susanna's aid as the fat man caught her foot and pulled her back across the bed. The action shoved her dress up, revealing she wore no undergarments.

"Ah! Now we are getting somewhere."

Red-faced and humiliated, Susanna twisted around and tried to kick the man in the face.

The fat man grabbed that foot, too. He laughed. "Sorry, Miss, but you're not dallying with one of your young men."

Susanna gave up all thought of escape and

concentrated on holding down her dress. She was not very successful.

"Oh, my," said the man with a lecherous grin, "you are quite becoming, young lady, and becoming quite exposed!" He laughed again and jerked her from the bed.

Susanna's bottom thumped to the bare floor and her head hit the bed rail. Stunned, she lay there wiping the tears away as the fat man stood over her, unbuttoning his pants.

"Oh, yes, let's do begin—wherever we might find ourselves!"

But before they could, a huge blade bit into the bedroom door, then into the jamb. The fat man watched the door fall back on its hinges, and as if to make sure the door offered no further resistance, the broadsword bit into the door again, scattering pieces to the floor. The fat man became very busy re-buttoning his buttons.

Pulling the huge sword from the frame, a stocky and thoroughly sunburnt man stepped into the room, allowing Susanna to see the man behind him, a pale-skinned man wearing a strange brown suit and carrying a longbow. Behind them, lights flickered against the wall of the hallway and screams came from the ground floor.

The house was on fire!

Susanna scrambled to her feet, climbed to the windowsill, and leapt into the arms of the young man floating outside the window.

Four

In the alley behind the bordello, Susanna shrugged into a cape offered by the handsome young man. His companion, similarly pale-faced and with ruby lips but of smaller stature, grinned at her. The smaller man didn't speak but simply grinned.

Susanna saw the ladder leaning against the building.

So that's how they'd done it. She'd been silly to think anyone had hung in the air outside the window. Still, the handsome young man was uncommonly strong and had easily plucked her from the air when she leapt from the second-story window.

"Miss," said Lucius Fallows, bowing graciously after introducing himself, "we must hurry if we are to reach the ship before it sails."

"Ship?" asked Susanna, remembering to curtsy. "Sail?"

"All shall be explained aboard the *Mary Stewart.*"

"Would that be your ship?"

24

"No, Miss Chase. Donato and I are merely passengers."

His partner gestured upward, and when the three of them looked up, they saw two men leaning out the second-story window. Donato grinned and saluted the two men.

"We must go now," continued Fallows. "When we reach the wharf, you may choose to remain ashore, but Donato and I must sail for the New World."

He nodded to his companion, and Donato went ahead of them, sloshing through the mud and kicking a few pigs in the process. Before they reached the street, a cluster of brightly colored gowns fluttered down from a second-story window. Someone was saving clothing before saving her own life.

Bizarre, thought Susanna.

Fallows snatched one of the gowns from the air and led her into the street—which was total chaos. Bells rang, men shouted orders, and women screamed, all because of the fire at the front of the bordello.

"Stay close, Miss." When he took her hand, his skin felt oddly cold.

Well, he had been standing in the alley for some time. But how had he known she was inside? Or known she needed to be rescued?

Men and women bumped into them, and a bucket brigade formed near the harbor. Soon pails of water were passing from hand to hand in an attempt to save the building. Susanna gripped Fallows' hand as they followed Donato through the crowd. Once, when sailors didn't move fast enough, the smaller man snarled, and larger men fell back and made way.

Strange, thought Susanna.

When the crowd thinned out, she saw a three-mast
ship outlined against the night sky. In comparison to
others in the harbor, this one had an extremely long
hull and sat much lower in the water, its masts empty
and tall in the moonlight.

A lantern lit the foot of the gangplank, but Fallows
ignored the gangway and led Susanna down the wharf
while Donato waited in the light. A boy clutching flags
on sticks reached the gangway, hesitated when he
saw Donato, and then raced past the grinning man
and onto the ship. When Lucius released her hand,
Susanna tucked it inside the cape for warmth. The
wharf was relatively empty with only a few sailors to
cast off lines.

Susanna saw three men headed in her direction. One
of the three, a black man, stopped when questioned
by a sailor, but the man with the broadsword and the
man with the longbow continued down the wharf and
proceeded up the gangway.

"This is where we leave you," said Fallows. "If you
choose to sail for the New World, all you need do is
board this ship." He pointed to the bow where a lantern
lit up the name: *Mary Stewart.* "Donato and I are
members of a troupe with an invitation to perform in
Charles Town in the crown colony of South Carolina.
If you choose not to travel with us, you may keep the
cloak."

Staring from the railing, a blond woman and man,
also with pale skin and ruby red lips, studied her.

Fallows held out the dress plucked from the air.
"You may wish to change into something a little less
recognizable than the one you wear. In the house you

have just left, white is not such a common color."

Susanna flushed and stuck the rolled-up dress under her arm.

"Do not squander your good fortune, Miss Chase." Fallows bowed before taking his leave.

"Oh, no, sir," said Susanna, hurrying after him. "I'm with you."

She followed Fallows over to the gangway where Donato favored her with another mad grin—enough to cause Susanna to falter before putting her foot on the gangway.

The man with the broadsword and his companion with the longbow stared down at her from the deck. A third young man joined them, speaking to one man, then the other, but always glancing in her direction.

"You should feel right at home," said Fallows, striding up the gangway. "I do believe there are others on this ship . . ."

He became aware that she had not followed him. He stopped and looked down at her. "Miss Chase?"

Susanna was staring at the fire. She had no doubt that the bordello had become a raging inferno threatening the rest of Liverpool, and though she knew no one on this ship, if she remained here, someone would be coming for her: the magistrate, the madam, or the heir to the Worthington estate.

Ignoring Donato's mad grin, Susanna put her foot down on the gangway and followed Lucius Fallows aboard the ship.

FIVE

At the head of the gangway, James Stuart turned over his broadsword to Billy then grasped the boy's arm. "A moment of your time, lad. I want you to hear what I tell the first mate."

Martin Chase was a brown-haired man with skin burned as dark as Stuart's, and he appeared genuinely excited at the appearance of the girl on the wharf.

Martin's anticipation turned into puzzlement. "She's boarding with Fallows? Why's that?"

"Don't ask me. I'm just the captain."

As Stuart related their misadventures to his first mate, Martin became visibly distraught. He regained some degree of composure when he heard Stuart tell Billy that the cabin boy would feel the sting of the broadsword if he related a word of the girl's misadventures to other members of the crew.

"Do as I say or I'll feed you to the sharks. Do you understand, lad?"

The archer bent down to the boy. "Just a whiff of

a rumor, that's all it takes to ruin any young lady's reputation, a joke, an offhand remark. Let the girl bring ruin to herself. Don't you have a hand in it."

Billy nodded rapidly. There was little chance a boy his age could survive aboard a ship without the protection of its captain and his senior staff. When Stuart released Billy's arm, the cabin boy took the broadsword, crossed the deck, and disappeared through the center door of three stern-side cabins.

Sailors were everywhere, shouting orders, double-checking lines, testing and climbing the rigging, assisting passengers and their luggage to their cabins below. Many passengers stood about idly, most at the railing, staring at the fire raging not far away.

When Stuart saw the first mate's concern was primarily for the girl coming up the gangway, he raised his voice to the passengers on the main deck. "It's dark, people, and there's nothing more to see. Report to your cabins so we can account for everyone before setting sail."

Lucius Fallows preceded the girl aboard and stepped aside, allowing her to curtsy. Donato saluted Stuart in the manner of an officer reporting aboard, then strolled away, grinning once again.

Stuart introduced the girl to John Belle, who, because of his longbow and arrows, received more than a cursory glance. "And give me leave to present your cousin, Martin," said the sea captain, "my first mate and the party responsible for us being in Liverpool this evening."

Martin had been pumping everyone's hands and thanking them for a job well done. As first mate, Martin was accountable for the ship and hardly ever went ashore.

He turned to the girl. "Good to meet you, Miss Chase."

"And you, sir." Another bow and curtsy. "This is true? You are my cousin?"

"From South Carolina. Please call me Martin."

Looking around, the girl saw that each sailor, though busy, had plenty of time to glance her way. "Alas, but at this time, I fear I cannot. That doesn't mean I don't appreciate what you've done."

Stuart excused himself to make ready to sail, and John Belle accompanied him. Both men headed for the helm, leaving the newfound cousins to get to know each other.

The archer gestured with his bow at Donato, who had stopped at the forward mast where he stared at those huddled in the bow: nine dirty, ragged young men ordered to remain in the bow throughout the voyage. Once all nine heads finally looked in his direction, Donato broke off his stare, grinned at Stuart and Belle, and crossed the deck to disappear down the below-deck stairs.

"If anyone needs reassurance that there's life after death," said John, "the complexion of these fellows should reassure them."

"That's the pot calling the kettle black." Stuart was referring to Belle's pale skin, black hair, and blue eyes, features that marked him as a member of the Belle family of Charles Town.

"*Au contraire, mon capitaine,* though those actors' skin is as pale as mine, you'd have a better chance of finding a vein on a Belle than one of them. All in all, I'd rather haul pure cargo."

"Oh, I'm to take advice from a man who believed fire was the answer to our predicament? Fire, John? What were you thinking?"

"Someone moved in front of my target. It caused me to pull my shot."

Stuart looked down the wharf in the direction of the fire. "Your distaste for city life will be your undoing, John."

But Belle was looking at the girl. Gown soiled, especially around the hem, and she was shoeless and needed a scarf to gather her reddish-blond hair. But she was all woman, and not even Fallows' cape could hide her endowments.

"A winsome girl on board for the next month with what?" mused Belle. "Over a hundred men. You do have your work cut out for you. Any idea how Fallows and Donato learned of the girl's whereabouts?"

Before Stuart could reply, another young man sporting a pale complexion and black hair clapped Belle on the shoulder.

"Well, brother, where have you been?"

"Stretching my legs before we cast off."

"With your bow and arrows?" His hand dropped from John's shoulder as he peered down the wharf. "What's that?"

"A bordello, Phillippe. I burned it to the ground so you wouldn't stray."

Stuart cast a sharp look in John's direction.

"Oh," said Phillippe, chuckling. "But I'm not that easily tempted."

"That may be, but I'm still suspicious of how easy it was to convince you to leave your law studies at the Middle Temple and return to Charles Town."

"I still don't believe Mother's dying, but if what she says can draw you out of the woods, then her cause must be true."

Stuart had his own point to make. "You delay this ship one more time, Phillippe, and John won't have to track you down. He'll find you in irons in the brig. I'm being paid to deliver you to Charles Town, and I don't think your mother cares whether you arrive in chains or not."

Phillippe did not appear to hear him. He had seen the girl. Shoulders slumped, she had begun to cry. Martin reached out to touch her and thought better of it. He made his excuses and left her with Fallows. The actor glanced around, shifting from one foot to the other.

"Now if there was ever a woman in need of comforting . . . Gentlemen . . ." Phillippe bowed and headed for the girl.

"She shouldn't be all that unhappy," said John. "After all, we did save her from a fate worse than death."

"Perhaps," said Stuart, grinning as his first mate joined him, "she's unhappy to learn she's Martin's cousin."

"Well," said the first mate, "she doesn't really know me."

John laughed. "And that's reason enough to leave her in the company of some actor?"

"But your brother's also with her," protested Martin. "You don't really think—"

"I think," said the archer, "that whenever my brother's about, all women are in danger, even great-grandmothers."

Their attention was drawn to the African striding up

the gangway, followed by the magistrate. As Alexander crossed the deck, he inclined his head toward the wharf. Stuart, Belle, and Chase looked that way. Posted at the foot of the gangway were two marines at parade rest.

"I thought you'd gotten rid of that magistrate," said John.

"It's why I brought the farmer's wife along." Stuart looked at the barouche parked on the wharf where Agnes Withering sat, stiff necked and looking straight ahead. "He's responsible for her now."

"Not with a couple of marines in his employ."

Six

Stuart introduced the man in black to his companions. The magistrate acknowledged the others but took extra time to evaluate the woodsman's clothing.

"What is that fabric? I've never seen anything like it before."

"Buckskin," replied John Belle.

"Oh, yes. I've heard of this—made from the skin of a deer." The magistrate reached out, caught himself, and asked, "May I?"

John nodded. He was used to strangers wanting to know more about his clothing, even touch it. In a world where everyone aspired to wear high-status black suits, buckskin was a novelty and created an informal atmosphere for John Belle, whether he desired it or not.

Rubbing the fabric between his thumb and forefinger, the magistrate exclaimed, "Why, it is very soft indeed, and appears quite pliable."

"I killed and skinned the animal myself. Tanned and

scraped the skin, and worked the fabric with my own hands into this condition."

"Amazing." Nothing in the magistrate's closet fitted so well, nor felt so soft.

"But it's not suitable for shipboard duty," said Stuart. "Sooner or later, we'll run into a storm, and when the sun reappears, John's buckskin will shrink. But you didn't come aboard to view the latest fashions from the colonies, did you?"

The magistrate released his hold on the buckskin. "That would be correct. You cannot sail until an investigation into the fire is completed."

"Pardon me," asked Martin Chase, "but the citizens of Liverpool actually care what happens to a brothel?"

"It's still someone's property," said the magistrate, "and there will be questions as to who is responsible for the fire."

Glancing at Belle, Stuart said, "I daresay the wives of Liverpool will award him a medal; that is, if they can find him."

Stuart knew John had pulled several arrows from the brothel's porch before they raced upstairs to find the girl, but given enough time to consider what had happened, someone would remember those glorious days when English armies strode across Europe, arrows from longbows preceding their soldiers and falling on their foes like dark rain.

The magistrate gestured at the harbor where the only light, other than the smoldering fire, came from a lantern here and there. "Of course, it's much too dark to sail, so the point is moot. Still, I have posted marines at your gangway so there is no question in the matter."

"This is foolishness of the highest caliber," growled Alexander. "I've never met a wife who regretted the loss of a brothel."

"Be that as it may, sir, the *Mary Stewart* is not to depart Liverpool until I say so."

"Magistrate," said Stuart, "a good number of businesses in the colonies depend on the goods in my hold, and any delay is another expense they must bear—actually, a hidden tax levied by your local government on my fellow colonials."

"I understand, but my order stands until rescinded by a higher authority."

The magistrate left them but stopped at the gangway to speak to the girl.

He touched his tricorn hat. "Good luck in America, Miss Chase. Our prayers are with you."

John Belle watched the magistrate descend the gangway. *"Mon capitaine,* you know where to find me." Belle strapped the bow over his shoulder and disappeared into the darkness of the rigging overhead.

"Well, Captain," asked Martin, "do we sail or not?"

Stuart watched Belle go and felt a twinge of envy. John's brother returned, escorting the girl. Trailing them was Lucius Fallows.

Fascinated by Belle's disappearance into the rigging, the girl asked, "Why'd he do that?"

Stuart glanced at her. "It's often where he goes, especially when the responsibilities of citizenship bear down on him."

Phillippe Belle, who couldn't care less about his younger brother's behavior, actually found it embarrassing, said, "Miss Chase needs a cabin, James, and I thought you or Martin might have thought to provide her with the proper accommodations."

"Phillippe," said Martin, "James Stuart is the captain of this ship and he is to be addressed as such."

"Of course. I was simply—"

Turning to his first mate, Stuart asked, "Martin, have you had enough of transporting Virginia tobacco to Liverpool?"

"Captain, I have had enough of Virginians whether they ship tobacco or not. Those people remind me too much of the ones living in Charles Town. But whatever you are thinking, we cannot sail. If we were already moored outside the harbor, I'd be all for it."

Stuart gazed at the harbor entrance. Like many seafaring men, Stuart wished to be a bold man of action, but it had been his father who sailed the Spanish Main, while the son was cursed to ferry, back and forth across the North Atlantic, the most rudimentary items of everyday life. Even a fattening purse could not relieve the tedium of such work.

"I'm with Martin." Alexander had sailed with Stuart's father and understood the young man's itch, but this was not the time, nor place, to scratch it. "Whatever foolishness the magistrate has in store is not worth risking the keel of the *Mary Stewart*."

Stuart watched the magistrate climb into the carriage box of the barouche and snap his whip across the horse's flank. Soon, he and the farmer's wife had disappeared up the cobblestone street. But before Stuart could turn away, another carriage pulled by two black horses raced in their direction.

"Captain Stuart?" asked Fallows.

"Yes," snapped Stuart. "What is it?"

"Would you be able to take the *Mary Stewart* out if you knew the way was clear to blue water?"

Stuart didn't appear to understand the question.

"What I mean is, many of our troupe see quite well at night, and if you'd like, we'd be happy to give navigational aid."

Stuart looked from Alexander to Martin and back to Alexander again. Phillippe and the girl he ignored.

The African evaluated the actor. Alexander had seen few plays in his lifetime, but the one's he'd seen had always been candlelit. "I'd chance it, Captain, if what Mr. Fallows says is true, and if we use our sweepers to clear the harbor and not our canvas."

"I can guarantee it," said Fallows.

Stuart wasn't so sure. He didn't trust landsmen when they spoke with such confidence about blue water. Still, it was tempting. He did not care to lose two or three days in this harbor. Neither did he wish to lose his keel.

Stuart hated being reasonable. Earlier this evening, swinging his father's broadsword had been exhilarating and something he'd never before had the opportunity to do. But if he sailed without the magistrate's permission . . .

The new carriage, and this was a closed one, stopped at the gangway and a British officer climbed down when the footman opened the door. The redcoat requested permission to come aboard, and Alexander stepped over to the railing and bellowed for the marines to make way.

The marines stepped aside and presented arms. The officer returned their salute. Behind him, the footman took up a position at the open door of the carriage, and a feminine shape leaned forward and peered through the opening.

"See what that fool wants," snapped Stuart.

"Aye, aye, sir." Alexander headed to the gangway.

"Captain," repeated Phillippe, "whether we sail tonight or not, Miss Chase will still need accommodations."

Stuart was staring at the redcoat coming up the gangway. "What?" he asked, distractedly. "Oh, have her placed in my cabin."

Susanna instantly colored. "Sir, if I might say, your cabin hardly seems an appropriate place for me to sleep tonight."

"Oh," said Stuart, turning to the girl, "I meant no insult, Miss Chase. The ship's cabins are full, but I will gladly yield my berth."

"You are too kind, sir." Again Susanna curtsied, but before she did, she saw the flicker of irritation in the man's eye.

Alexander returned from the gangway where he had left the redcoat. "Captain, we are quite fortunate, indeed. The major has orders for New York and on to Albany."

Stuart brightened for the first time since departing London several days earlier. "Oh, he does, does he?"

"That he does, and the magistrate said the *Mary Stewart* could sail if his order was rescinded by a higher authority, and I would say, from what we know about Indian activity around Albany, that this major does fill the bill."

Seven

Below deck, in the passengers' quarters, Lucius Fallows nodded to a burly young man who sat in a chair outside a cabin door. The young man's solid shoulders, large hands, and plain clothing made him appear to be any another sailor, but he was Lucius Fallows' manservant.

The young man rose and bowed. "They are all inside, my lord, just as you requested."

"Very well, Oren."

A heated argument stopped when the cabin door opened. Oren closed the cabin door behind Lucius and retook his seat. Several passengers stared at Oren as he sat down again, but he ignored them.

As Lucius came through the door, Donato gave him an exaggerated bow. Matching closets and single beds took up most of the space, and both beds were raised an additional eight inches off the deck to accommodate low, wide pull-out drawers with heavy brass handles. The drawers were said to have been installed by the acting troupe in London to hold additional costumes for their performances in Charles Town.

The narrow room had a drop-down table on the far wall at the foot of the two beds, and the room's only light came from a candle in a brass holder that sat on the table. Lanterns and pipe smoking were forbidden below deck, and privacy was guaranteed to all occupants unless one of the ship's officers believed the danger of a fire existed.

On one bed sat an attractive young blond woman, and facing her, a blond man scowled at Lucius from the opposite bed. Ostensibly to give Lucius more room, Donato took a seat on the bed next to the woman. Everyone in the cabin was dressed exquisitely. All had pale skin, coiffed hair, and ruby red lips.

"Here's the great man," said the blond man sitting on the edge of the bed. "What are your orders now, my lord? Rescue more damsels in distress? Would you care to tell me what that accomplished?"

"We are now one step closer to the New World, Gabriel. This ship would not have left England without the girl."

"We'd be a week closer if you'd allowed me to have a free hand with these feebleminded folk. I say we seize the ship and sail straight for Philadelphia."

"And who shall sail the ship? I don't remember anyone in our party qualified to sail a ship, especially during daylight hours."

Gabriel muttered that he'd get this ship moving, and the whole project would move much faster if he was in control.

"Dear brother," said the woman sitting across from

him, "can't you see Lucius only has our best interests at heart?"

Gabriel glared at Lucius, but his sister continued to smile.

"You know as well as I that we've faced some insurmountable obstacles, and each time Lucius produced a solution."

Gabriel shifted around on the opposite bed. "There are those on this ship, weak-minded seamen and thieves being transported to the colonies, that we could dominate from below deck."

"But only if you have the capacity to concentrate on any subject for more than a few hours," said Lucius with a touch of sarcasm in his voice.

Gabriel straightened up on his bed. "You are not to speak to me in such a manner!"

"And what will you do? Will you seize control of our little group?"

At this, Gabriel looked away.

"I've observed this Captain Stuart, and young though he may be, he has a fierce center that would take all my concentration to make him submit to my will."

"Your will, perhaps."

"Oh, please. The invitation from the theatre on Dock Street, the crossing of over three-thousand-miles of saltwater to the American colonies, and the reason given why we're never topside during the daylight hours—what solutions did you contribute to these problems?"

The scowling man did not answer.

"Many aboard this ship have access to the highest levels of colonial society, and you want to throw all that away because of your impatience? Admission is everything. Admission means invitations from one party to another, from one private dance to—"

"I will listen no longer!" Gabriel leapt to his feet, pushed past Lucius, and left the cabin, slamming the door behind him.

The others watched him go. A moment later, Oren stuck his head inside, but was dismissed with a wave of the hand by Lucius.

Once the door closed again, he said, "Portia, you must talk some sense into your brother. Gabriel's emotions place our entire project in danger. Once we are established in the New World, our people can expand, just as the British colonies are expanding westward. But we must reach the New World first."

Lucius took a seat across from Portia and took the young woman's hands. This caused a frown to grow on Donato's face.

"Putting aside the fact that this ship has the fastest crossing times in the history of transatlantic trips, making Gabriel's demands to seize the ship all the more irrational, the Spanish empire is finished and any of our kind who remain aligned with Spain are finished. They may enjoy the decadence of the coming decades, even revel in it, but that decadence is a distraction to our future. The future is the Mississippi River valley area, with a river said to be as long as the Nile, but with a wealth of furs and bottomland those in Europe can only dream about."

Donato leaned over. "Listen to Lucius, my dear. He has studied the way of our fellow Europeans and believes the English will eventually march across this

New World, opening the way for our kind. Why, they will never know we are among them—"

"Unless Gabriel brings us to ruin," said Lucius, still leaning forward. "I selected each of you because of your gifts. You, my dear, can blind men with your charm, and Gabriel was chosen because of his incredible singing ability, a voice that brings tears to the eyes of those who hear him."

"Your brother will sing our way into the social circles of Charles Town," interjected Donato, "and then, by invitation, up the coast through Philadelphia, New York, and Boston—all will fall under his spell, then ours."

"But, my dear," added Lucius, "we must first reach Charles Town if we are to turn your brother's voice loose on the English colonies."

Portia looked from one man to the other. "I shall speak to him, but Gabriel's passions have governed his life, and they are why my brother and I are here today."

She straightened up and pulled her hands away from Lucius. "But who is this girl you and Donato rescued? I was at the railing when she came aboard and I saw nothing special about her."

Donato grinned. "Lucius must've found something special in this girl. I've never seen him so nervous. What's wrong, Lucius? Couldn't you fill her mind with your thoughts as you're able to do with so many other young ladies? You've never had that much trouble with Portia."

Unable to blush, Portia simply looked away.

"She was important to the crew," said Lucius. "And what's important to the crew is important to us."

"Is this why you spend so much time with the captain," asked Donato, "or are Portia and I to worry that you have longings for him, too?"

"I have no such longings. I am completely devoted to the mission." Lucius got to his feet. "Donato, the ship cannot leave the harbor unless the crew knows the way is clear to blue water."

"Blue water?" asked the woman. "What is this blue water I hear so much about?"

"Oh, the ocean, the sea," said Lucius, dismissively. "Donato, I want you to go ahead of the ship . . ."

But Donato was staring at Portia.

Lucius let out a long sigh. "Just join me on the bow in your own good time."

"Yes, yes," said Donato, getting to his feet.

"And what's to become of me?" asked Portia, looking up from the bed. "Am I to remain downstairs day *and* night?"

"Below deck," corrected Lucius.

Portia dismissed the correction with the wave of her hand. "Downstairs or below deck, the Atlantic Ocean instead of blue water—it is these people who are out of step. They're just a bunch of narrow-minded sailors."

"But," said Lucius, hand on the cabin door, "what your brother doesn't understand is that we are at the mercy of these people for the next month, and it might be best if you cultivated a friend or two. It is, after all, a very long voyage."

"Lucius," said Portia, smiling up at him, "I can have as many friends as I choose to have on this ship."

"No, my dear, only one. Just as I have concentrated on the captain, you are to focus on the young woman who has just boarded the ship. Learn what there is about this girl that makes her so unique, because one day, as your brother suggests, we may have to seize control of this ship, and on that fateful day, none of us would care to learn that this young woman is some sort of huntress."

Eight

Smartly dressed in his red uniform, the officer issued orders in a clipped manner. To Alexander, he said, "You there, have our luggage brought aboard."

"Aye, aye, sir."

Alexander barked an order and two sailors, busy leaning against the ship's railing, hustled down the gangway.

"They'll treat your luggage with every respect, Major."

"See that they do." The officer stepped to the railing and shouted at those on the wharf. "Marines!"

The marines came to attention and looked up at the officer.

"I hold you personally responsible for the transfer of our luggage to this ship."

"Yes, sir!"

"And my wife shall be boarding. See that the sailors mind their manners."

"Yes, sir!"

The officer followed Alexander to the knot of men standing near the helm. He spied Susanna and gave her a swift, appraising glance, taking in the cape covering her soiled gown, her shoeless feet, and tousled hair.

"Miss, see to it that my wife's comfort is attended to."

"Sir," objected Phillippe Belle, "Miss Chase is a passenger on this ship just as you and your lady are."

The officer looked around. "Then where's her luggage?"

"It will be along shortly," said Alexander.

"Sir," said Susanna, curtsying, "I was formerly employed at Lord Worthington's estate and am indentured to a good family in Charles Town. I can attend to your wife's every need."

"Very well, Miss Chase. Until we dock in Charles Town consider yourself in service to my wife."

"Major, I don't think—" started Phillippe.

"Cousin," said Susanna, turning to Martin, "will you introduce Captain Stuart and welcome the major and his wife aboard the . . ." She looked to Stuart for assistance.

Taken with the girl's self-assurance, it was a moment before Stuart got out, "The *Mary Stewart.*"

"You, sir," asked the officer of Stuart, "are a Papist?"

"Worse than that, Major," said Martin, finding his tongue. "The captain's father was a Scot."

"Oh, well, we are all part of the same empire now." Looking Stuart over, head to toe, the major asked, "Then you, young man, are captain of this ship?"

"That I am, sir."

"Very well. I understand that there are few trained men in the colonies. This is why I am being sent overseas." The officer pulled a letter from his tunic. "My orders, sir. I am Major Edmund A. Ladd of the 35th Regiment Afoot."

Stuart opened the envelope, slipped out the sheet of paper, and glanced at the orders. In Albany, Ladd was to be joined by a colonial militia officer by the name of George Washington. Stuart did not recognize the name.

"My lady and I expect the best shipboard accommodations. I assume that will be your cabin, Captain."

"It shall be. Martin, would you and your cousin attend to the Ladds' every comfort?"

"Aye, aye, Captain."

Martin and Susanna left, nodding and curtsying to the major's lady as she came up the gangway. Everyone eyed the woman. Mrs. Ladd's dress was of a quilted fabric suitable for cold-weather traveling, with extra fullness and warmth. Elbow-length gloves covered her arms, and on her head sat a pinner, a lace-bordered cap worn on the crown of the head.

"How soon do we depart, Captain?" asked Ladd.

"Major, that might be a problem."

"Problem? Are you prepared to sail or not?"

"We are, indeed." Stuart beckoned Ladd to the railing where the officer could see the lines still attached to the wharf.

"A local magistrate wishes to seize a couple of my men and try them for public drunkenness and disorderly conduct."

"You can't be serious. Sailors are supposed to be drunk and disorderly when ashore."

"Sir, I'm quite serious."

"Who is this fool?"

Stuart looked up the wharf. "Actually, you passed him on your way here. I'm sorry if this in any way inconveniences you or your lady, but you know how difficult these petty bureaucrats can be."

"And you tolerate this?"

"Sir," said Stuart, straightening up, "once my ship enters any harbor, I'm subject to the rules and regulations of that harbor. The civil authorities, too."

"This is ridiculous! You've seen my orders, and you must understand I have a pressing assignment in the colonies. I was told that one of the speediest ships would be departing Liverpool this very evening, and that is why we are here."

"I'm sorry, Major, but there is little I can do."

Ladd eyed Stuart. "Can you identify the members of your crew whom the magistrate wishes to arrest?"

"Sir, I will not."

"Edmund," asked his wife, joining them at the railing, "is there a problem?"

"Captain Stuart, this is my wife, Katherine."

"Captain Stuart," said Mrs. Ladd with a smile and a curtsy, "pleased to make your acquaintance."

Stuart returned her attention with a nod.

Mrs. Ladd gestured at the closed carriage on the wharf. The driver, footman, and two marines were watching sailors from the *Mary Stewart* haul the Ladds' luggage aboard.

"Though it ruffled my nerves, my husband insisted

we reach Liverpool before you sailed."

"And, my dear, we arrived just in time. The *Mary* . . . the ship was just about to sail."

"Is that your decision, Major?" asked Stuart. "Your order?"

"Of course," said Ladd with a wink and a nod. "We military men must stick together."

Nine

While Captain Stuart and Major Ladd worked out the protocol for the departure of the *Mary Stewart* from Liverpool, Martin Chase led his cousin over to where three cabins were located across the rear of the main deck. Phillippe Belle trailed along, and this caused Martin to ask Belle if he could spend some time with his cousin. "You know, to acquaint her with the ship."

"Of course," said Phillippe, clearing his throat. "I just thought she might need an escort."

"I think I can handle it," said Martin with a smile.

Susanna curtsied to the retiring gentleman. "I want to thank you for everything you've done, Mr. Belle. I can honestly say that you've made me feel much more comfortable on this ship."

"Well, yes," said Phillippe, "any gentleman would." He bowed and backed away. "Your servant, *mademoiselle.*"

Though this end of the deck was sheltered by an overhang, in the darkness off the Irish Sea the air was still chilly. Illumination was provided by an overhead lantern, and lines creaked and groaned from wharf side.

Susanna tightened the cape around her. Her reddish-blond hair fluttered about and she had no way to control it. She needed a pinner or a scarf. Two sailors placed the Ladds' heavy, ornate sea chests in front of the cabins and waited for further instructions, all the while ogling Susanna. Martin would have none of that and ordered them to their stations.

Once the sailors left, Martin lowered his voice. "Sorry to entangle you in this, Susanna. I had no idea a redcoat would be joining us."

"Think nothing of it, cousin. I've always been someone's maid, and several of my masters have tried . . ." Instantly, she colored and looked away. "Not that they were successful."

Martin flushed. "I understand."

She stared in the direction of the smoldering blaze. "I must say England has become rather inhospitable of late, and I'm looking forward to life in Charles Town. Would you perchance know the kind of people to whom I'm indentured?"

"I shall have a copy of the articles of indentureship brought to your cabin."

"And I shall sign them." She glanced at the main deck that included the bow, a wheel, and two more masts, along with cannon arrays on both sides. "Of course, I have little choice."

Susanna realized this was not the mood to set. "Thank you for all you have done, Martin. In truth, I have always dreamed of traveling to the colonies. Of course, because of my circumstances, I always thought it was just that, a dream."

Martin had to clear his throat. This girl might be his cousin, but she was also the most winsome young woman he'd ever met. Susanna wouldn't have any problem finding a husband. A line would spring up wherever she stood and would run around the corner of any street in Charles Town.

Martin shifted his gaze to the two sea chests. "I don't know what you're to do for clothing. I should've prepared for such an eventuality."

"Which one?" asked Susanna with a laugh. "Being dismissed from the Worthington estate or escaping from . . . that place with only the clothes on my back?" She opened the cape. "And this dress."

She held out the dress tossed from a window of the bordello and given to her by Lucius Fallows. "I'll have you know, Martin Chase, that I sew all my own clothes. I've even sewn dresses for Lady Worthington for everyday wear. All I need is cloth, shears, a needle, and, oh, yes, a piece of chalk."

She glanced toward the fire and let out a breath. She must slow down. Her nerves were running away with her tongue.

"You shall have all you need," said Martin, "and you shan't pay a shilling."

"I shall pay, cousin. I've always worked for my keep."

Martin heard chattering among the crew. The major's wife was coming up the gangway. Martin looked to the railing and saw the exasperated look on the major's face as Ladd stood with James Stuart. Once Ladd's wife had joined the two men at the railing and introductions had been exchanged, Stuart nodded to Martin over Ladd's shoulder.

"Wait here, Susanna, if you please."

Martin hurried to the far cabin and thumped on the door. "Rise and shine, Kyrla, and report to the helm."

Hearing no answer, he thumped on the door again.

"Go away, Martin," said a hoarse voice. "I've pulled back the curtain. It's too dark to leave the harbor."

Martin thumped on the door until the voice promised to report to the helm; then he returned to Susanna. "Helmsmen can be rather hardheaded, but it's a good helmsman you need in any storm." He raised the latch of the middle cabin. "Have you ever sailed before, Susanna?"

But the girl was staring at James Stuart at the railing with the Ladds. "Martin, how old is the captain?"

"What?" He glanced at his friend. "Four and twenty, but you have nothing to fear. He went to sea as a cabin boy and has over three years of experience as captain. Besides, Alexander sailed with his father. Susanna, have you ever sailed before?"

"I've never been in a rowboat. I can't even swim."

"Well, your education begins now, and pay attention for it could save your life. Starboard is the right side of the ship and that is where you will sleep, but we must first prepare accommodations for the Ladds." Martin released the latch on the middle door. "Port is the left side of the ship."

Susanna held up her left hand. "I know my left from my right, and the cabin you just knocked on to raise the helmsman, or the third cabin, is on the left side . . . or port side of the ship."

"Face the bow. That way it'll make more sense."

The girl looked around, looked everywhere. "The bow?"

"Oh, sorry," he said, chuckling. "Face the front of the ship. That's the bow. The rear of the ship is called the stern."

Susanna faced the bow. "Now cabin number three is on the star . . . What do you call it?"

"Starboard. The opposite side is port, though you may hear some of the sailors refer to it as the larboard side."

Bewildered, the girl asked, "Is there somewhere all of this is written down? I *can* read, you know. I've read the Bible all the way through."

Martin laughed, opened the door to the middle cabin, and disappeared inside. And very quickly stepped back out again.

"Susanna, you are to avoid the bow at all times—understand?"

"Yes, yes." The girl looked forward. "Is there a better chance I might fall overboard there? The front of a ship, I mean the bow, is narrower than the rest."

Martin shook his head. "There are nine, dirty, ragged young men ordered by the captain to remain there throughout the voyage. Transportees are never permitted to leave the bow. The Crown pays their passage to the colonies, but those men have no trade but a knack for thievery; they're swindlers, cheats, and have nothing to look forward to but a short life, ending with a quick drop at the end of a very short rope. None of them will survive a year in America."

Susanna could not believe what she was hearing. "The colonists will . . ."

Martin nodded. "So give the bow a wide berth. Those men have a history of making fools of young girls. And worse." Very quickly, he disappeared through the center door again.

Susanna was still staring toward the bow when Martin called from the interior of the cabin. "Open the door and meet me inside."

She looked from the door where Martin had disappeared to the door in front of her. It wasn't that she didn't trust her cousin; she simply didn't trust any man, and here she was on this ship with all sorts of new dangers.

"Susanna, I said open the door and come inside."

She tightened the cape around her shoulders, loosened the latch, and pulled back the door.

In light from an overhead lantern, she saw a narrow, unmade bed, its headboard at a window opening on the . . . stern. Also a window on the . . . Susanna faced the bow . . . on the port side of this particular cabin. The two stern windows wrapped around the corner of the cabin in the shape of an "L." Through them, Susanna could see lights flickering on shore. Clothes lay in disarray on the bed, more on the floor, rather, the deck, along with a pair of boots on their sides. This was definitely a man's room. Or cabin. The closet at her left had no door and was full of pants, shirts, and shoes. And a fresh stack of linen.

Susanna realized Martin was on the other side of the same cabin, more or less in the shadows. On Martin's side sat a table with several chairs, crossed broadswords hung on the wall, and under them was mounted a shelf of books.

Books on a ship! Susanna never would've imagined. Could she dare ask to read one?

Using his foot, Martin pushed a chair toward her. "That's your first chore, sailor. Make that bed. You'll find clean sheets in the closet. They were delivered an hour ago." Martin smiled. "But now that we have you aboard, we won't have to take our laundry ashore, will we?"

"No, no. You shouldn't have to."

"And empty the chamber pot over the side, but before you do, you must find the wind." Martin wet his finger by sticking it into his mouth and holding it up. "With a wet finger you can find the wind's direction, then choose your railing. It's not the same as emptying a chamber pot out a window into the street below."

Susanna nodded. Her cousin appeared to be a goodhearted man, just trying to help out.

She turned to the closet—and found a boy her age at the open cabin door. Susanna stepped back and pulled tight the cape around her. She felt so vulnerable. Her undergarments had been taken away in the bordello. The towheaded boy stepped inside, and she backed further away.

"Here now, Martin," said the boy, "I heard what you said, and you're giving this girl all my chores."

"Susanna, this is Billy, the cabin boy for these cabins. If you need him, you can usually find him on the poop deck."

"The poop deck?" asked the girl, flustered.

"The overhead deck."

"But why? Why not just call it the uppermost deck?"

Martin laughed. "I really don't know."

"I say here," said Billy, "all this claptrap is fine and dandy, but the girl's still taking my chores."

"Actually, Billy, I had some other jobs in mind, a trial promotion during the return voyage."

The boy perked up. "A promotion? What kind of promotion?"

"Can we speak of it later? I have to repair this cabin."

"Aye, aye, sir." And without a glance at Susanna, he disappeared out the door.

"As I said, that was Billy, and he'll come in handy." Martin's voice became serious. "Still, Susanna, you are not to roam this ship alone, do you understand?"

"Of course. I would never go anywhere without an escort."

"That may not always be practical, but Billy can go anywhere and may forget you're a girl."

"Martin, who's the black man?"

"What? Oh, that's Alexander."

"I never met an African. I read of them before but had never seen one. He doesn't eat people, does he?"

"Hardly," said Martin with a laugh. "Alexander's just like any other sailor on this ship, just long on experience, and that's why you don't have to worry about the captain. Alexander has more than enough experience to make up for anyone's shortcomings, even the captain's."

The first mate reached into the wall on his side of the cabin, and soon there came a noise from the other side of the bulkhead.

Martin was pulling on something—what? A rope?

As his hands moved hand over hand, a narrow portion of the floor opened the entire length of the cabin, and then fell back on Martin's side. A wall rose from the floor, and Susanna stepped back. On the false wall was mounted a sizeable piece of glass with several holes beside it.

Raising his voice over the rumbling noise, Martin said, "The captain doesn't give up his room easily. That's why there are two doors on the deck that open into this room." The first mate hooked a table leg with a foot and pulled the table completely to his side before the lip of the table caught on the rising wall. "Your side of the cabin is simply a diversion."

"Soldiers usually travel on this ship?"

"We can't refuse them, and in truth, they're welcome aboard. Newspapers from Philadelphia report a build-up of French troops in the colony of New York."

"The middle colonies," said Susanna, again trying to orient herself to more than simply the ship.

"The French and their Indian allies would like nothing better than to split us in half."

"Will there be war?"

"Isn't there always with the French?"

Before Martin disappeared behind the new wall, he tossed several pegs in her direction. The wooden pegs hit the deck, making a ringing sound, then rolling to her feet.

"Insert those pegs on either side of the mirror." Her cousin disappeared behind the movable wall once it met the ceiling.

Soon the sound of pounding came from Martin's side, and over the sound of a mallet striking wood, someone spoke behind her, causing Susanna to jump.

"And just who the devil are you?"

Ten

The voice came from a woman with bright red hair, plenty of freckles, and square shoulders. She wore men's pants, a man's shirt, a pair of gray lace-up boots, and a wide-brim hat; but she definitely was a woman. Her beefy arms were crossed over her considerable stomach, her feet spread, and on one side of her belt strapped a belaying pin. The other side held a sheath complete with knife, and not necessarily one for eating. The substantial woman barred the doorway of the cabin, and Susanna knew that if this woman did not wish her to leave this cabin, she, indeed, would not be able to do so.

"Susanna's my cousin," said Martin, appearing at the door to stand beside the redhead. Martin carried the wooden mallet and the lantern. "Kyrla Stuart, Susanna Chase."

The woman unfolded her arms and peered at the girl. "What you mean, she's your cousin? You told me they were all killed by the plague." Involuntarily, Kyrla crossed herself, as did Susanna.

Martin handed both the lantern and the mallet to Susanna. "Leave the overhead lantern for the Ladds, and hit those pegs a lick or two, once you've fit them into the wall next to the mirror."

Susanna took the mallet, and soon she was pounding pegs into the wall by the light of the lantern hanging from an above deck beam.

"You sure of this, Martin?" asked the redhead.

For some reason, the first mate instantly heated up. "What does it matter if she's not my cousin? Her passage is paid to Charles Town, and if you don't remember, that's what Stuart and Company is all about: making money."

"Hey, hey," said the redhead, backing off, "you act as if she's your lady, though she certainly doesn't look like one."

Susanna stopped pounding the pegs and faced the cabin door. Her grip tightened on the mallet, and she smacked the flat head of the mallet into the palm of her hand, once, then twice.

"Kyrla, don't you have to report to the helm?"

The redhead stepped from under the overhang and scanned the nighttime sky, seeing stars and a waxing moon. The masts were empty of canvas, and when she looked toward the bow, she saw only the inky darkness of the harbor, leading to the Irish Sea.

"Not likely," she said.

Her fellow crewmates caught a glimpse of her and began to clap and chant her name. Once Kyrla acknowledged the cheers and chants, she returned her attention to the first mate.

"If you expect her to be treated like a gentlewoman,

you'd best find her a bonnet. She doesn't look a day over fourteen."

Turning back around, Kyrla gave an excessive bow to the sailors, who continued to clap and chant, and when she did, more cheers rained down on her. At the railing, the Ladds stared at her. Kyrla ignored their stares and headed for the helm.

Susanna stepped from the cabin, bringing along the mallet. "Why is she on this ship, Martin? A woman, I mean."

"Kyrla's a helmsman, and as good as her father before her."

"Then she's not the captain's wife?"

"She's Stuart's sister—well, adopted sister. The Stuarts took her in and raised her after her parents died. Stuart's mother wanted Kyrla to learn a trade."

"You mean put her in service to a gentlewoman?"

Martin shrugged. He didn't see Alexander approaching from behind him. "More likely wanted her to work in the company store or in the warehouse, but Kyrla's been sailing Charles Town harbor in her own skiff since she was five. The girl has saltwater in her veins."

"But she's a woman . . ."

Her cousin smiled. "Well, we try to overlook that."

"Martin, am I really your cousin?"

"Of course, you're Martin's cousin," said the one-armed man, scowling at the first mate.

Martin faced the African.

"And I'm not surprised to find him socializing," said the African, "instead of informing you of your current status. You're aware that the major and his wife are right behind me?"

Susanna glanced beyond the huge man. "I see them."

"There's much to learn—besides whether you are Martin's cousin or not. Martin, would you escort the Ladds over here?"

Looking properly chastened, the first mate left them.

"Martin's father operates Stuart and Company, a shipper of wholesale goods from the American colonies to England and back again. Stuart and Company has agents in each English port and their colonies, and when our agent in Liverpool informed Martin's father of the deaths in your family, Samuel—his father—worked out an indentureship with the Belle family. That would be the family of John and Phillippe, the archer, and his brother, the rake. Because Phillippe is a rake, he has not been told to whom you are indentured. The Belles have an estate on the Cooper River outside Charles Town, an estate larger than anything you've ever seen, and they owed Samuel Chase a rather large favor."

Susanna tried to use her eyes to caution the African that the Ladds and her cousin were standing behind him, but Alexander was too caught up in imparting a good bit of information quickly.

"Despite this evening's adventures, your reputation—"

Martin Chase cleared his throat. "I don't think that's an appropriate topic to discuss with a young lady."

"Quite appropriate," said the major, "if this young lady is to be put in service to my wife."

Alexander jerked around. "Oh, sir, you and your lady's quarters are over here. Miss Chase has just started repairing them."

"Be that as it may, I'd hoped to hear the answers to some of the questions you raised with Miss Chase."

The African appeared surprised.

Ladd gestured at one of his ears. "Excellent hearing." He pointed to the overhang. "Especially when assisted by the superstructure of this ship."

His wife studied everyone, especially the girl.

"Well," asked the major, "is the young lady the first mate's cousin or not?"

"Of course she is, though this is the first time they've met. Martin, allow me to introduce you to Mrs. Ladd."

"Ma'am," said the first mate, nodding to the woman.

Susanna curtsied. "I already met the major when he came aboard. Good evening, Mrs. Ladd."

"Miss Chase, I understand you are indentured to the Belle family of Charles Town."

"I have just learned that myself. My cousin, Martin, has the documents."

"Well, you can count your lucky stars. Lord Ashley, the current Lord Ashley, that is, thinks highly of the Belle family."

Susanna didn't know what to say so she said nothing.

"And your age, young lady, if I may ask?"

"Mrs. Ladd," cut in Alexander, "Miss Chase has agreed to serve as your personal attendant during the voyage, and Captain Stuart has asked I remind you that there should be some sort of remuneration for Miss Chase's service."

"I will discuss that with the captain," said the major.

"This is not a matter for ladies to discuss."

"That, Edmund, is just what I'm trying to ascertain: whether Miss Chase is a suitable servant or not. What is your age, child, and where is your clothing?"

Susanna stared at the deck as Martin Chase informed the Ladds that such questions should be referred to the captain, but if there was a question of virtue—

"There certainly is," said Mrs. Ladd. "Anyone can see Miss Chase doesn't have suitable clothing for sea travel, and the clothing she wears is soiled and torn. How did that come about?"

"And she has no shoes," pointed out the major.

Alexander tried to intervene, but Mrs. Ladd would not allow it. "What does her appearance tell the sailors, and indirectly, tell them about me? You heard the outpouring of enthusiasm for that redheaded woman, and she wears pants."

"Mrs. Ladd," said Martin, "those chants are the crew's way of dealing with the fact that the captain will lash anyone who besmirches the reputation of any woman aboard this ship."

"Sir!" said Ladd. "You forget yourself."

"Sir," said Martin, taking a step forward, "I take the protection of the gentler sex as seriously as any other Englishman. That redheaded woman is the captain's sister."

Mrs. Ladd put her hand on her husband's arm. "Edmund, please . . ."

Ladd stared at Martin. Martin stared at Ladd. In the major's hand, a glove flipped back and forth.

Seeing the glove, Alexander said, "Gentlemen, I do not believe it's in anyone's interest to fight a duel over which one of you is the greater defender of the gentler sex."

The word "duel" stopped the conversation cold. Contrary to common belief, men did not run around looking for duels. Well, perhaps in South Carolina they did, but this was aboard ship and every hand was necessary, even passengers if the ship should face distress at sea.

"Mr. Chase," said Mrs. Ladd, playing the role of peacemaker, "my husband and I are willing to take your word about the virtue of your cousin."

"Madam, it is not my word, but Lord Worthington's; he wrote the letter and had it notarized."

"A notarized letter? Why didn't you say so? If the issue of Miss Chase's chastity has been settled in the mind of Lord Worthington, it's good enough for us. Isn't that so, Edmund?"

When her husband continued to glare at the first mate, she repeated, "Edmund, dear, isn't that so?"

"Yes. That is so."

But it didn't stop the two men from glaring at each other.

"As for the adventures I referred to," said Alexander, chuckling, "I'm sure that was one of the fastest rides Miss Chase has ever taken in a carriage down to the harbor."

"Oh, yes," said Susanna, head bobbing. "I don't remember ever taking a faster ride."

"And during the ride," said Alexander, smiling all around, "her sea chest was lost at one of the switchbacks. The captain has sent one of the crew to recover it."

He turned to the girl. "We apologize for that, Miss Chase, but at the moment we truly thought we'd sail with the tide and had to make haste. Unfortunately, that's not to be. The magistrate believes there's a fugitive aboard."

Mrs. Ladd gripped her husband's arm. "Edmund, this is too much to bear. You simply must do something."

"My dear, all is taken care of."

"Are you sure?"

"The captain and I have discussed the matter and come to a happy resolution." Now it was Major Ladd's turn to pat his wife's arm. "Nothing for you to worry about, my dear."

Returning his attention to the first mate, Ladd asked, "Mr. Chase, if you would, show us to our cabin."

"Of course," said Martin, stepping back and letting out a breath.

Chase led them over to cabin number one, but did not accompany them inside. The room was much too small to allow Martin to join them without creating a forced state of intimacy.

"A bed, a chair, and a mirror? Is this all there is?"

Though Mrs. Ladd did not mention it, a privacy screen occupied one corner and a window overlooked the stern and the port side making a wraparound "L" in the corner. The room was illuminated by a lantern from an above deck beam.

"Why, we shall be stepping all over each other," said Mrs. Ladd. She pointed at the two chests outside the door. "What shall I do with all my clothing?"

Martin reached around the door jamb and pointed to the open locker. "Your clothing goes in here, Mrs.

Ladd." He leaned farther in. "That is, once the captain's garments have been removed."

Mrs. Ladd could only stare. Inside the closet were shoes, pants, and shirts, and not much room.

"Is there something else your ladyship requires?"

"Well," said the major, "if a table and chair are not too much to ask."

"But, Edmund, I'm used to having my personal servant sleep on a pallet at the end of my bed." Again, she surveyed the room. "Edmund, where shall you sleep?"

The major looked to the first mate.

"I'm sorry, Major, but there's only this one cabin."

"Are we to sleep together then?" Mrs. Ladd shook her head. "Oh, no. That will not do. That will not do at all."

"If you'd like, sir, you can bunk with the captain, but he does keep rather irregular hours."

"And where are those quarters?"

"A better question is: Where's that servant girl? This room needs a great deal of work and she needs to begin immediately."

Eleven

"**S**usanna," said Alexander, "you'll billet in this cabin."

The African opened the door to cabin number three on the opposite side of the deck from the Ladds' cabin. "You'll share a cabin with Kyrla Stuart, one of the helmsmen."

"Mr. Alexander, I've met the woman and I don't believe she'll agree to such an arrangement."

"It's just Alexander, and Kyrla's responsible for sailing this ship, not where you bunk."

"Then who's responsible for me?"

"The captain, but we'll all help out."

Susanna scanned the main deck. "There appears much to be learned."

"There is, but even more to learn about oneself."

Susanna didn't understand.

"On this ship you're sixteen years of age."

"That's not possible. Even with the new calendar, I will be only fifteen this fall."

Alexander snorted. "The Gregorian calendar will be the ruin of commerce, losing eleven days in a single year. But really, do you want to wear the bonnet for the next month? A ship is not a safe place for any young lady under normal circumstances, and there will be times when you'll find yourself unescorted."

Susanna considered the close bonnet worn by girls until reaching sixteen. With such a deep brim hiding her face, it would be impossible to see anyone but those in front of her, or off her bow, in nautical terms.

"You're correct. I'd prefer to be sixteen and enjoy the freedoms that come with my majority." She smiled at the black man. "Which includes being able to speak to young men. No woman would turn down such an opportunity."

"And Martin thinks Mrs. Ladd is being too harsh with you. Susanna, on this ship you'll have plenty of sailors to choose from, but be warned that many of those men are not as they appear."

"That does not come as a surprise to any woman."

"Yes, well, I'm sure you can find one who suits your fancy, and that's what concerns Mrs. Ladd."

"Is her concern for me or for herself?"

"I would think they are one and the same, but anyone who has questions is to be referred to the captain. Am I clear on this?"

"Even I can see the value in only one person relating my history to those who might question it." Susanna curtsied. "Thank you, Alexander, and I hope I have a chance to repay you and Captain Stuart for your kindness."

There came a shout from sailors in the rigging, and a

rat-faced man strode up the gangway, his arms wrapped around an armful of clothing. Over his shoulder was tied a pair of shoes.

The rat-faced face man spied the first mate and strode over. "Here you are, Martin," he said, dropping the clothing and shoes to the deck, "and a fine piece of goods they are. Seven in all, plus a few petticoats and these shoes." The sailor's teeth were yellow, his skin sunburned black, and his clothing faded and torn.

"Those clothes!" shouted Mrs. Ladd who had stepped out of her cabin. "That is no way to treat a lady's clothing."

The rat-faced man turned to the woman, but before he could explain, Alexander backhanded him across the face. "Jenkins, have you no respect for the ladies?"

Jenkins sat down hard. Heads turned in their direction, and all chatter ceased on the main deck and in the nearby rigging.

"Edmund, do something. This display is quite disgraceful."

"You rascal," said the major, moving to stand over the man. "I've a good mind to thrash you."

Jenkins tried to speak, but Alexander placed a boot on the sailor's chest. Martin picked up the gowns, brushed them off, and handed them to Susanna.

"I believe these belong to you, cousin."

Susanna didn't know what to do but claim the dresses, the petticoats, and the pair of shoes. Quickly, she hid the petticoats under one of the gowns.

"Major Ladd," said Alexander, "Jenkins is one of the men for whom the magistrate is looking. It would be a good idea if you summoned a marine from the wharf to take this man into custody. It would not surprise me if Jenkins planned to sell what he found of Miss Chase's clothing and thought he could include me in the proposition."

From amidships came the call to shove off, and the first mate left them, heading for the helm. The African removed his boot from Jenkins' chest, and once the sailor caught his breath, he tried to open his mouth.

Alexander kicked him in the hip. "Oh, shut up, Jenkins. You are such a complainer."

Hoisted to his feet, one of Jenkins' arms was wrenched behind his back and he was frog-marched across the deck to the gangway. Along the way, the rat-faced man protested against such false accusations.

"Then," asked the major, accompanying Jenkins and Alexander, "you deny you're the sailor the magistrate is looking for?"

Jenkins said he was not.

"Major, I have shipped out with this man many times before and you cannot trust a word he says."

Jenkins said he was no liar but an honest seaman.

Alexander pushed Jenkins down the gangway. "On your way!" To the marine coming up the gangway, he added, "Don't let that sailor slip away or the magistrate will have you in the stocks."

Billy, the cabin boy, handed Jenkins' kit to the African, and in one motion, Alexander turned and tossed the kit to the wharf.

"No one shall ever say we stole from a thief!"

Jenkins and the marine had barely reached the wharf when the gangway was hauled aboard. As the lines were cast off, Jenkins shook his fist at the *Mary*

The Charleston Vampire

Stewart, cursed Alexander for the one-armed fool he was, then raved about his rights as an Englishman, saying he had expected better of an officer in service to the Crown.

Ladd realized he had become the object of Jenkins' wrath, and when he turned from the railing, he saw sailors lined up to release the sails from their yards. Everyone appeared to be staring at him.

"Sweepers, Mr. Chase," said Stuart.

"Sweepers to your oars!" shouted the first mate.

A group of sailors rushed below deck, and long oars were thrust out of the below-deck gun ports and began to move the ship away from the wharf. Working in unison, the sweepers moved the *Mary Stewart* toward the harbor's entrance.

"Ready topsails and jibs."

"Ready topsails and jibs!" shouted Martin Chase.

Men raced up the rigging to attack the canvas as Major Ladd returned to the stern and shooed the two women toward the cabins.

"Nothing for you ladies to see here."

His wife glanced over her shoulder. "But, Edmund, why would Jenkins return those gowns if he was stealing them?"

Twelve

They had just cleared the harbor, and James Stuart was standing beside his sister at the wheel—when from each side of the deck rushed a figure from the darkness. Together they knocked Stuart flat. The bosun, a tall man with ropy muscles and a sea-battered face, had gone below deck to order the sweepers to withdraw their oars. He never returned to the helm.

Startled, but only for a moment, Kyrla pulled the belaying pin from her belt, reached over, and popped one of the figures on the back of the head. The man slumped to the deck, collapsing on Stuart's arm. At the same time his partner pinned Stuart's other arm and brought up a knife. Its blade flashed in the moonlight.

Stuart bucked and thrashed around, making himself a difficult target. But the difference was made when his sister released the wheel, stepped over, and kicked the man in the side. The wheel began to spin, and the man trying to stab her brother took Kyrla's kick under his upraised arm, forcing the knife blade higher. Kyrla grabbed the upraised arm and held on tight.

For the few seconds Kyrla faced the stern, she saw two more figures drop from the roof of the stern-side cabins and force the latch on the Ladds' cabin. Very quickly, the two women were dragged from their quarters. Their screams caused Major Ladd to open the door of the middle cabin, evaluate the situation, and bring his sword to bear.

At the helm, Kyrla had given Stuart enough of an opening to bring around his arm, smashing his elbow into the face of his assailant. The man's nose exploded in blood and he dropped the knife. While reaching for the knife, Gabriel came from out of nowhere and threw himself on Stuart's attacker.

The singer growled, probably false bravado, thought Stuart. Still, the head butt to the bloody face of his assailant knocked the man backwards, across the deck, and into the railing. From the bow, Alexander shouted for Kyrla to hold steady to the original course.

While Kyrla returned her attention to the wheel, Stuart scrambled to his feet and scanned the deck for his assailant and Gabriel. Only the unconscious man lay at his feet, the one Kyrla had laid out with the belaying pin. Stuart used a foot to roll the man over, and immediately recognized him as the spokesman for the transported men who had been huddled in the bow when the lines had been cast off.

"See to the women!" shouted Kyrla.

At the stern-side cabins, under the overhang, Susanna fought with two men, one of which finally threw her to the deck. Major Ladd already lay facedown, his sword on the deck, his wife kneeling beside him—that is, until the second man, a rather tall man, turned his attention to Mrs. Ladd.

How the transported personnel had reached the stern without him or his sister seeing them, Stuart couldn't fathom. That, plus the sudden attack, caused him pause. Something wasn't right, and it wasn't just the tall man taking Mrs. Ladd by the hair, pulling her head back, and trying to kiss her on the side of the neck.

The door to the middle cabin opened, and Billy appeared with Stuart's broadsword. The boy was too small to even raise the weapon. But he was bold. He shouted at the man molesting Mrs. Ladd and charged.

In response, the tall man backhanded the boy, knocking him away, then returned to trying to kiss Mrs. Ladd on the neck.

The broadsword dropped from the boy's hands, and Billy fell back, bounced off the bulkhead, and came at the man again. The molester let go of Mrs. Ladd once again, grabbed Billy, and with an ease that amazed Stuart, pitched the cabin boy across the deck, over the side, and into the water.

"No!"

Stuart raced to where Billy had disappeared. At the railing, he picked up the end of a coil of line, tied it off, and threw the line over the side. Then, in a matter of steps, he recrossed the deck and drove a shoulder into the tall man, knocking him off Mrs. Ladd's neck. When the two men rolled to a stop, Stuart came up with his knife—which he immediately plunged into the tall man's chest.

That made little difference. On his feet again, the tall man pushed Stuart away, then withdrew the knife, leaving a wound that leaked little or no blood. The transportee smiled, dropped the weapon to the deck, and advanced on Stuart—until an arrow struck him, piercing the top of his shoulder. Ignoring his wound again, the man turned to see where the shaft of wood had come from. When he did, another arrow passed through his chest. The tall man went down, screaming and thrashing about.

Major Ladd was on his feet again and he slashed at the man with his sword, practically decapitating the transportee. Once again, remarkably little blood appeared, but the body stopped thrashing about.

Ladd and Stuart turned their attention to the girl in time to see the man straddling Susanna leap to his feet and back away, only to come within range of Col. Ladd's sword.

Another head toppled to the deck.

"Secure the women in your wife's cabin and stand guard at the door!" ordered Stuart.

Ladd shot his sword into its sheath, and while he ushered his wife and the girl into the cabin, Stuart raced to the railing. The rope lay limp in the water.

Billy was gone!

Alexander was there, clapping Stuart on the back. When he did, Stuart came up with his knife.

"Avast there, Captain! It's me, Alexander."

Stuart put away his knife and wiped his sleeve across his face. "You all right?"

"Much better now. I was in the bow waiting for that actor to run us aground when the transportees turned on me like mad dogs. They didn't seem interested in slicing me up, more like ripping me to pieces with their teeth."

"Were you injured?"

"Only a few scratches, but I made sure they lost a lot of their teeth. Though I must say that didn't appear to bother them."

"How many were there?"

"Four or five."

"And you escaped—how?"

The African put his one arm around his friend and turned Stuart to face the bow. On the deck lay five transportees, twitching in the darkness. Each of them had at least one arrow through his torso, some two or more.

As Stuart and Alexander passed the helm, Kyrla smiled a weak smile. "That actor did what he said he'd do, Captain. We've reached blue water."

"Turn the ship around," ordered Stuart, after explaining Billy's fate.

"But, James, we can't do that!"

"I'm the captain and I say we bring her about."

Kyrla returned her attention to the wheel but directed her comments to the African. "You'd better talk some sense into him, Alexander. I start maneuvering a ship this size around in these waters, and we're going to rip out that hull everyone was so concerned about only a few minutes ago."

"I want Billy found! It was my fault that . . ."

Stuart could not tell them what he thought he'd seen: Billy being casually thrown over the side by one of the transported men.

"It was my fault," he repeated.

"It doesn't matter whose fault it was," said Alexander. "Kyrla is correct. We cannot return to Liverpool."

Stuart shook his head. "This is not right."

John Belle dropped to the deck, bow in hand, quiver empty. "Everyone all right?"

"I wouldn't be if you weren't such a good shot." Alexander glanced amidships. "You finished them all."

"They don't look dead." Belle gestured with his bow at the bodies twitching amidships.

Lucius and Donato appeared out of the darkness of the bow, and as they passed the five bodies, they grimaced.

"What happened here?" asked Lucius.

"The transported men tried to seize control of the ship."

Donato surveyed the twitching bodies with arrows through their torsos, then studied the woodsman and his bow.

"Good shooting, Belle," said Lucius.

"I'll check on Portia," said Donato. "She planned to take a turn around the deck after dark."

"And thank Gabriel," said Stuart. "He saved my life."

In this particular instance, Donato failed to flash one of his evil grins before walking away.

Martin Chase appeared from below deck.

"Where were you?" demanded Stuart.

"Doing what I always do once we shove off: taking a count of the passengers and looking for stowaways. The bosun's still checking the hull. I wanted to see if we'd cleared the harbor."

"We could've used you topside."

"Used me for what?"

Stuart waved him off. "Never mind."

Martin saw the twitching bodies. "What happened to them?"

"Stay away!" warned Lucius. "They appear to have contracted the plague."

Everyone but Fallows stepped back.

"Donato," called out Fallows, halting the small man before he disappeared below deck, "send Oren topside to assist in ridding the deck of this garbage."

Stuart studied the actor. "What are you saying, Fallows?"

"Throw them over the side."

Everyone looked at the actor.

He pointed at the five men. "Look at how they shake. They have fever and chills, and they're coughing up blood."

Soon, all nine bodies were over the side, including the two decapitated ones, along with their heads. Before the dead men went over the side, John Belle pulled his arrows from the bodies and observed there was little blood. That observation did not slow down the process, and once the bodies went into the ocean, Martin called for Billy to fetch a couple of bottles of whiskey from the captain's locker.

Stuart had to tell his first mate that the boy had been shoved over the side when he tried to stop one of the transportees from attacking Mrs. Ladd. Stuart was not yet ready to admit that one of the transportees had simply flung the boy over the side from amidships. Again Stuart scanned the deck.

Not a single hand or passenger topside.

Where was everyone? Had no one been disturbed?

He looked up. Not a sound from the crow's nest.

Where the devil was the watch commander?

Martin returned with the bottles, and they doused their hands with whiskey. Alexander poured liquor on his scratches and the major wiped his wife's neck liberally with the liquid. Everyone took a long pull from the bottles, though both women appeared embarrassed by drinking from a common bottle, repeatedly wiping off the mouth. Susanna didn't appear to have ever drunk anything so strong. She coughed and hacked until Mrs. Ladd slapped her on the back a couple of times.

Lucius looked at them quizzically.

Martin explained. "I never met a drunk who contracted the plague."

Lucius nodded, and Oren, after glancing at Lucius and receiving a nodding agreement, stuck out his hands, allowing Martin to pour the remaining whiskey over his hands. No one, not even Mrs. Ladd, complained this was a waste of good whiskey.

Susanna and the Ladds joined a short ceremony performed at the railing for the souls of the transportees. Mrs. Ladd said thanks for Billy and prayed for his soul, and everyone with the exception of Lucius Fallows made the sign of the cross.

Watching the bodies disappear into the wake, Martin said, "Let's hope the Crown never learns of this."

Alexander shrugged. "What better solution than to take the dregs of the empire and dump them at sea."

"Mr. Belle," said Lucius, speaking to the woodsman,

"if you don't want to spread the plague, I recommend you toss those arrows over the side."

John looked at James Stuart.

The sea captain shrugged. "You can always make more arrows."

The wooden arrows went over the side.

Fallows watched them go. "You should hunt in my homeland, Mr. Belle. The Carpathian Mountains are the largest mountains in Europe, and there you will find more bears and wolves than you'll have arrows for."

"Miss Chase," asked Stuart, "if you don't mind my asking, how did you get that man off you? One moment he was straddling you and the next he was on his feet and backing away."

"And into Major Ladd's sword," said Alexander, grinning.

"Please," said Mrs. Ladd, "think of what you're asking this young lady."

Susanna only stared at the deck.

Lucius stepped to her, his arms going around her shoulders. "Miss Chase, if you don't care to discuss . . ."

Susanna backed away, breaking contact with the hot breath she felt on her neck. She looked into the dark pools that were Lucius Fallows' eyes. She shivered.

"My apologies, Miss Chase," said Lucius, stepping back. "You do not need to be rescued again." Lucius returned to the railing where he had stood during the ceremony for the souls of the transportees.

Susanna stared at Fallows, then shook like a dog coming out of water.

Stuart also apologized, adding, "I mistook you for a fellow sailor. It was rude of me to ask such a question."

Susanna looked him. "A fellow sailor, you say?"

Stuart only smiled at her.

"Still," said Alexander, "despite Mrs. Ladd's objections, we'd like to know how you did it, since we made such a poor showing ourselves."

"What—what do you mean?"

"I mean the crew was dead asleep, even the night watch, and none of us appeared able to put even one of these men on his back. Oh, yes, Major Ladd and the woodsman did so, but none of us experienced seamen held up our end of the bargain."

"I—I don't know what I did." She stared at the deck once again. "I was resolved to my fate."

"My dear, if you are uncomfortable—" started Mrs. Ladd.

"No, no," said the girl, head coming up, "the captain must know he can depend on me. I am a member of the crew now."

At this declaration, a hint of a smile appeared at the corners of Stuart's mouth.

Susanna cleared her throat. "I closed my eyes and begin quoting the Twenty-third Psalm. Oh, and there was my necklace, the one with the gold cross you returned to me. I held it up between me and the man. Silly to think it would do any good."

From down the railing, Lucius laughed. "You are so right, Miss Chase."

Mrs. Ladd cleared her throat, and her husband spoke sharply to the actor. "Don't blaspheme, young man."

Lucius leveled his gaze at the Ladds and stared at the couple with such cold hatred that Mrs. Ladd wasn't the only one who trembled.

From overhead came a sonorous voice, a voice such

as might be heard in the best choirs in Europe.

Everyone looked up. Susanna gripped Stuart's arm.

"What's that?" asked Martin, peering into the rigging.

"Gabriel," said Lucius. "From time to time he's so overcome with joy that he breaks into song."

Thirteen

Stuart was ashamed of what had happened. Ships were believed to be a safe haven in a stormy world. At least that's what Stuart and his crew believed. Once a ship was over the horizon, mainland problems were left ashore, one of the attractions of life at sea. But the *Mary Stewart*, his ship, had exploded into anarchy. Because of this, Stuart almost forgot to thank Lucius Fallows for successfully maneuvering the *Mary Stewart* out of the harbor.

Fallows took this opportunity to remind Stuart that his troupe would not vary its routine, but would sleep during the day and make its first appearance the following evening. In the coming weeks, there would be performances of *Hamlet, Macbeth, Romeo & Juliet,* and a crowd favorite: *The Taming of the Shrew.* All this negotiated before the troupe had been invited aboard.

With dawn breaking, Stuart summoned Martin, Alexander, and Kyrla to the center stern-side cabin where Stuart now billeted to break out yet another bottle of whiskey. All four of them were red-eyed and exhausted, and they stank of whiskey.

"Besides Billy," reported the first mate, "I have confirmed that there are two other crew members missing."

Kyrla took the whiskey from the captain's locker and thumped the bottle on the table. Taking down mugs from a shelf, Alexander set them out and took a seat on the other side of the table from Kyrla. Martin joined him in the adjoining chair and poured the whiskey. Kyrla took her mug, downed it in one gulp, and clumped the mug on the table.

"Again!" she ordered.

Martin glanced at Stuart, who sat at the head of the table, puffing on his pipe with the stern window propped open.

"Stuart is my brother," said Kyrla, "not my father."

The first mate poured more whiskey, and Kyrla downed it again and placed the mug upside down on the table. She burped and leaned against the mirror on the false wall.

From the other side came the sounds of the Ladds preparing for bed—or simply trying to calm down. Mrs. Ladd had insisted her husband, not her maid, sleep at the foot of her bed tonight. Her husband had not argued the point.

Stuart looked up at his sister and the pipe came out of his mouth. "Girl down for the night?"

"I took care of it."

Martin put down his mug. "I don't like the way you put that."

"I still don't believe she's your cousin."

"You know, Kyrla, one day I'm going to forget you're a woman."

The redhead rolled off the wall and the hilts of a pair of knives dropped into both hands. "Then I'll help you remember."

Martin glanced at the knives, picked up his mug, and sipped from it. "Fight with a fool . . ."

"Don't worry, Martin dear. John Belle's planted outside our cabin door like a tall stalk of corn." Kyrla put away her knives.

"John wouldn't like being compared to anything as domesticated as a stalk of corn," said Stuart. "Sometimes I think he's about ready to pop, sitting on that platform all day."

"He already has popped," said Alexander, "and there are nine bodies to prove it. How does a man loose that many arrows so quickly?"

"His record is nineteen," said Martin, glumly.

"Nineteen?" asked the African.

"In one minute," said the first mate, not looking up from his mug. "Nineteen arrows in one minute."

They stared at him.

Martin noticed. "In an upcountry contest, which included some Cherokees, he once—"

There came a knock at the door. It was Phillippe Belle asking to join them. He was sent away.

"And don't bother your brother," called out Martin, since John Belle was posted outside the next-door cabin.

Stuart asked Alexander, "You take care of Jenkins?"

"He took the money with a smile. Well, a crooked smile where I'd popped him. He had no problem remaining behind. One of his wives lives in Liverpool."

"Where did he find those dresses?" asked Martin.

"Right outside the window where I dropped them." Alexander glanced at the redheaded woman, then looked into his mug. "I just hope the girl's handy with a needle and thread."

"Right outside where?" asked Kyrla, rolling off the wall again. "Where'd the girl's dresses come from?"

Picking up on what Stuart had begun to say, Martin asked the helmsman. "Are you handy with a needle and thread, Kyrla?"

"I don't have to be handy with a needle and thread."

"That's a shame," said Martin, "because it's all that's keeping me from asking your brother for your hand in marriage."

"I wouldn't marry you if you were the last man on earth." The redhead looked around the table. "All of you know something you're not sharing with me."

"We know lots of things we don't tell you."

"James?"

Her brother puffed away on his pipe.

She looked at the African.

Alexander continued to stare into his mug.

"Kyrla," said Stuart, "you wanted me to promote you to sailing master and I did. Worry about that the remainder of the voyage. It's your first trip as master."

"I don't know where Donato came from," said Alexander, turning to Stuart. "Fallows asked me to stand aside, so I left the bow. I didn't pass Donato leaving the bow, and yet he must've been there when the transportees attacked me."

"Four or five men in a coordinated attack—how would you notice anything?"

Across the narrow cabin, Kyrla continued to steam.

"Does anyone understand what just happened?" asked Martin. "We've had transportees aboard before, and they've made their play for the ship, but those nine men acted in unison. You'd think they were marines."

"A thoroughly trained squad of marines focused on their objective," added Stuart. "They went for the helm, the captain, and Alexander on the bow. Not to mention they knew how to draw out Major Ladd."

The room was quiet. Eventually, Martin said, "I have to say that it was good to have Fallows and his troupe aboard."

"Still, I never would have figured Gabriel for a fighter," said Alexander.

"He didn't so much fight as run into the fellow and knock him over the side." Stuart shook his head. "Poor Billy."

"Still," said Alexander, "if choosing sides, I never would've picked Gabriel."

"But why seize the ship when we were barely out of the harbor?" asked Martin.

Alexander played with his mug. "They might've been so nervous their leader had to strike."

"We were all dead men," said Stuart, staring at the pipe in his hand. "They planned to offload the goods nearby, perhaps Ireland, and scuttle the ship."

"But wouldn't it be more profitable to sell the goods in the colonies?" asked Kyrla, finally joining the discussion.

"Not if you received the goods for free."

Martin shook his head. "They would've come below and killed me while I was taking a count of the passengers, and I wouldn't have known why. Crazy."

After another pull on his pipe, Stuart asked, "Did you see what the girl did? She frightened off that man with a gold cross and saying the Twenty-third Psalm."

"I don't believe her," commented Kyrla.

"No surprise there," said the first mate, "but she's a good girl. She asked for a Bible before turning in."

Stuart removed his pipe from his mouth again. "I'd ask for a Bible after what we've just been through."

"So," said Alexander, grinning at Martin, "you'd pick the girl for your side."

Kyrla rolled her eyes. "I'm off to bed. I'm not spending what's left of the night with a bunch of bucks in season."

The three men watched her go, and once the cabin door closed behind her, a smile spread across each man's face. Martin chuckled and reached for the bottle.

Alexander held out his mug. "You have to admit Susanna's a pretty young thing."

Martin looked up, about to pour the African a drink. "She's my cousin, for goodness sake."

"Oh, as if cousins haven't married before."

"She's trouble," said Stuart, puffing on his pipe again. "A girl that pretty onboard is nothing but trouble."

"She may be, Captain," said Alexander, grinning, "but that's only because she's not *your* cousin."

Fourteen

Lucius Fallows pushed open the cabin door without ceremony or Oren's assistance. He found everyone sitting on the narrow bunks just as they had during their earlier conversation.

Gabriel smiled at him from the corner. "Put your girlfriend to bed, did you, Lucius? Is that what kept you?"

One moment Fallows was closing the door, the next he was across the small cabin, where he pulled Gabriel off the bed and held him off his feet by the throat.

"Stupid! Stupid! Stupid!"

The other members of the troupe jumped to their feet with Donato and Portia pleading with Lucius to release the singer.

Gabriel tried to pry Lucius' hands loose; his feet kicked, but his only sound was a gurgling noise.

"Please, Lucius," pleaded Portia, "don't hurt him."

"I could tear him limb from limb!"

Donato put a hand on Fallows' shoulder. "Not his throat, Lucius. Not his throat."

When Lucius did not desist, Donato called to Oren, who immediately opened the door and entered the cabin.

Lucius explained. "Gabriel's the one behind the mutiny!"

The singer continued to struggle, feet kicking, fists slamming into Fallows' hands and shoulders, and soon into Lucius' face. Gabriel's own face did not turn red but remained constantly pale. The same could be said of Fallows.

"Oren, assist us here," said Donato.

Oren squeezed past the small man and the woman and put a hand on his master's shoulder. "My lord, please . . ."

Fallows did not appear to hear him.

"You're a fool, Gabriel! Just what did you think you'd accomplish with that little performance?"

When Gabriel only gurgled, Portia said, "He was hungry, Lucius. We're all hungry."

"Master?" asked the burly man again.

"Oren, remove your hand from my shoulder."

Oren did, and Gabriel continued to sputter and struggle as he hung in the air.

"Portia's right, Lucius," said Donato. "None of us could wait until we learned which member of the crew should accidentally fall overboard and drown, and would not be missed."

"Yes, my lord," agreed Oren, "but now there's enough food for a whole week. I've stowed it away where none of these people will find it."

"Please, Lucius," begged Portia, "not all of us are as strong as you are."

There was a knock at the door.

All heads turned toward the cabin door.

"Mr. Fallows?" It was the girl.

Lucius dropped Gabriel to the bed, on top of what appeared to be a pile of dirty laundry. Oren went to the door and opened it, at least enough to see.

"One moment, Miss." He closed the door. "It is the girl, my lord, the object of your attention."

Oren made way for Lucius, and he and Donato took seats on either side of Gabriel and opposite Portia. Both men pulled the woozy man to an upright position.

Fallows surveyed the room. Everyone appeared normal, except for Gabriel, who struggled to catch his breath, hacking and coughing.

He opened the door.

Susanna stood in the hallway, holding Fallows' cape. She curtsied and held out the cape. Though tired, the girl appeared pleased to see him.

"Just returning your garment, sir. I've even brushed it."

She glanced into the cabin, but all she could see was Portia sitting on the edge of one of the beds. The woman smiled condescendingly. Someone coughed and cleared his throat.

"Oh, I didn't mean to interrupt."

Lucius took the cape. "Are you sure you don't need this, Miss Chase? After all, you came aboard with very little clothing."

A sneer from Portia. Her nose elevated.

Susanna held out her arms, displaying her new gown, which, with its high neckline, covered the necklace. Truth be known, she was euphoric from surviving—with honor—the most treacherous night of her life.

"Remember where this came from?" Susanna brought down her arms. A hand rose to her mouth. "I'm sorry. That was rather prideful of me."

She crossed herself, and Lucius stepped back and took a deep breath. From inside the cabin, Portia hissed.

Susanna didn't appear to notice. She had bent over to pick up a basket sitting by the cabin door. "I was on my way downstairs—er, the hold, to bring up some eggs for breakfast. Which is very soon. It's breaking dawn."

She curtsied, then was off down the passageway, heading for the ladder leading to the hold. Behind her, Lucius tossed the cape to Oren and hurried after her.

"Miss Chase, may I accompany you? The hold's not the sort of place a young lady should go unaccompanied."

Susanna smiled over her shoulder. "I guess you're right. I'm used to running out to the barn and picking up a few eggs."

"Miss Chase," said Lucius, catching up with her at the ladder and insisting that he precede her down the ladder, "I can assure you that this ship is not any barn."

"That may be true," said Susanna, peering into the hold. "I've been told there are hogs down there, even a cow or two."

At the other end of the passageway, Martin turned the corner and saw Lucius and Susanna disappear down the ladder. The first mate hurried after them, then stopped, wondering what business it was of his. Having stopped, Martin overheard what was being said in one of the cabins.

A voice coughed, then cleared his throat. "I've got the boy. Let's eat."

Martin wasn't sure he'd heard properly, so, as those on the other side of the door noisily bit into their meal, he hurried along the passageway in the direction of the ladder.

FIFTEEN

The following morning, Stuart slept late, slept deeply, and slept in a nightshirt. His trousers lay over the back of a chair, his shoes under the chair, ready to be put on at a moment's notice. Sword and pistols hung from grommets on the bulkhead. Still, whenever a watch was called, Stuart woke, glanced at the wind vane in the deck beams above, pulled back the curtain covering the stern window, and fell back to sleep, reassured by the passage of the *Mary Stewart* through blue water, the ship filling all its canvas.

Until someone knocked on the door.

"Captain Stuart! Captain Stuart!"

Stuart raised his head and stared at the door. A book lay open on his chest, *Plutarch's Lives,* and light came through the edges of the curtain on the stern window. Still, the *Mary Stewart* moved easily through the water. Nothing sounded out of harmony.

"Yes?" he called out, sitting up and sticking his bare white legs over the side of the bed. They stuck out from under his nightshirt. *"Yes?"*

The Charleston Vampire

The girl opened the door, saw his white legs, and closed it, well, almost closed it.

"I'm sorry, Captain. I really am."

"No," said Stuart, wrestling to his feet, a struggle because he slept in a trundle bed that slid from the wall and rolled across the floor, out from under Kyrla's bed in the adjoining cabin.

With the assistance of the table, Stuart balanced himself to pull on his pants. He felt rotten, and he desperately wished it had been the whiskey from last night.

It was not.

It was Billy.

They should've gone back for the boy.

Finally able to stand, Stuart padded the few steps across the room and opened the door, which had remained cracked. The girl stood there with a plate of food and cup of tea.

He didn't see any of that. "What's wrong, Miss Chase?" Sticking his head out, he glanced left and right, then toward the bow, upward toward the rigging.

"No, no, Captain," said Susanna, holding the plate and cup of tea where he could see. "Breakfast." She wore a bib apron over her dress. A head scarf gathered her reddish-blond hair.

Rarely having food served in his cabin unless served to his whole staff, Stuart could only stare at the plate.

Kyrla appeared, and in her hoarse voice, demanded, "Why are you bothering the captain? There's no emergency."

Susanna turned her head away as if expecting a blow. "It's—it's . . ."

98

Steve Brown

"It's breakfast," said the first mate, crossing the deck
to the stern-side cabins. In Martin's hand was his own
mug of steaming tea. "And it's quite good, so stand
aside, Kyrla, or report to your duty station."

"I don't have duty. I woke up and found your cousin
gone."

Martin noticed Kyrla was dressed, complete with
boots. "You didn't sleep in those clothes."

"What business is it of yours what I sleep in?"

"Silence!" ordered Stuart. "It's too early for you two
to be at it again."

Stuart gestured Susanna to step inside. She did,
but when he closed the door behind them—to shut out
Kyrla and Martin's bickering—she immediately asked:
"Sir, would you mind leaving that door open?"

It took a moment, but Stuart grasped what she
meant. He jerked open the door and ordered her from
the cabin.

"You may leave the food."

Susanna put down the plate and cup and left the
cabin, head bowed.

"Thank you," said Stuart, coming to the door.

She turned and smiled. "Oh, you're quite welcome,
sir."

Kyrla and Martin were still going at it, so Susanna
gave them a wide berth and headed for the below-deck
stairs.

"Is it possible you two could take this somewhere
else?"

Stuart closed the door, sat down, and stared at the
food. Suddenly, he pushed back the chair, went to the
door, and flung it open. The girl was gone.

"Find the girl!"

Martin and Kyrla stared at him.

"I said: Find the girl!"

They did, and Kyrla returned with Susanna in tow. She knocked on the cabin door and opened it, shooing Susanna inside ahead of her.

"What's she done, James? If she won't tell, I'll get it out of her—woman to woman."

Martin appeared at the door again. "What's this?"

Kyrla explained that his cousin had wronged her brother. "What'd she do, James?" she repeated.

While Kyrla talked, Stuart continued to eat. Now, he looked up at the girl, head hanging, hands clasped in front of her, close to tears.

"Miss Chase, who told you to bring this food to my cabin?"

Without looking up, Susanna whispered, "The cook."

"Now see here, girl, you can't bother the captain unless there's an emergency." When Kyrla tried to go on, Stuart told his sister to shut up.

"Miss Chase, do you know there's a rule not to bother the captain unless there's an emergency?"

"I do now."

"Do you know *why* there's such a rule?"

"Well," said Susanna, looking at him from under her eyebrows, "I guess because you're so important."

Stuart laughed. "Wish that were so."

Slicing into the eggs, he found something inside and included the piece of meat in his bite. "Captains never sleep. Oh, they go to bed, but there's always one last thing to check, then another to check, then another.

For that reason, the captain is afforded the luxury of not being bothered unless it's truly an emergency."

Susanna's cheeks became spots of red. "That's why the cook said to knock hard and to speak loudly. He said you were a sound sleeper."

"And now you're aware that there are those on this ship you cannot fully trust for they will lead you astray."

Susanna said nothing.

"For example," said Stuart, returning to his eggs, "you can trust your cousin, but you cannot trust my sister."

Kyrla exploded in a torrent of curses.

Stuart shot a look at Susanna, who appeared stunned to hear such language. He told them all to get out.

They did.

A few moments later, the first mate knocked on the door and reentered the cabin.

Stuart didn't look up from his plate as Martin took a seat at the table. "Why don't you marry the woman? Then you can leave her ashore."

"Are you crazy? Kyrla's much too difficult to live with. You, yourself, should know that. She's your sister."

"I know nothing of the sort. I left home before she became of age, and if she couldn't do the job, she'd be ashore this very moment." He stared at the door. "And Kyrla may have made her last North Atlantic run for Stuart and Company."

"I wouldn't be so hard on her. It's just women squabbling."

"I didn't see the girl squabbling, nor cursing. I've

warned Kyrla about such language. There are civilians aboard."

"Well . . ."

"Then, at the pain of repeating myself, why don't you marry my sister?"

Martin started with his explanation, but Stuart interrupted. "It was a rhetorical question. Is there something you wanted?" Stuart took another bite of eggs. "You know, these aren't half bad. They have something in them."

"It's a ham omelet, and I had to fight for my share. Susanna said she cooked it with fresh eggs."

Stuart's head came up. "You let her go below?"

"Fallows accompanied her."

"Fallows was up this morning?"

"Only to go below with Susanna. I haven't seen anything of them this morning."

Stuart said nothing, only gazed off in the distance. Fallows had told Stuart that he and his troupe hailed from the Carpathian Mountains, a place where the sun rarely shone, and for that reason the bright sunlight of the North Atlantic troubled their eyes. The actor also said he'd had a difficult time convincing the troupe to make the trip. In London, everyone felt comfortable in all the fog.

Martin broke into his thoughts. "You look rotten."

"I feel rotten, and every time I drop off, I see Billy at the window, pounding on the glass, asking to come aboard." Stuart paused. "The last thing I told him was that I'd feed him to the sharks if he revealed where we found the girl."

"Oh, come on," said Martin, leaning on the table,

"you can't hold yourself responsible for what happens during a mutiny."

"I do."

There was nothing either of them could say to that, so the two men sat quietly, each sipping his tea.

Eventually, Martin said, "I don't envy your conversation with Billy's parents."

"They knew the danger. We all know the danger."

"No, we don't," said Martin, putting down his tea. "We just think we do. Anyway, despite what occurred last night, the *Mary Stewart* appears to be shipshape."

"Perhaps," said Stuart rather thoughtfully, "you should lower men over the side to check the hull."

Martin chuckled. "I'm sure we'll know about it when one of the seams parts."

Stuart ate his potatoes and followed that with a biscuit and another sip of tea. "And not a single passenger or crew member came topside."

"Not to help out—no. But, like me, they didn't know anything was amiss. And there's more disturbing news."

Stuart put down his cup and pinched the top of his nose. "What is it this time?"

"Mrs. Ladd heard the night watch was to be brought up on charges, so she's requested, through her husband, that while your court of inquiry is in session, that you, as commanding officer of the *Mary Stewart*, hold an inquiry into the virtue of one Susanna Chase."

"Why, for God's sake?"

"It seems not only did Susanna come aboard without any clothing last night, she also wore no undergarments."

Sixteen

Once Stuart finished breakfast, he shaved, dressed, and then strolled the main deck, content for a while; that is, until thoughts of Billy the cabin boy reoccurred. Stuart didn't know why he'd taken the death of one child more seriously than any other. Children died all the time, their parents too, but he suspected it had to do with last night's chaos. As Martin had asked: Why did the nine men act in unison?

Yes. Why?

Many of the passengers were taking some air, but fortunately, he did not see the Bentley family. Given the enthusiasm of its matriarch, Stuart wouldn't be surprised if, in his capacity as ship's captain, he didn't officiate at the marriage of at least one of the Bentley girls before they docked in Charles Town.

After nodding to passengers taking some air, and answering the usual questions about the differences between sharks and porpoises, Stuart checked the status of the lines. All had been re-coiled, and a badly painted sign alerted the boys on the ship that the lines were not playthings. He found a couple of places where the rigging needed to be rewoven and mentioned this to the bosun, the officer in charge of ship's maintenance. The bosun added the reweaving to his list and reported that there was the usual dampness inside the keel but no seams had opened.

Rounding the stern for the first time, Susanna appeared topside with a steaming cup. She curtsied. "Tea, Captain?"

"Thank you." He nodded and took the cup.

"Sorry to have alarmed you this morning, sir. I can promise that won't happen again."

"Any new sailor will be the butt of many jokes and that was simply your first. On my part, I would like to apologize for my sister's language, and as a result, you may find her on her knees more often than not in your billet."

"Oh, but it was no matter." Still, the girl crossed herself.

"You betray your agreement by crossing yourself."

Stuart continued toward the head of the ship, stepping out onto the bow. He encouraged Susanna to accompany him, and gave her a hand as she stepped over a variety of pulley blocks with associated ropes or cables for hoisting.

"Does this mean I can trust your sister, Captain Stuart?"

"You can now."

They stood there watching the ship slice through the water on a beautiful September day of blue sky and blue sea. The *Mary Stewart* had reached the Atlantic swells and seas ran at four feet, visibility was to the horizon, with no clouds, and a strong wind blew at their backs—information gathered by Stuart without thinking.

Something else he gathered—how relaxed he felt around this girl. Why not? The breakfast had been delicious.

Stuart cut off the thought. He had infinitely more responsibilities than this one girl, no matter how winsome she was.

Referring to their earlier conversation, he said, "The *Mary Stewart* is a new world for you, Miss Chase, and there will be errors. Just don't repeat the same one twice."

"Oh, no, sir, I would not."

Without warning, a gust of wind cut across the bow, and Susanna had to fight to keep her dress and apron down.

Gesturing with his cup at her dilemma, Stuart said, "See your cousin for some shot. Sew the shot into your hem, and the breeze, which is constant on a ship, will hardly trouble you. If the shot is rolled in animal fat, it won't rust either. Your dress may have a soiled look at the hem, but the dirt will come out easier."

"Thank you, sir."

And they returned to watching the *Mary Stewart* slice through the water. The ocean was blue, flat, and endless, with only the bowsprit ahead of them.

"Oh, my," said the girl, sounding breathless. "Whoever stands here, with their back to the rest of the ship, might think they were the king of the world."

Stuart chuckled. "If they weren't responsible for

all that's behind them, yes, they might have such feelings."

A few minutes later they returned to their stroll on the main deck, which had begun to shake itself out and take on a sense of normalcy. Earlier that morning religious services had been conducted by a Presbyterian minister on his way to the South Carolina upcountry, and Stuart had to figure, by the number of Presbyterian ministers he had ferried to Charles Town, the South Carolina upcountry had to be filled with plenty of Presbyterians or members of other denominations proselytized by them. And below deck, out of sight of the preacher and away from any breeze, a cabin had been set aside for card playing, mostly whist.

A man played a guitar, another played a fife, a third, a fiddle—and watched the young women taking their daily constitutional. Alicia Bentley appeared topside and began escorting two of her sisters around the main deck, hooking one sister by each arm, the two sisters' free hands each bearing parasols shading all three girls. Alicia had to keep a tight rein on Katie Bentley, who wished to stop and speak with every young man, sailor, or passenger. The youngest of the sisters, Lindy, remained below deck, as her family did not wish to offend other passengers with the sight of her pregnancy. When the Bentleys strolled past, Katie focused her smile on the captain, while Alicia had eyes only for Susanna. Marion Bentley, who was hardly ever seen without a book, gestured toward the railing.

"It's not that you couldn't reach America by only using sails, but there are sea currents that make the trip much faster. What you must do is sail south and catch the current from the Canary Islands, then onto . . ."

When the Bentleys made the turn at the bow—a more cordial place now with the transportees gone—the three women passed boys down on their hands and knees playing jacks and young girls jumping one long rope and chanting: "Rich man, poor man, beggar man, thief . . ." As the Bentleys strolled by on the far side of the main deck, the man playing the guitar broke into song:

"Young ladies are coming to the colonies, and in the afternoons, I can see them walking . . ."

The Bentleys laughed and pressed on, passing Alexander demonstrating to older boys how to fire a cannon. The cannon would be fired the following week, and fired at a target built and set adrift by these same boys, but today the African was giving the boys instruction, and more importantly, something to look forward to. The following evening Alexander would entertain children of all ages with stories of Blackbeard the pirate. Alexander had once been marooned by Blackbeard, but for some reason, that episode of the African's life never made it into any of his tales.

Oak benches and tables had been set forward of the helm, and at these tables, under tarpaulins made from discarded sails, sat male passengers arguing politics and religion, drinking tea or hot chocolate, and sharing a noontime meal of cold ham, pork, and salad, all shore-side staples that would not be as readily available as the voyage progressed toward America. Among those at the tables were Major Ladd and Phillippe Belle.

Voices drifted over on the wind to where Susanna and Stuart leaned against the starboard railing, snatches of arguments over original sin versus the doctrine that replaced it: a benevolent God who, having set the universe in motion, had given human beings the power to reason. Now it was up to humans to comprehend the orderly working of his creation.

"Therefore," said Phillippe Belle, raising his voice and his cup, and smiling in Susanna's direction, "it's the responsibility of right-thinking men and women to make certain that the church and state conform to these natural laws."

Many said they would drink to that, and did.

Because of Phillippe's direct stare, it took a moment before Susanna could question what she'd heard.

"Right-thinking women, Captain?"

"Evidently so. Mrs. Ladd has confiscated my cabin for a tea club and the opportunity to squabble over these same issues, only in a more polite manner."

"Sir, I have heard such discussions in the Worthingtons' study and billiards room, but none among the female friends of Mrs. Worthington."

The sea captain smiled. "Perhaps Mrs. Worthington knew how to properly conduct a tea club."

Stuart saw Major Ladd rise from one of the tables and head in their direction. "But I wouldn't worry. Such conversations are rarely heard in America. In America, everything takes a backseat to the accumulation of money."

"The accumulation of money? Are you serious?"

"Oh, yes. Colonists look for anything that will turn an extra shilling."

"Isn't that rather crass?"

"If it is, then avarice has affected everyone in the colony of South Carolina."

Once Major Ladd made his good mornings, he asked, "Are you prepared to do your moral duty, Captain?"

Ladd glanced at Susanna, who had curtsied and now stared at her feet, hands held in front of her.

"At six bells, Major." To Susanna, he said, "That would be three o'clock, Miss Chase. And Miss Chase, Major Ladd and I may need your assistance, so maintain your availability."

Susanna nodded but did not look up.

Ladd glanced at the men at the tables. "I, myself, have opinions about philosophy and the natural sciences."

About to take a sip of his tea, Stuart looked over his cup at the officer. "And are we to hear those ideas now, Major?"

"I daresay not." Ladd glanced at Susanna. "Science, mathematics, or philosophy, what interest would these subjects hold for a young woman? But I must say I am looking forward to meeting this Benjamin Franklin of Philadelphia. He appears quite remarkable for a colonial. Flying a kite in a storm to conduct a scientific inquiry. He's fortunate he wasn't killed."

Stuart looked into the rigging. "There's a great deal you could learn from John Belle, and he's a passenger on this ship."

Ladd shaded his eyes from the noonday sun and peered at the platform halfway up the forward mast. "Strange man, Belle."

Ladd brought down his hand. "But I really doubt any colonial has something to teach a member of the British Army."

"He could teach you Indian fighting. The French have allies within the Indian nations who are encouraged to take out their restlessness on us colonials."

"Oh, yes, the Red Man. Looking forward to seeing some of those, too."

"You may do so, sir, and not in the manner you expect. During King George's War, the French and their Indian allies destroyed Saratoga, killing and capturing more than one hundred inhabitants. As a result, all settlements north of Albany were abandoned, and I can promise you, Major, those settlements were not abandoned because of the fear of an invasion by France."

"Yes, yes, another subject of little interest to the gentler sex." Ladd drew himself up. "Sir, I have been told that you play an exceedingly good game of chess, and this is one of the reasons I booked passage on your ship. Perhaps a match later this evening?"

"With the business to be conducted this afternoon, perhaps another time, Major. There are many long nights ahead of us, and I'd be pleased to face you over a chessboard. That is, if your wife and her friends have not commandeered my cabin for her tea club."

"Well, the ladies must have their diversions."

"This is truer than you may believe. Soon, we shall all desire a diversion or two and come to see the evening's entertainments as the high point of our day, though I've heard Gabriel won't be able to sing tonight. He has a sore throat."

Ladd glanced at the girl again. "Very well, then I will see you at three." He doffed his hat and left them at the railing.

"So," muttered Stuart, "I must yield half my cabin because of my reputation as a chess player?"

Susanna chuckled. "Perhaps it's because of your reputation as a pirate hunter. That is, if you don't mind my expressing interest in a subject holding little interest for my sex."

Stuart eyed the girl. "You certainly don't have the demeanor of a scullery maid, Miss Chase."

"I was a personal maid, sir, and when you lose your family, you become an excellent listener and remember a great deal. Am I speaking too boldly?"

"Not at all. Are you planning on remembering everything you learn aboard the *Mary Stewart?*"

"As much as you are willing to teach me, sir."

He chuckled. "That would make you a formidable woman."

"But the man who killed Blackbeard should fear no woman."

"I did not kill Blackbeard, though I do not discourage such gossip. My father did the deed. I, myself, am no more than a glorified bookkeeper, steering a barge filled with barrels of rice to England and returning with pewter plates, bowls, and mugs."

As if to make this point, Martin Chase interrupted to report a missing pig. There was a nod from Martin and a modified curtsy from Susanna.

"We've searched high and low, Captain."

"I would rather think—regarding the hiding place of the pig—that it would require only searching low."

The first mate rolled his eyes, and Susanna hid a chuckle behind her hand.

Stuart realized he was trying to impress the girl and his tone became more serious. "The count must've been wrong when we sailed from London."

"I, myself, Captain, made the count."

Susanna tried to excuse herself, but Stuart objected.

"Miss Chase, please do not fly at the first hint of unpleasantness."

"Yes, sir." The girl remained, hands clasped in front of her, head down.

"Then a thorough search for the remains is in order."

"That it is, Captain, and I have men doing just that, but all we've found is a blood trail and no pig."

Stuart scanned the main deck. "If someone butchered a pig, why have we not smelled the smoke? No one eats pig meat raw, and raw pork will not keep more than a couple of days."

"It's a puzzle, Captain, and why I brought it to your attention."

"Anything else?"

"I'm sorry to say I must report Ingram in his cups again."

"Then pay him off, give him a small bonus, and put him ashore at Charles Town. I will not suffer drunks aboard my ship."

"The fault is mine, sir, and for that I apologize."

Stuart clapped his friend on the shoulder. "Miss Chase, your cousin is much too affable to be a first mate, and we are endeavoring to prove that to him."

"More likely I am proving that to myself," groused Martin. After nodding to Susanna, he took his leave.

"A missing pig?" she asked.

"And a much more serious issue than any seaman found drunk. If you don't stamp out thievery when you find it, such occasions can, and will, eventually affect the safety of the ship. Thus, you see me as I am, Miss Chase, a glorified pig wrangler."

"Oh," said Susanna, with a laugh, "but that cannot be. You sail the Seven Seas."

"Only one, Miss Chase, only one."

They both looked out to sea.

"Captain?"

"Yes?"

"Who is Mary Stewart?"

"My grandmother. She was killed in Glasgow the same day my father shipped out for America. Probably a good idea since my father had just murdered the man who killed her, but their name was spelled as the French do: Stuart, as is mine. My grandfather was a Highlander."

"A Catholic?" Susanna's family was Catholic and she had been cautioned to never tell anyone. Ever.

About 1700, Stuart's grandfather kidnapped a woman from the Scottish Lowlands who became Stuart's grandmother. He'd taken her to the Highlands, where Stuart's father was born. When the grandfather died in battle and the women were being divided up during a drinking bout, the grandmother took the opportunity to slip away with her son, not to the Lowlands of Scotland but to disappear in Glasgow, the ship-building capital of the British Empire.

"And," said Susanna, "you spell the name of your ship in the English style because of the low regard Englishmen have for Mary Stuart."

"Well," said Stuart, smiling, "Catholic Mary did cause a good bit of trouble for us Protestants."

"Yes. Mary, Queen of Scots. I believe they chopped off her head."

Susanna wondered if her cousin Martin was a Catholic but would never dare ask. Still, late at night when she could not sleep, she pondered whether her family had been wiped out by the plague because of their Catholicism. And what did that mean for her? Susanna said her morning and evening prayers in Latin, under her breath.

"Being gone all these months must be difficult for your family."

"I have no family, Miss Chase. My wife died giving birth."

"Sir," said Susanna, crossing herself, "I am truly sorry for your loss. I should not have inquired."

Stuart shook his head. "I should not have married the girl. She had always been a sickly child."

"But still you did."

"Well, there's no accounting for matters of the heart, is there?"

Susanna returned his smile. "I certainly hope not."

"Still, each time I return to Charles Town, I have an opportunity to visit my children."

"Oh, there were children? I was afraid to ask."

"I am the father of a boy and a girl five years of age. Twins run in the Belle family. They reside in my mother's house."

"Twins?"

"My father married a Belle."

"Then you are related to John and Phillippe?"

"They are my cousins, as Martin is yours."

"Truly, Charles Town must be a very small place."

She gripped the railing. "I look forward to meeting your children, sir. I know a few games I might teach them. I've substituted for many a nanny."

Stuart may not have heard this. He was scanning the deck and the overhead. Sailors were reworking the rigging or sewing canvas or leaning against the railing and smoking pipes. Still, none could resist a glance at the girl.

"Er—yes. Breakfast was delicious, Miss Chase. I understand you and Mr. Fallows went below to personally select the eggs."

"I don't think Mr. Fallows has that much interest in eggs, sir, but he was kind enough to accompany me."

"Miss Chase, there are many dark corners on any ship."

"As Mr. Fallows instructed, and I will make sure someone accompanies me whenever I go below. You know, the hold is a rather dark place for chickens to roost, pigs to wallow, and cows never to be able to stretch their legs."

"The chickens are only sequestered there until they calm down, though I haven't seen Mr. Fallows on the list of those to sup with me at my table."

"They are an odd bunch, sir. Oh, that makes me sound like an old gossip." She made the sign of the cross in front of a chest tightly wrapped and looking quite different from last night when rescued from the brothel.

"Oh! What was that?" Susanna pointed at a fin. "A shark?"

"Porpoises. Unlike sharks they travel in packs."

"Oh, look how they leap!"

And they watched the porpoises leap and swim alongside the *Mary Stewart* until Stuart asked, "Miss Chase, I'm of the impression that you are quite devout, is that not true?"

"I try, sir, and I thank you for the Bible. I said my prayers last night and again this morning."

"This is not the point I wish to make, but do not mention your past to anyone on the ship, other than your experiences on the Worthington estate. As you learned earlier today, there are those who would lay traps to snare you."

Susanna looked Stuart in the eye. She could not understand why she felt so comfortable around this man. True, he'd saved her life, but she had no such feelings for Lucius Fallows. It must be something about being in command of such a large ship or perhaps the loss of his poor wife. And those two children without a parent. James Stuart should quit this ship immediately upon reaching Charles Town and remain ashore with his children.

Stuart was speaking. ". . . while that gesture proves you are devout, there are a good number . . ."

Stuart became aware of the crew staring at them, and asked, in a loud and irritable voice, if they didn't have tasks to perform. The men returned to their work or their pipes, at least until their captain turned away.

He went on to add: "What I'm trying to say is crossing yourself is an excellent practice, Miss Chase, but you are no longer a child. You no longer wear the bonnet."

"Thank you for that, sir. Onboard a ship, it would be an unwieldy garment."

"Yes, yes. And by reducing the number of times you make the sign of the cross, I'm sure you'll acquire some gentlemen friends."

"In truth, Captain, I care little of what other gentlemen may think of me, but I would not wish to lose your high regard, if you hold me in such regard."

"That I do. From the very moment you came aboard, Miss Chase, I have admired your courage and steadfastness." He reached for her neck, "Pardon me, but that's not the proper way to wear that piece of jewelry around so many sailors."

Susanna's head jerked back as Stuart fingered the chain and ran his finger down it until the gold cross appeared. The cross fell across the bodice, but it was his touch . . .

Unnoticed by them, Phillippe Belle had left the tables and now joined them. "And what are you doing, Captain, if I might be so bold as to ask?"

Stuart jerked his hand away. "Not that it's any of your business, Mr. Belle, but I was encouraging Miss Chase to wear her cross outside her garment as a reminder to the young men onboard this ship that she remains pious and virtuous. Would you be one of those young men, Mr. Belle? One who must be reminded of this young woman's piousness and virtuousness?"

Phillippe drew himself up. "I would not, sir. Women hold a place of honor in my life."

More people crossed the deck and joined them at the railing; Alexander with the sextant, a rolled-up chart under his arm, and a pencil stuck behind an ear. In Alexander's company were two of the Bentley sisters, Katie, the flirt, and Marion, the bookworm. Katie carried

Stuart's diary, Marion his almanac. Marion's scissor-glasses had a ring in the end of the handle through which a ribbon was placed, and hung around her neck, always there for easy pick up and focus.

The girls curtsied, and Katie smiled. "We are here for our lesson in . . . ?" She glanced at her sister.

"Celestial navigation," said Marion Bentley. She explained to Susanna: "Using angular measurements, or sights, between the sun and the horizon. The moon is used at night."

Susanna had no idea what they were talking about and her pang of jealousy confused her even more.

"Miss Bentley, have you checked the calibration of the instrument?"

"Aye, aye, sir. When I placed the shades on the device, I checked the alignment of the mirrors."

Stuart returned the teacup to Susanna. "With your permission, Miss Chase."

He nodded, Susanna curtsied, and from the rigging, several sailors gathered overhead, fascinated that an instrument could actually tell their captain where their ship was on this wide and featureless ocean. Such readings were something akin to witchcraft.

"Of course," continued Marion as they walked away, "if you shoot the moon at night, there is no horizon, and the captain would use the horizon on the instrument."

Before Stuart followed them, he reminded Susanna of her responsibilities to the galley and Mrs. Ladd.

Glancing at Phillippe Belle, Stuart added, "Those responsibilities may call even now."

Phillippe chuckled as Stuart walked away. "We seem

to have both a guide and a ship's captain all in one."

Susanna did not comment, but only watched the Bentley girls stroll away with James Stuart.

Seventeen

The court of inquiry was convened by Stuart at six bells, and the jury was made up of John Belle and Lucius Fallows. Stuart wished to have Fallows included in the two-man jury because he believed the man had displayed exceptionally clear thinking for a foreigner. In deference to the Romanian's difficulty with the sunlight of the North Atlantic, Alexander escorted Fallows from below and quickly across the deck under a parasol and into Stuart's modified cabin where the curtains had been pulled and a lantern hung from an above-deck beam. Martin Chase ran the ship, and Alexander, as sergeant at arms, was posted at the door inside Stuart's cabin.

Stuart sat at the head of the table behind a small, portable, wedged-shaped writing desk that provided a raised and slightly angled surface. Inside a compartment under the lid were writing materials, and on top of the angular surface sat a mallet. A Bible lay on the table across from the jury.

To the two-man jury, he said, "If any of those men who mutinied had survived, even one of them, they would've been hanged by the neck until dead. That's the penalty for mutiny."

Belle and Fallows nodded, as did the sergeant at arms, though Alexander, technically, did not have a vote.

Stuart picked up the mallet and brought it down. "First case."

The sailor, a usually reliable man, was marched in, dragging his chains. The two jury members sat on one side of the table facing the sailor, whose back was against the mirror on the opposite wall.

Stuart asked the sailor if he had fallen asleep during his watch. The sailor said that he must have done so because the first mate had found him asleep.

"Do you have anything else to add in your defense?"

"No, sir, I do not."

"Then I shall pass sentence."

Lucius shifted in his chair. "Captain, may I ask a question?"

"Is it a question regarding procedure?"

"Actually, I wondered if there was any chance of leniency."

"That is determined by the captain."

"What I mean is, is the court open to mitigating circumstances?"

"When the safety of the ship is at question, sir, there are no mitigating circumstances."

Fallows nodded and leaned back in his chair. He found it astonishing that someone so young could be in charge of a three-mast ship, but Lucius had heard that those living in the British colonies believed they could do anything, perform any act—with no hindrance from a lack of age, class, or education.

"Twenty lashes administered by the sergeant at arms once this court concludes." Stuart whacked the table with the mallet again. "Next case!"

The sailor dragged his chains out of the cabin, where he was taken into custody by two other sailors.

Lucius said, "I doubt anyone in my party would be able to stand the sight of that much blood."

"Mr. Fallows, none of the passengers will be allowed topside during the punishment. This is not some form of entertainment."

Alexander opened the cabin door and Major Ladd stepped inside, coming to attention at the opposite end of the table. His complaint: His wife had discovered her personal maid, Susanna Chase, wore no undergarments and must not have worn any when she boarded the *Mary Stewart.*

"Does the jury understand this is a question of virtue?" asked Stuart of Fallows and Belle, both having participated in the rescue of Susanna from the brothel.

Belle and Fallows nodded.

"Does everyone understand that if the proceedings of this inquiry should become general knowledge, I, as captain, if I'm able to prove who spread such gossip, will bring the transgressor before this court where he shall suffer the same fate as the man who fell asleep on watch?"

Everyone nodded, including the major, who wore his uniform.

Stuart looked at Fallows. "But the lashing of the gossiper will take place in public as the conversation in this room shall have become common knowledge, so the punishment shall match the crime. Is this understood?"

Once again, all four men nodded.

"And everyone at this table realizes a captain reigns supreme on his ship, no matter how many redcoats board this vessel."

Again, all four men nodded, with Fallows and John Belle glancing at the major.

"Major, as you have probably noted from last night, the *Mary Stewart* is not an English country village."

"Which makes it even more important that the basic rules of decorum be preserved."

"This is true, sir, but my advice would be not to press points of honor beyond a certain degree."

Ladd drew himself up. "Sir, there can be no shades of honor."

"Then consider the matter in another light. If you are dead, or incapacitated, who shall defend your wife's honor? Ashore that would be done through the rule of law, or a family member."

"Sir, are you threatening me or my wife?"

"I am not, but there are many chores to be performed and I do not wish to add to that list. So, Major, I must ask: Do you still wish to proceed with this inquiry?"

"That I do, sir. The girl's conduct is a reflection upon my wife's honor."

"And a serious affair for both women. Now we come to the crux of the matter: Are you willing to take the word of this young woman if she swears on the Bible?"

"I would, sir."

Stuart nodded to Alexander, who left the cabin, went next door, and escorted Susanna into the presence of the jury.

Anxious, the girl dry washed her hands as she stepped to the opposite side of the table. She wore the same white gown, albeit cleaned, that she had worn when she first boarded the ship. There was no scarf on her head, but, as Stuart had requested, she wore the shoes dropped by Alexander from the bordello window.

"Miss Chase, we believe something has gone missing—"

"Sir! I am no thief!"

"Miss Chase, would you please wait for my explanation."

The girl's breath came quickly. Color filled her face. She straightened up and nodded several times but did not look around.

"No one is accusing you of anything, Miss Chase. You will simply be asked some questions and then be dismissed. Do you understand that you are in no way on trial for thievery?"

Susanna's chin trembled. "Yes—yes, sir."

"Very well, place your hand on the Bible."

Susanna did.

"When you place your hand on the Bible, you are swearing to answer truthfully any question submitted to you by anyone in this court. Once again, do you understand?"

Susanna glanced at the other three men. "I understand."

"And you are not allowed to elaborate. Most of your questions will be answered simply 'yes' or 'no.' This court has other matters to handle and will not listen to chattering from some scullery maid."

"Sir, as I told you . . ." The girl's eyes narrowed, then hardened. "I understand your instructions."

"Very well. Are you dressed exactly as you were the night you first boarded this ship?"

"Yes, sir."

"Exactly? Really, Miss Chase, you must tell the truth."

Susanna appeared puzzled, but her entire life she had been asked odd and compromising questions by men in a position to lord over her. There were always traps, and this man's traps were no different than other traps sprung on her before.

She glanced at the Bible. "May I be excused, sir?"

"Yes. Return when you are willing to answer the question truthfully, but you must not tarry."

"Yes, sir."

Alexander opened the door, and while Susanna was gone, no one spoke or even looked at each other.

Minutes later, the girl returned and took her place across from Belle and Fallows. Now she no longer wore the shoes, and her chest was no longer flat but had a pleasant roundness to it.

"I am clothed as I was when I came aboard, sir."

"Very well. What is your name?"

"Susanna Chase."

"Where were you born?"

"Liverpool. Liverpool, England, that is."

"Were you employed on Lord Worthington's estate?"

"Yes, sir."

"For how many years?"

"Ever since I can remember. My family worked there until cholera—"

"What were your duties?"

"I was a maid, sir, a personal maid."

"Were you fired or reprimanded in the performance of you duties?"

"Never!" The red spots returned to her cheeks.

"But you were separated from the estate, correct?"

"Yes, sir, but that I can—"

"Miss Chase, how many other girls like yourself were employed on the Worthington estate?"

"There were three, including me: Bridgette and—"

"To the best of your knowledge, how many young ladies are employed there today?"

Susanna had no answer for that.

"To the best of your knowledge, Miss Chase."

"None, sir."

"Where are they now, Miss Chase?"

"Scattered, sir."

"Scattered?"

"I don't know where they are."

"Do the other girls know where *you* are?"

Susanna said nothing.

"Again, to the best of your knowledge, Miss Chase."

"In that case, I don't think they know where I am. Sir."

"So everyone is scattered, is this correct?"

Fallows leaned forward, saw the Bible across from him, and leaned back. John Belle remained upright next to him. At the door Alexander stared over Stuart's head. Ladd stared at the girl.

"Yes, sir. The girls are all scattered."

"Miss Chase, we must not slander anyone."

"Oh, no, sir, I would not."

"So you understand the definition of slander?"

That stopped her.

"Major," asked Stuart, "if you please, define slander."

"To utter a false claim against another party," said the man in the red uniform.

Susanna shook her head. "Oh, no, sir, I would never do that."

"Miss Chase," asked Stuart, "will you tell us the truth about how you took your leave from the Worthington estate?"

Susanna nodded. "Sir, I was—"

"Miss Chase, I asked you a question? Will you tell the truth?"

"Yes, sir."

"Then answer the following questions, and please remember the definition of slander. Major, if you would be so kind?"

"Do not utter a false claim against anyone, Miss Chase."

"Oh, no, sir," she said to Ladd. "I swore on the Bible."

"Miss Chase," asked Stuart, "is Mrs. Worthington still living?"

"No, sir, she died when—"

"Please do not ramble."

"No, sir. I mean, yes, sir."

"Is Mrs. Worthington alive?"

"No, sir. The cholera took her."

"Is Mr. Worthington living?"

"Yes, sir."

"Is Mr. Worthington healthy?"

"No, sir. He doesn't have long . . ." The girl's voice trailed off. She looked at her bare feet.

"Is there an heir to the Worthington estate?"

Susanna looked up. "Er—yes, sir."

"The Worthingtons have sons?"

"Just the one."

"And his age?"

"I think two and twenty. I'm not really sure."

"Has the son always lived on the estate?"

"No, sir."

"Where has he lived—recently?"

"In London, studying law at the Middle Temple."

"When did he return?"

"A few days before we were—"

"Scattered?"

"Yes, sir."

"Is the heir healthy?"

"Yes, sir."

"Is he vigorous?"

The girl looked at him, head canted to one side.

"Does he ride, fence, dance, all the normal activities of a young man?"

"Oh, yes, sir," said Susanna, nodding, "he is quite vigorous."

"Is the heir engaged to be married?"

"No, sir," replied Susanna, puzzled again.

"Prospects?"

"Oh, I could not say."

"But Miss Chase must say, mustn't she, Major, and she must not slander."

Ladd nodded from his end of the table.

"Does the heir have prospects, Miss Chase?" asked Stuart.

"Not that I know of."

"Well, perhaps the heir is too vigorous?"

Susanna glanced at Major Ladd, then at John Belle and Lucius Fallows.

Lucius leaned back in his chair and regarded the girl. And that's what she was, a mere girl, no one of any consequence. Certainly no huntress.

"Miss Chase," said Stuart, "I will have the truth about the vigor of the heir to the Worthington estate."

"Yes, sir. The heir is very . . . vigorous."

"And how soon were you girls scattered once the Worthington heir returned from London?"

"Two days, sir. The first day was the Sabbath, so there was no chance to pack until—"

"Who was responsible for the scattering? Would that have been the magistrate?"

"Well, for me, it was, sir."

"Do you miss the other girls, Miss Chase?"

Major Ladd had drifted off, but now he returned his attention to the girl.

"Yes, sir. They were good friends of mine."

"Were you told not to try to find them?"

"We swore on the Bible." She gestured at the book on the table. "Like now."

"And the magistrate placed you in the home of your nearest living relative, did he?"

"He did." An edge came into the girl's voice.

Stuart scooted forward in his chair, putting his arms on the writing platform. "Pay attention to my next question, Miss Chase. Do not anticipate the question, and make sure you answer clearly. Are these instructions clear?"

"They are."

"Did someone come to you two nights ago . . . come to you in the middle of the night and inform you that you must leave the home of your nearest relative?"

The girl stared at Stuart. Her eyes were cautious, watchful.

"The truth, Miss Chase! We shall have the truth! Did a woman come to you in the middle of the night and inform you that you must leave the home of your nearest relative and must do so immediately?"

The girl's eyes brightened. "That's exactly what I was told, that I must leave immediately."

"So, the house where you had been sent to live, that very house had become unsafe?"

"Yes," said the girl, nodding. "Very unsafe."

Ladd broke in. "Because the heir had located you?"

"Major, please! Wait your turn."

Ladd nodded and returned to a relaxed position.

Staring at the major, the sea captain asked, "Do you remember the definition of slander?" When the girl did not answer, Stuart said, "That question is for you, Miss Chase." Still, Stuart did not stop staring at Ladd.

"I remember the definition, Captain Stuart."

"Very well. Now tell me, how did you and the other girls know the heir was vigorous"—the words tumbled out of Stuart's mouth—"if you had known him for only two days, and one of those days was the Sabbath, and not a day when the heir would be employed in vigorous activity?"

"We knew!"

The girl's chin quivered. The men held their breath. Major Ladd continued to study her.

Stuart leaned back. "You will have to admit, and you have sworn on the Bible, Miss Chase, that the heir's reputation for being vigorous preceded him."

"Oh, yes, sir. We knew the heir was very . . . healthy." She tried a smile on James Stuart.

It did not work. "Miss Chase, do not get ahead of me."

"No, sir. I will not."

"So, tell me, Miss Chase, is it possible that this woman who spirited you away, that the reputation of the heir could have possibly been known by this woman?"

Susanna hesitated.

"Miss Chase," said Major Ladd, "it is not a lie or slander for you to speculate whether the woman who spirited you away from your new home might, and this is the key word, might have known the reputation of the heir of the Worthington estate."

"Actually," said Stuart, "the major will agree that you could be mistaken in your evaluation, and it still would not be a lie. It would only be your opinion."

"That is correct. You may speculate, Miss Chase."

"Oh, yes," said Susanna, nodding vigorously, "it is quite possible that the woman who took me away from my new home knew of the heir's reputation."

The major came to parade rest. "I think we are quite through, Captain Stuart, and if you have no further questions, there are chores for Miss Chase."

"If you insist, Major, but we must honor the jury."

"Of course."

"Any questions?" asked Stuart of Fallows and Belle.

Both men shook their heads. They did not speak, nor did they look at the girl.

"And, Captain Stuart," said Ladd, "you shall hear no more of this matter from either me or my wife."

"The Ladds understand this inquiry is at an end. Does the jury understand this matter is concluded once and for all?"

Belle and Fallows nodded.

"Then this court is dismissed!" And Stuart slammed the wooden mallet against the elevated desktop.

Once everyone had left and the door closed behind them, Stuart let out a long sigh and collapsed back in his chair.

Alexander leaned against the closed door and smiled. "You'll have to take care, Captain, or someone will mistake you for being human."

"Well," said Stuart, "if anyone does, it probably won't be *that* young lady."

Eighteen

Everyone had supped, the lanterns were lit, sunset had been spectacular, and privacy screens had been assembled to create a backdrop for the performance. Every passenger, save those suffering from seasickness, brought chairs, pillows, and comforters topside to watch the performance. The actors, from that faraway land where the sun rarely shines, performed for almost an hour with Gabriel leading off as Richard III:

"Now is the winter of our discontent, made glorious summer by this sun of York; and all the clouds that lour'd upon our house in the deep bosom of the ocean buried . . ."

Donato as the villain, Claudius, followed with the soliloquy from *Hamlet,* "O, my offense is rank . . ."

Later, Portia and Gabriel went back and forth as Desdemona and Othello, that is, until Gabriel's voice faltered and Donato had to replace him, and Portia's words of love appeared to bring genuine rapture to the face of the smaller man. And because the role of

Desdemona had been played on the stage by Margaret Hughes more than fifty years earlier, tonight's performance brought few mutterings of "shameful exposure" over the role of a woman being played by Portia.

The last performance of the evening was a three-man chorus of Oren, Donato, and Lucius fronted by Portia, who sang "The Willow Song."

Most of the crew hung on every word sung or spoken by the beautiful actress, many dangling from the rigging or sitting along the ship's railing. The candlelit backdrop made the woman's countenance radiant, her yellow hair and red lips lustrous, her face graven pale. The gown she chose to wear: emerald green.

When Stuart approached Fallows after the performance, he asked Lucius why he appeared only in the chorus.

"I'm the money."

Seeing the sea captain's puzzled look, Fallows added, "Plays cannot go on without backing. It's the same as during the days of Shakespeare. There always has to be the money."

"Just like any other business."

"No," said Fallows, "entertainments are not like any other business." A tight smile crossed his face. "You have to be a fool to think you can make money entertaining, and I am . . ." He looked across the deck where Portia stood, taking the congratulations of both passengers and crew. "I am a fool for that woman."

"Er—yes," said Stuart, surprised at the man's sudden revelation. "I know the feeling. It afflicted me once."

"And the outcome?"

"She's dead. The children are with my mother. Charles Town is more disease-ridden than any ship of the line."

Fallows studied Stuart. "So now what do you live for?"

"Not for some woman. I've suffered enough in the past."

"Yes, if one could only live forever . . ."

"To live forever would be quite agreeable. I have a business to run, and a good number of family members dependent on me."

"Well, don't let your business cuckold you as Portia has cuckolded me."

The Bentleys, including three of their girls, broke away from those surrounding the actress and approached the two men.

"And, Captain Stuart, if you want to avoid another romantic entanglement, you'd be wise to keep your distance from Alicia Bentley. Of the lot, she's the cleverest by far."

Stuart studied the Bentleys: mother, father, and girls all dressed in the latest fashion. Only the youngest was not topside but sentenced by pregnancy to remain below deck, out of the public eye. Also sentenced to that below-deck purgatory was a woman who freckled in the sunlight, but who had sneaked a look at tonight's performance by wearing the close bonnet.

Oren began to break down the props and return the privacy screens to their cabins, and Lucius, noticing a pleading look from Portia, bid Stuart adieu.

With considerable sarcasm, Lucius added, "So I may attend to my lady's every need and desire."

The pale man strode away, only to be introduced to the girls by Mrs. Bentley, a short, stout woman. It took another moment to break away, but Lucius finally did, and the Bentleys continued in Stuart's direction.

Stuart had been joined by Martin and Alexander, who each reported on the security of the ship: Martin below deck, Alexander topside. All three were anxious for the safety of their passengers, but everything appeared in order. Still, watches would be doubled, and Alexander would wander the deck, kicking anyone found sleeping.

"Any sign of the pig?" asked Stuart.

"No, sir," said Martin.

A sailor in charge of catching rats approached, tentatively.

Stuart looked at him, but the rat catcher only shook his head.

"Then why do we have you along?" Stuart's eyes narrowed. "You're not eating them again, are you? Or the missing pig?"

"Oh, no, sir!" said the rat catcher, shaking his head. "I would never do that, Captain." And he scurried away before having to answer even more questions.

Eight bells rang, or four bells rang in pairs, signaling the end of the last dog watch, eight o'clock.

Once the ringing subsided, Mrs. Bentley spoke for her entire clan. "Captain Stuart, I want to thank you for that excellent cold luncheon served this afternoon and followed by such a wonderful performance tonight. The reputation of your ship preceded you. I know my husband presented himself when we first came aboard, as was proper, but I wanted you to meet my girls—the ones who are not married, that is, Alicia, Marion, and Katie. Judith remains with her husband in England. She is a Buckley now, but all the others are very eligible."

The girls and their mother curtsied, their father bowed, and Stuart and his crew returned the gesture.

"Oh, but we have already met the captain," said Katie with some glee. "We shot the sun with him today."

Mrs. Bentley glanced at Katie, then looked to Stuart for an explanation. Stuart smiled at Marion Bentley, who, as usual, took much too long explaining celestial navigation.

"Yes, yes, my dear. As I was saying, all of my girls are available and looking for husbands, but for Lindy, who is to meet her lieutenant in Boston. We are taking a tour of the colonies, and I would not be surprised if my girls didn't return with several engagements to rich colonials."

Stuart introduced his first mate, Martin, and Alexander, the ship's quartermaster. The usual stares at the missing arm occurred, but Alicia Bentley looked in the direction of the stern-side cabins.

"I certainly hope you're enjoying your voyage," said Stuart, smiling. "No sickness?"

"Oh, no, but Lindy does have her moments . . . because of her condition. She would dearly love to have been in the audience, but you know how people would talk."

"Mrs. Bentley," injected Martin, "Lindy is welcome topside anytime she pleases. The many rules of landsmen simply do not apply at sea, especially for a voyage of such duration."

Both Stuart and Mrs. Bentley turned on Martin and assured him that all the rules of proper society remained in effect no matter what circumstances a young woman might find herself in.

"Captain Stuart," asked Katie, "will the troupe be acting for our enjoyment every night while we are at sea?"

"Certainly not Sundays," corrected her mother.

"Oh, no. I meant the other nights."

"At least three nights each week," said Stuart. "That was the agreement for their passage to Charles Town."

"Three?" Still, Katie seemed pleased instead of disappointed. "Then may we have a ball—I mean, a dance, Captain Stuart?"

"Katie Bentley!" said both Mrs. Bentley and Alicia. Mr. Bentley only shook his head and strolled away.

"Please excuse my daughter. I'm afraid Katie is more accustomed to activities ashore."

But Katie would not be reined in. "Captain Stuart, is it not true the voyage will last several weeks?"

"At least a month. It depends on the wind."

Katie turned to her mother. "Then why shouldn't we dance on this boat?"

"It's called a ship," said Marion. Her scissor-glasses hung around her neck on a ribbon and in a hand she carried a copy of Shakespeare's sonnets. "A ship is a large seagoing vessel. A boat is much smaller."

"That is correct, Miss Bentley," said Phillippe Belle, joining them upon Portia's retirement for the evening. "You travel on a ship."

Katie Bentley was not about to allow this conversation

to be hijacked by a discussion of maritime terminology. She gestured at the main deck. "And you have a large enough floor."

"Deck, not floor," corrected Marion. "You would dance on the deck of a ship." Marion saw her mother and Alicia staring at her. "That is, if the captain permits."

"I dare say Captain Stuart understands my point," said Katie.

"Of course, he does," said Phillippe. "There's plenty of room with the tables and benches moved aside."

"But only if my first mate can round up the proper instruments," cautioned Stuart.

Katie clasped her hands together as if praying and turned her attention to the first mate. "Oh, please try, Mr. Chase, please, please try!"

"Katie Bentley, you must not be so bold."

Katie ignored the advice and canted her head and smiled up at Martin. "I'm sure you'll find what we need. This is a very large boat—I mean, ship."

"Certainly, Miss Bentley," said Martin, clearing his throat, "but only if you'll allow me the first two dances."

"Oh, I will, I will!" squealed the girl, and she indicated that she and Martin should walk over to the railing and further discuss the matter, including the possibility of passengers putting on their own plays. "We have done that back home, ever since we were children. Alicia is the very best writer in our family."

They were followed by Marion and Mrs. Bentley, leaving Alicia to inquire, "Captain, I've recently been informed of Miss Chase's sudden illness. Pray tell, is this true?"

"I would be most honored to escort you to Miss Chase's cabin," said Phillippe, gesturing toward the bow, "but first, perhaps a turn around the deck. As a gentlewoman, you may not be aware of Miss Chase's background."

"Alexander," cut in Stuart, "escort Miss Bentley to Miss Chase's cabin and report back to me as to the latter's physical condition. I did not know it to be so serious."

"Aye, aye, Captain." And the African gestured in the direction opposite of where Phillippe Belle was preparing to go.

Walking away, Alicia asked, "Do you know what ails her?"

Smiling over his shoulder at Stuart, Alexander said, "I do believe, before the evening meal, something upset her stomach."

Phillippe began to complain, but Stuart cut him off.

"If you have any information to impart to others on this ship about Miss Chase's background, take it up with Major Ladd. As Miss Chase is in service to his wife, the major is thoroughly acquainted with the matter."

And with that, Stuart turned on his heel and left Phillippe standing alone.

Nineteen

Alicia knocked on the cabin door.

From inside came a female voice. "Go away, please!"

Alicia stood under the overhang of the three cabins at the stern of the ship. Alexander had returned to the helm, but before reaching there, one sailor after another stopped the African, asking his good opinion.

This is very odd, thought Alicia. This black man is asked more questions than the ship's own captain.

"Susanna, it's me, Alicia Bentley."

Long pause, then: "Come in, Miss Bentley."

Alicia pushed back the door and stepped inside.

It was dark inside the cabin, even though the curtain over the stern windows was pulled back. Very little light came through the stern-side windows when a ship was at sea. What light there was came from the stern lantern, and in its red glow Alicia could make out Susanna lying facedown on her bed. A chair stood between the two beds, and Alicia made her way in that direction, feeling her way with her hands.

"I heard you were seasick."

Susanna rolled over and sat up, sliding her feet over the side of the bed. She brushed back her hair. In the light from the stern lantern her face glowed red.

"My cousin told everyone I was seasick so I wouldn't have to work in the kitchen tonight. I really don't want to be seen on this ship again."

Alicia took a seat in the chair and made herself comfortable. "That's going to be rather difficult. We still have several weeks at sea. Why didn't you want to work in the kitchen tonight? The cook wasn't forward again, was he?"

Susanna told her about the joke played on her that caused her to awaken the captain early. "He only did it because I won't speak with him. But he's much too vulgar and suggestive to have more than formal contact with."

"I agree. In our current situation, as women, we must be selective in—"

"His joke amused Kyrla Stuart the most."

Susanna did not mention the court of inquiry, nor had she believed Martin when he stuck his head in the door before the performance and said all was well, she was not to worry, and come out and enjoy the show.

"Kyrla Stuart frightens me," said Alicia.

"Me, too, and I share a cabin with her."

"She could sit on me and squash me like a bug." Alicia's smile turned to a genuine look of concern. "She strides around this ship like . . . like . . ."

"Like she owns it. Well, she does. She's a member of the Stuart family."

"No, no, I didn't mean that. I know her family owns this ship. It's just that . . ."

Alicia stared at the cabin door as if seeing beyond it. "I know this sounds strange, but Kyrla Stuart strides, and I think that's the correct word, strides around the ship. Women walk or stroll. Men stride, and that's how Kyrla acts, as if she belongs here. What I mean is women like Mary Read and Anne Bonny dressed like men and ran away to sea to be pirates, and that plays to our fancy, but we're women and this is not our place. Only men belong on the *Mary Stewart*. Still, somehow, and for some reason, Kyrla feels she belongs here."

"Kyrla wears pants. You think she's a man dressed in women's clothing?"

Alicia burst into laughter and couldn't stop laughing. Tears ran down her cheeks, and she was helpless to stop them. But when she saw the growing dismay on Susanna's face, how the stern lantern turned the girl's features a ghoulish red in the light through the window, Alicia reached over and touched the younger woman's knee. The image of Kyrla Stuart being a man had been so real, so absurd . . .

"No, no." Alicia wiped the tears away. "What I meant is where does Kyrla Stuart find the nerve to act like a man?"

"Well," said Susanna, leaning back on her elbows, "I once worked in the kitchen with a really large woman, and you had to stay out of her way or she'd run you over, knock you into the stove if you didn't watch out. She did that more than once to one of the smaller girls. She had the worst burns."

"But with Kyrla Stuart it's different, and I don't think it has anything to do with her size. Where did she gain such confidence?"

"I don't know," said Susanna, tiring of this line of inquiry. "Was she at the entertainment this evening? She wasn't in here."

"You did miss a very pleasing show."

Alicia pulled her legs into the seat of the chair and wrapped her arms around her knees. She found it fun talking to Susanna. The girl was a bit younger and a lot less sophisticated, but, in a pinch, she'd do. In truth, Alicia missed her older sister. They'd had such pleasant conversations under the covers before Judith had married and left home.

A stab of pain struck through Alicia. Judith belonged to another world, a world Alicia would never see again, and *she* belonged to this new world, whatever that might be.

Alicia understood a woman's identity came from being in the bosom of her loving family, but her parents were clearly out of their depth, her mother foolish, and her father a bookish recluse. So what did this mean for their family in this new world? Was it her duty to marry the richest man she could find? Someone who could provide for her *and* her family? Someone like Phillippe Belle?

There was hardly a hundred pounds a year to live on, and while she dearly loved her sisters, they could be so embarrassing.

Imagine demanding a dance be held!

What next? A regular seat at the captain's table?

The letters of introduction garnered before leaving England had to work. They just had to.

Once again, Alicia became aware of Susanna staring at her. "Sorry. My mind wandered. My sister bothered the captain to have a dance on the main deck."

"A dance? I didn't know there were that many gentlewomen and gentlemen aboard."

"I don't think there are, but I wouldn't be surprised if some of the crew joined in. You can't really believe every sailor will be happy watching us passengers have all the fun."

"But sailors dancing with gentlewomen? I would rather think I could dance with the—"

"The captain?"

Susanna shook her head. "Oh, no, not him!"

"Why not? He's rather handsome."

"Why, er—he's much too old for me."

"Really? I believe the captain to be four and twenty, and you're at least sixteen or you'd be wearing the bonnet."

Alicia grinned and wondered if the red light through the stern window made her look as ghoulish as Susanna had when she'd become dismayed at Alicia's excessive laughter.

"It's just a dance, Susanna. You're not marrying him."

"Oh, no, Miss Bentley, I wouldn't consider it."

Susanna looked away.

Oh, my, thought Alicia, she's taken a fancy to the captain, and her feelings have not been reciprocated.

But instead of pursuing that line of thought, which might prove embarrassing, Alicia said, "I really would like to have heard Gabriel sing tonight. Everyone says he has the most wonderful voice. A real nightingale."

Susanna shivered and wrapped her arms around herself. She remembered the dismissive look from Portia, the hissing sound issued from Fallows' cabin the night before. "His sister—she's . . . frightening."

Again Alicia laughed, but this time she recognized the laugh for what it was: the farther they sailed from England, the more anxious she became. She looked around and resolved to leave this red cave and take this girl with her. Susanna should not be alone with her thoughts tonight. As for her, she desperately needed that turn around the deck suggested by Phillippe Belle.

"So," said Alicia, "both Kyrla and Portia frighten us so much that we're afraid to leave this cabin."

Walking the main deck, the two girls huddled together like schoolgirls, and their conversation was quite similar.

"Susanna, you simply must tell me what you know about this man called the woodsman who sits on that platform in the rigging and rarely ever comes down."

John Belle intrigued Alicia because she thought him either a simpleton or extremely reflective, given all the time he spent alone. And since men and women did not dine together unless invited to do so, Alicia was at a loss as to how to meet this intriguing young man. The one time she had suggested her family invite the Belle brothers to dinner, only Phillippe joined them.

Susanna glanced up as they passed under the forward mast. "That's John Belle. He has a brother traveling with us, and they could not be more different. John is for the forest and has lived among the Red Men, while Phillippe is for the city and considered a rake. Phillippe is returning from studying law at the Temple because his mother is on her death bed. He's to inherit an estate on the Ashley or Cooper River, I don't remember which."

"Both rivers were named for Lord Ashley Cooper?"

"That's what I'm told, but what does it matter? The woman Phillippe Belle marries will be rich beyond belief."

Alicia was relieved to see Susanna regain her vitality and congeniality. All it took was a discussion of possible beaus, a subject that had the same effect on her.

James Stuart appeared out of the darkness and nodded to the young women. "Miss Chase, good to see you out and about again." Stuart doffed his hat. "Miss Bentley."

Alicia curtsied. "Captain."

Beyond her curtsy, Susanna made no reply.

As the girls continued toward the bow, Stuart said, "Hope to see you in the galley again, Miss Chase."

Alicia tried to prod the younger girl into an acknowledgment, saying Susanna should not wish to be considered peevish.

The younger girl only shook her head and whispered. "He holds no charms for me."

The Ladds were taking their evening stroll, and when Mrs. Ladd recognized them from across the deck, she led her husband in the girl's direction. Once again, the women curtsied, the major doffed his hat.

"If you're feeling better, Miss Chase, there are tasks to be performed. The chamber pot hasn't been emptied for two days."

"Yes, ma'am, I will take care of that."

As the girls strolled away, Mrs. Ladd's voice followed them. "Now, Miss Chase, if you don't mind. My husband will see Miss Bentley below."

Another form appeared out of the darkness: Phillippe Belle.

"That's not necessary, Major Ladd," said Phillippe. "Miss Bentley and I are acquainted. I shall see her home tonight."

Ladd looked at the Bentley girl, who merely stared at the deck, giving no sign of regret or enthusiasm.

"If the young lady has no objections . . ."

Alicia looked up and smiled. What else could she do? To refuse a stroll with Phillippe Belle would give offense—to a Belle of Charles Town. And she would never hear the end of it from her mother.

It was quite a while before Alicia could free herself of Phillippe's attentions, the main deck having become a center of social intercourse for the young people on the ship. As a result, Alicia sequestered herself in her cabin for several days, even taking her meals there, a great sacrifice for such a dedicated walker.

Which led to her mother's entreaties to bring her parasol and return to the main deck, and the attentions of Phillippe Belle, a young man of significant means.

Which led Alicia to make a rather bold move, something she would never have done back in England.

But I no longer live in England, do I?

She would employ Mrs. Ladd in her effort to gain an introduction to John Belle. Not only did Mrs. Ladd have a position in ship's society created by spending several weeks at sea, she commanded respect as the wife of a military leader.

So, scheduling her daily walk to coincide with that

of the Ladds, Alicia returned to the main deck and fell in stride with the couple, only to be joined by Phillippe Belle.

The next day, she tried again, and was ambushed by Phillippe Belle once again.

Mrs. Ladd was not stupid. "Mr. Belle, if you please!"

Phillippe stopped walking. He even stopped bragging about the size of Cooper Hill, the family plantation in the Low Country famous for its rice and indigo.

"Sir," said Mrs. Ladd, "you must state your intentions."

Phillippe glanced at Alicia hidden by her parasol. "I, like Miss Bentley, enjoy a stroll this time of day."

"But every day, sir?"

Major Ladd, who also knew his duty, took the young man's arm, walked him over to the nearest cannon, and began to explain the differences between the huge cannon on the deck and the much smaller swivel gun mounted on a shaft and extending over the railing.

"You look here, Belle, if you need to rake an opposing position—rather, rake the decks of an opposing ship. Sorry there, wrong terminology, me being in the infantry and all that."

Mrs. Ladd took the young woman by the arm. Protected from the sun by their parasols, they continued along the deck. It did not take long for Mrs. Ladd to come to the point.

"Yes, child, what may I do for you?"

"Your husband knows quite a bit about warfare, doesn't he?"

"It is his chosen profession, though why a young

woman of breeding would bring up such a topic, I can not understand."

Alicia glanced at the foremast top as they passed underneath. "I am given to understand that Mr. John Belle is acquainted with the tactics of Indian fighting, and I thought your husband might benefit from such an exposure to the topic."

Mrs. Ladd stopped and stared at her. Were all members of the Bentley family quite mad?

"But there's little chance of Mr. Belle teaching Major Ladd anything about the Red Man if your husband never meets him."

Mrs. Ladd glanced at the top. "I, for one, can't believe Mr. Belle might have anything of importance to impart to my husband." An eyebrow arched. "Or is there someone else aboard this ship who might wish to be addressed by John Belle?"

Alicia twirled her parasol and looked out to sea. "I simply thought your husband might benefit from the knowledge of Mr. Belle during his travels into the upcountry of South Carolina. Once we dock at Charles Town, Mr. Belle will return to the upcountry and your husband will never see him again."

"You know, Miss Bentley, I never thought about it like that."

Alicia gave the older woman a warm smile. "I must say I have given the matter a great deal of thought."

Mrs. Ladd glanced at the foremast. "Yes, I can see that you have."

The encounter did not go according to plan. Though John Belle was requested to come down from the top, and the young man patiently answered Major Ladd's questions about Indian fighting, it appeared the major did not agree with John's notions of the Red Man's abilities.

The British soldier, said the major, was the finest fighting man the world had ever seen, and these Red Men would soon learn this if they dared engage a redcoat army on the field of battle.

And as Alicia watched John Belle bristle at being preached to about a subject he knew intimately, she realized John included the Ladds, his brother, and *her* as fellow travelers on this ship of fools.

What was she to do?

Evidently, stroll the main deck with Phillippe, for not long after the conclusion of the discussion, John made his good-byes, leaped into the rigging, and returned to the platform on the foremast.

Twenty

In desperation, two days later, Alicia asked Alexander how she could learn to climb the rigging. They ran into each other in the passageway, a happenstance Alicia engineered.

Alexander wasn't sure he'd heard correctly. "Pardon, miss?"

"Mr. Alexander—"

"It's just Alexander."

"Alexander, I want to learn to climb the rigging."

The African glanced down the passageway in the direction of the Bentley cabins. "Miss, is this something of which your parents would approve?"

"Probably not."

"Then I cannot be a party to it." He turned to walk away.

Alicia followed him and the words spilled out of her. "I did a great deal of walking in England, but on this ship I am unable to do so, and this dreadful situation shall continue for several more weeks, making this a rather torturous trip."

Alexander stopped, but before he could question her, a couple came down the above-deck ladder and passed them. The black man and the white girl made way, Alexander nodding, Alicia curtsying.

"Susanna Chase roams this ship as if she's a member of the crew."

"Miss Chase *is* a member of the crew. She hired herself to Mrs. Ladd as a maidservant for the duration of the voyage, and also she works in the kitchen at the behest of the captain." The African smiled. "Miss Chase is a very good cook—if you are so inclined. A ship cannot have too many cooks."

Alicia ignored his offer of employment and plunged ahead. "I have milked the cow in the hold, gathered eggs from the poop deck, served meals from the kitchen—er, I mean, the galley, entertained children for hours, visited those incapacitated by illness or injury, and have assisted the doctor with smashed fingers and broken limbs. I've even joined the captain in shooting the sun, and the bosun has instructed me how to repair canvas and reweave rigging."

She did not dare tell this man, nor any other man, that she kept a diary: *Journey to a New World.* Instead, she simply smiled and added, "The bosun was kind enough to have a pair of gloves sewn for me. In any event, Alexander, I believe boredom to be the greatest enemy on such a long passage and these are the steps I have taken."

"You would be correct, Miss Bentley. Boredom leads to accidents, and nerves lead to arguments settled with fists, guns, or knives."

"Of this, I am aware. In the whist room, while waiting my turn at a game of backgammon, I read the captain's notice that there were no duels to be fought until the *Mary Stewart* reaches Charles Town. Anyway, I have read every book on this vessel, some of them twice, met everyone with the exception of John Belle, and whatever one's opinion of Mr. Belle, he has a remarkable way of dealing with this very long voyage."

"So," said Alexander, smiling, "climbing the rigging is nothing more than your investigating another area of the ship."

She ignored his suspicion. "I've thought about this considerably, and besides learning how to climb, which I assume is much like learning to ride a horse, I must have the proper clothing, such as the gloves sewn for me by the bosun. Perhaps the correct clothing would be the proper expression."

"What about a pair of men's pants?"

Alicia flushed and looked away. "I could never wear pants. I'm quite aware of the low regard with which my mother holds Kyrla Stuart."

"And you believe others won't hold you in the same regard if you scale the rigging?"

"Sir, you do have influence with the crew."

"So," said Alexander, smiling, "I'm to go about the ship knocking heads to gain you favorable treatment from the crew in this endeavor."

Alicia straightened up. "I've been on this ship almost two weeks, sir, but I believe you were knocking heads, as you put it, well before my family ever booked passage on the *Mary Stewart.*"

He continued to smile. "I can handle the sailors, but there will be those who don't care for my good opinion."

"And I shall not care for theirs either, but I doubt

I shall ever see these people again once I reach the American colonies."

A scrawny, dirty sailor stuck his head out of the hold and placed two small cages, one by one, at Alexander's feet before finishing his climb up the ladder.

Alicia stepped back. She knew this nasty man was in charge of catching rats. Fortunately, she had not seen a rat or been bitten by a bedbug, two plagues normally visited on most ships.

Both cages were empty.

"You can see they work just fine." The rat catcher became aware of the woman. "Oh, sorry, miss." And he took the two empty cages and crept down the ladder, returning to the hold.

Alicia held a handkerchief to her nose and put out a hand to steady herself against the bulkhead.

"You all right, miss?" asked Alexander.

"Yes, yes. I've seen the cages before."

"Still," said the African, "this investigation of the rigging is a very serious step to take."

"I do not need to be preached to on this matter, sir. I am quite aware of the consequences." After checking the passageway as well as the stairs to the main deck, she said in a lower voice, "But one word from you and I will quit this exercise, if you can truthfully say my reputation would be damaged if I became acquainted with Mr. John Belle."

"I would never say that about John, but Phillippe would be another matter."

To this, the girl said nothing.

"If you must do this, Miss Bentley, there may be only one way to accomplish it."

When the black man would not go on, she encouraged him.

"Very well. I once met a woman who took one of her dresses and sliced up the skirt and petticoat, front and rear."

Alicia colored at the idea and turned away.

"Shall I go on, miss?"

Not looking at him, she said, "Yes, yes. Please do."

"In this way, sewn together front and rear, the pieces could be worn as pants. And these women did not sew those new legs tight or remove the extra material, but allowed the separate pieces to flow together whenever they stood."

"Which made it appear to be a dress once again," said Alicia, regaining the nerve to look at the man.

"And if you climb the rigging, whatever you do, don't look down. You'll be busy enough holding on to Jacob's ladder, and as you've seen, Jacob's ladder practically swings free. It is like no other part of the ship you've been to."

Alicia thanked him and remained in the passageway long after the African had disappeared into the hold, then she returned to her cabin and began sorting through her old dresses and petticoats.

Another couple of days passed before Alicia garnered enough nerve to approach the rigging. Using her hand to shelter her eyes, because she had determined to do this without a parasol, she peered at the wood-and-rope ladder winding its way around the top. And one had to look closely at the rigging to make out one's path. Strung over the deck was a maze of ropes, netting, and spars.

Just tell yourself you're nine years old and climbing the apple tree in the backyard of the family estate. Or what was formerly the family estate, and the reason for this exercise.

Phillippe Belle was there, asking if she had a question about the ship's rigging or one of its masts.

"Not at all, sir," said Alicia, pulling on her gloves crafted by the bosun. "If I did, I'm sure my sister Marion knows more than enough to enlighten me."

And up the rigging she went—to the astonishment of Belle and several other passengers. Crew members stopped and stared, then broke into cheers. They were quickly silenced by Alexander issuing commands through a speaking trumpet.

Stuart rushed from his cabin and passed the helm. "What's going on here?"

Alexander gestured at Alicia with the trumpet.

"What's she doing up there?"

"Climbing the rigging."

"Well, come help me talk her down." Stuart headed for the foremast. "She could be injured."

"She seems to be doing quite well, as if she climbed a lot of apple trees when much younger."

Female passengers drifted over and lowered their parasols to gaze upward. Men used their hands to shelter their eyes, and more than one wondered aloud how the girl kept her dress down.

Stuart shook his head. "Of all the trouble I thought women could create on a ship, I must say I never thought of this."

"James, she's a walker with nowhere to walk."

"Ridiculous! The *Mary Stewart* has enough room for the lady to walk her legs off."

At his comment, people turned and stared.

"Sir," said Phillippe Belle, "please don't be so vulgar and cease speaking of the young lady's legs."

Children snickered, women blushed, and men turned away from the spectacle, but only at the encouragement of their wives.

Stuart took Alexander's arm and pulled him away from the foremast. "I hope I won't find you had a hand in this."

"James, it's 1752. The world is changing. Women are changing."

Stuart watched Alicia reach the foot of Jacob's ladder. He shook his head. "I'd hoped the Empire would survive me, but this may be the end of it. Come on, Alexander, we need to decide what to tell the crew."

"Don't worry, James, it's all been taken care of."

John Belle's solitude was disturbed by cheers, then someone huffing and puffing their way up Jacob's ladder. Moments later, Alicia Bentley stuck her head over the edge of the platform located one-third up the forward mast. Jacob's ladder was a rope-and-wood affair around the top, or platform, and farther up the foretop, or forward mast, to reach the uppermost sails.

Flashing an anxious smile, bonnet blown back into a half-circle around her face, she held on tightly to the free-swinging ladder with her gloved hands. "A bit of help, please?"

Closing his mouth, which had most certainly fallen open, John Belle scrambled to his feet, grabbed the rope ladder, and steadied it with one hand. Using his other hand, he assisted the girl to the platform. Bending over to catch her breath, it was a moment before Alicia was able to stand upright.

"Thank you, kind sir."

"Just what in the devil are you doing up here?"

Alicia did not hear the question. All she heard was the roaring in her ears, and her eyes widened as she saw the ocean stretching flat and distant to her left and right. In her head, she quickly calculated the distance from where she stood to the deck below. She had done what Alexander had warned her not to. She'd looked down.

Alicia's head spun, she lost her balance, and she threw her hands out to grab . . . nothing. No lines, no mast . . .

John Belle seized her around the waist and pulled her into him. He steadied her on the platform.

"You all right?" he asked, raising his voice over the breeze.

"Oh, my," said Alicia. Except for dancing, this was the tightest any man had ever held her.

John must have realized this and his hands came off. He took one of her gloved hands and wrapped it around a shroud, or line holding the mast upright. Her other gloved hand he slapped on the forward mast, upon which the platform, or top, was mounted.

"Now hold on!"

Alicia did.

"What are you doing up here, Miss Bentley?"

Alicia shivered with fear and could not speak. With her hands secured, both left and right, she'd been free to look around. And down.

Oh, my . . .

"Miss Bentley?"

"Sir, please help me sit down, and help me sit near one of these ropes so I might hold on."

"Lines," he corrected. "They're called lines."

The girl's face was pale, her legs weak. "If I do not sit down immediately, I shall faint and topple to the ground."

"Topple to the deck. It's called the deck."

"Sir . . ." His voice sounded so very far away.

John grabbed the girl and helped her sit down. For a second, he thought he should lay her across the narrow platform, then thought better of it. Again, he removed his hands from around the girl's waist.

Slowly, Alicia's color returned. She opened her eyes and smiled. "Thank you, Mr. Belle."

She glanced toward the edge but made no move to scoot over and have a better look. Actually, she could see much more than she cared to, as the top was slatted so water could not collect on it. Behind her bellied the mainsail, ahead of her the foremast, but to starboard and port the ocean stretched out forever, and in the constant breeze her bonnet remained a semicircle around her head. The man in the crow's nest, on the mainmast, stared down at them.

"I must say this is much higher than any apple tree in my family's backyard."

"Pardon?" asked Belle, cupping his ear.

Alicia repeated her comment in a much louder voice.

"You didn't answer my question, Miss Bentley. What are you doing up here?"

Oh, my, but he knows my name.

"I had to get some air." But he couldn't hear that until she spoke directly into his ear.

Turning to her ear, he pressed her for an answer. "Don't jest. Why'd you come up here?"

She explained how she knew the ship from its bow to its stern and that she had been in the hold more than once. All that was left was the rigging, and here she was—though her exercise might in someway have offended him.

"Do you wish for me to leave?" she asked.

"Perhaps not right away. I'm not sure you have your sea legs."

"And you would be correct, Mr. Belle."

Below them, the bosun piped half the crew to mess, and Alicia finally understood the purpose of the whistle. The whistle, or pipe, could be heard over any noise or weather. She certainly could not hear what was being said below, and that was probably for the best.

John had taken a seat, his legs hanging off the platform. He seemed very comfortable up here.

"Mr. Belle," asked Alicia, raising her voice, "might I ask you the same question? Why are you up here? Day and night?"

"I have nothing in common with those on deck."

"You have a brother below."

"I have brothers and sisters in Charles Town, but I don't see them very often." John looked out to sea as the ship cut its way through the endless blue water under a cloudless blue day.

"May I inquire why?"

"I don't care for the city."

Alicia laughed but remembered to grip the line and the forward mast. "Forgive me, sir, but I'd not heard that Charles Town had gained the status of a city."

"You may not think so, Miss Bentley, but soon the American colonies will become the center of the British Empire."

"Oh, really, and how would you account for that?"

John turned away, looking through the spars, or lines, and out over the ocean. He could not very well explain to a lady that the women in the colonies were birthing babies at a faster rate than those in England.

"I'm sorry, Miss Bentley. I misspoke. I apologize for my rudeness."

"This is your reply? You are not willing to debate the issue. Believe me, sir, I have debated issues with young men before."

"Of that, there can be no doubt."

And they sat in silence as the wind whipped through their hair and clothing. Alicia's bonnet remained pressed back and straight up whenever she looked into the wind.

She turned to him. "You like the quiet, don't you?"

"I do, but I can understand that a woman would not."

"Sir," said Alicia, chuckling, "I have spent a great deal of time in solitude. When you have four sisters and a garrulous mother, you search for such opportunities."

"Is that why you walked so much—back in England?"

Alicia nodded. "Something I shan't be able to do in

Charles Town, though the city now covers the entire peninsula. What a shame to cut down all those lovely trees. Without a forest, how would anyone find a moment's solitude?"

Twenty-one

"**F**or this reason I shall marry this man."

The final sentence came out in a rush. Still, the young woman could not face her mother. Alicia was not used to being disrespectful to adults.

But Alicia knew gossip travels fast, so here she was, confessing her transgression and insisting she would soon marry, though her intended might be unaware of *her* intentions.

"Philippe Belle has proposed? This is wonderful news."

Alicia realized she must not have told her mother which Belle she intended to marry, only that she would marry.

Oh, my, what have I said?

Think, girl, think!

Which was quite impossible. She shook with nervousness and could not remember exactly what words she had used.

"Oh, Mr. Bentley," said her mother with great

enthusiasm, "did you hear our daughter? She is to marry. She is to marry Mr. Belle." Mrs. Bentley clapped her hands together. "Oh, this is such delightful news."

Mrs. Bentley brought her hand under her chin in a thoughtful pose. "Now, who should I tell first, and this is no insignificant matter because to produce the most pleasure from such wonderful news—should I pay a call on the most influential woman on this ship or someone who will slowly pass along such delightful news, so as I might enjoy issuing my own happy tidings? Hmm. Will it be Major Ladd's wife or the invalid woman down the hall . . . ?"

Alicia faced her mother, hands behind her back for she could not stop them from shaking. Her stomach was quite unsettled. She could not believe she was being so disrespectful. The two women faced each other in the narrow area between the beds.

Falling back on words and phrases she had rehearsed, Alicia said, "Mama, I won't be a part of this charade any longer."

"Charade? What charade?"

Mrs. Bentley glanced at her husband propped up on his bed with *An Enquiry Concerning the Principles of Morals*, a book by Scottish philosopher David Hume. In his treatise, Hume argued that the foundations of morals lie in sentiment, not reason.

Mrs. Bentley sighed. So much of the girls' future left to her. Their eldest, Judith, was happily married and living in Hampshire, but in truth, the beautiful Judith had been a rather easy match.

"It's Mr. John Belle," blurted out Alicia.

Her mother seemed unable to place the name. "Who?"

"John Belle, the youngest member of the Belle family is the one I shall marry."

"Youngest? Not senior? Not entitled to any land? Not entitled to anything? But why would you do such a thing? If it is not to be Philippe Belle, you can certainly wait until we arrive in Charles Town. There you shall find many a suitable young man, since many of our fellow passengers have sons awaiting their fathers' arrival—and their good advice."

"But they are not my choice."

"Your choice? What do you mean by your choice?"

"I do not care for them."

"What does that have to do with anything?"

"I am not in love with Philippe Belle. My heart loves another . . ."

"Love? You think you're *in love?*"

Another glance at her husband and Mrs. Bentley knew she must continue to bear this tremendous responsibility alone. "Yes, yes, I understand, my dear. All we've seen for almost two weeks have been the sky, the clouds, and the sea—nothing of what I was led to believe was the romance of the ocean. For this reason, I can understand why you've developed an attachment to this young man in the middle of this oceanic . . . desert where nothing ever changes."

"Mother, are you determined to parade your daughters in front of every eligible bachelor in America?"

"If that's what it takes to find a suitable match. Remember, all it takes is one rich husband and this family shall be settled for life."

"But what if we took the remaining money from Judith's husband and let a house in Charles Town? Perhaps we could be comfortable there."

"So you can be near this man."

"This man, as you call him, will not remain in Charles Town. He shall travel inland almost as soon as the ship docks."

"Then what would be the advantage of our family remaining in Charles Town. After a few weeks, that is."

Alicia wrung her hands. "Oh, Mama, do you not think everyone is on to your plan?"

"Alicia, every mother on this ship, if she has daughters, has designs on every young man aboard, and especially those with an annual income."

"Oh, Mother!" Red-faced from frustration, Alicia turned away again.

From the cabin next door came the cries of one of her sisters as she was set upon or teased by another. Her sisters could not stand being cooped up so long anymore than she could.

"Oh, those girls . . ." To her husband, she said, "Mr. Bentley, please take your nose out of that book and explain to your daughter the depth of our predicament."

Mr. Bentley lowered his book. "I'm quite sure Ally understands the depth of our predicament, every time she sees the size of her sister's belly."

"Mr. Bentley! How can you be so indiscreet?"

"My dear, it is not I who have been indiscreet, but Lindy—by sharing her favors with a dishonorable officer in service to the Crown."

"Oh, Mr. Bentley, how can you speak of our baby in such a manner?"

"Because our baby is no longer a baby, but shall soon have a baby of her own."

Her father reached out and took his daughter's hand. Alicia glanced at their hands together and smiled nervously. She could always count on her father's support.

"My dear," asked her mother, "do you know who Philippe Belle is? He's a Belle of Charles Town and due to inherit Cooper Hill, a fabulous inland plantation which puts to shame many of the estates in England. Now, take Captain Stuart, if you must, while certainly not a gentleman, his family owns Stuart and Company and he has an annual income of thousands of pounds, or so I am told. My dear, you are surrounded by young men who would—"

The cabin door swung open, and Marion stood there, glasses hanging around her neck. "Mother, come quickly! Lindy's having her baby."

"But that's impossible. It's much too soon!"

The women hustled out of their cabin and into the next-door cabin where they found Lindy writhing in her bed, the sheets wet.

She looked up. "Mama, I have wet myself."

Then the pain hit her, and she cried out.

Mrs. Bentley took her daughter's hand and stroked her forehead. "Everything's fine, Lindy. Mama's here."

Mr. Bentley sought out the doctor and, with him in tow, returned to stand outside Lindy's door. The doctor asked everyone but Mrs. Bentley to leave. Outside the cabin, the three girls hovered around their father. Mr. Bentley put his arms around Marion and Katie, but Alicia stood alone, head leaning into the bulkhead. Passengers nodded, smiled, and continued on their way.

The back of Alicia's neck heated up. If they were at home their embarrassment would be limited to their household.

Oh, please, Alicia! That's nothing but a fairy tale! Back in England, we would never live down what Lindy has done to the family's reputation. Oh, Lord, there has to be some way I can put all this behind me.

Katie burst into tears and turned her face into her father's shoulder. "Will Lindy be all right, Papa?"

Her father tightened his grip on his daughter's shoulder. "Lindy will be just fine. Women have been having babies ever since the beginning of time."

Inside the cabin, the doctor asked how long it had been between pains.

Lindy didn't know.

"How much time?" repeated the physician to the mother.

Mrs. Bentley did not appear to understand.

"What have other physicians recommended? Is there anything I should know?"

Mrs. Bentley could not remember.

"I'll need an assistant."

"I have birthed five girls."

"But have you ever been a midwife?"

Mrs. Bentley appeared puzzled.

To the open door, the doctor asked, "Have no preparations been made? Mr. Bentley, your daughter's bleeding."

"I'm the girl's mother," said his wife, blocking the doctor's view of her husband. "It is my duty."

The physician ignored her. "Is there anyone on this ship who can assist me?"

Alicia Bentley spoke up. "One of the scullery maids has birthed babies before, or so she told me."

"Then find her and bring her to me."

Alicia headed down the passageway, and as she passed one of the cabins occupied by the acting troupe, she noticed Gabriel and Portia at the open door.

The two actors raised their chins, sniffed the air, and looked down the passageway. When they focused on the Bentley cabin as the object of their desire, savage grins appeared on their faces. Their upper lips rose and they bared their fangs.

Drawn by the noise outside his cabin, the passenger across the passageway opened his door and saw the actors baring their teeth. Both Gabriel and Portia struggled to be first from their cabin, jamming themselves in the open door frame. They snarled at each other.

The passenger didn't wait to see more. He slammed shut his cabin door, turned, and leaned against the door. His hand fumbled for the latch, missed it, and eventually secured the lock.

His wife did not look up from where she sat mending one of her husband's socks with needle, thread, and darning egg by the light of a flickering candle. "Well, is the Bentley girl birthing her bastard child or not?"

Twenty-Two

When Susanna was informed by Alicia that her sister was birthing her baby and the doctor needed assistance, she left the pot she was stirring, burst out of the galley, and turned the corner leading to the passenger cabins. As Susanna raced down the passageway, she cleared her way by waving a stirring spoon and shouting a phrase learned from the crew.

"Make way! Make way!"

Passengers saw the girl headed in their direction and got out of the way—even Gabriel and Portia, who held a passenger between them. Seeing the young woman with the golden cross bouncing off her chest and the stirring spoon in her hand, the actors released their prey and disappeared into their cabin. One moment they were in the passageway; the next, the door to their cabin slammed shut and bolted.

Susanna leapt over the passenger dropped to the deck, and at the Bentleys' cabin door, stumbled to a stop—into Katie Bentley. Katie shrieked, passengers stuck their heads out cabin doors, and Katie's father said: "See here now." Although the greater threat had vanished, no one knew that.

Lindy lay on the bunk, hair tangled and matted across her forehead, a rise in the sleeping gown at the abdomen. The doctor looked up from where he sat at the side of the bed. He held a small piece of ice to the head of the pregnant girl.

"And you are?" asked the physician.

"I'm Susanna Chase." She curtsied. "How may I be of service?" Her hand clasped the spoon, one end damp from the contents of a pot she had been stirring.

"I think not!" said Mrs. Bentley and closed the door, leaving Susanna in the passageway.

An argument ensued between the doctor and the mother. Then, from the other side of the cabin door, and over the whines of Mrs. Bentley, came the doctor's voice.

"Miss Chase, we shall need a pitcher of water, a bowl, and a sheet. Tear the sheet into strips."

"Yes, sir."

Susanna turned to go, but Alicia, having followed Susanna from the galley and listened at her sister's door, stopped her friend.

Alicia took the stirring spoon. "I'll find those. Remain here with my sister."

Susanna knocked on the cabin door. "I have sent someone for a pitcher of water, a bowl, and the sheets, Doctor."

"Very well. Now, find the father and bring him here."

"Bring him here?" shrieked Mrs. Bentley from the

other side of the door. "What do you mean bring him in here? This is no place for a man. Why he will only upset my poor Lindy."

Lucius Fallows was already upset and ready to display his rage as he approached the cabin shared by Gabriel and Portia. But he was put off his stride upon entering the room and finding not only Gabriel and Portia but also Oren and Donato. All four sat on the two beds, and everyone jumped as Lucius slammed shut the door. Gabriel could not stop shaking. Portia had her arm around her brother, trying to calm him.

"So close . . . so close," muttered Donato.

"Well, what is it this time?" demanded Lucius. "We're out of London no more than two weeks and all of you need a nursemaid."

"The girl . . . the girl . . ." In Gabriel's lap lay a silk handkerchief he twisted with his hands.

Portia looked up. "The girl is as you said: a huntress."

"And we are trapped on this ship with her." Donato held his head in his hands, weeping. "All is lost . . . all is lost . . ."

"We had such a good life in London—" started Gabriel.

"But would've had to move on. You don't age, Gabriel. How would you have explained that to your contemporaries? For that reason, we move every ten years."

They did not face him, only stared at the floor of the cabin.

"In America we can move west with the country. I

tell you the French will put up little resistance with the number—"

Donato's head snapped up. "Oh, put away your politics, Lucius. I, for one, have supported you from the beginning, but the girl came after us with a wooden stake."

"And—and she wore a cross," stuttered Gabriel.

Lucius shared a cabin with no one. He knew nothing of any wooden stake, but he knew enough to fear one.

Taking a seat next to Portia, he said, "Tell me all about it."

"Dead?" asked Mrs. Bentley. "My baby's baby is dead?"

"Has been dead," said the doctor, entering the cabin. "Her body flushed the child out."

For once Mrs. Bentley was at a loss for words. Her husband put his hand around his wife's shoulder as they sat on the bed in their cabin.

Mrs. Bentley gulped for air. "I—I don't understand."

Marion sobbed, Katie appeared stunned, and on the other side of Mrs. Bentley, Alicia gripped her mother's hand and held it tightly. Susanna remained with Lindy in the next-door cabin.

"But my baby, my grandbaby . . ." Her head appeared loose on her shoulders. Her eyes would not focus.

Taking a bottle from his bag, the doctor offered it to her. "Take a drink of this, madam. It's laudanum."

While Mrs. Bentley took a long pull on the bottle, the doctor explained. "The baby was stillborn. Miss Chase will keep the child sequestered until you can make your arrangements. I have asked the Presbyterian minister to pay a call. There is no Anglican priest aboard this ship."

"What was wrong with the child?" asked Alicia.

"The umbilical cord became wrapped around his neck. He suffocated to death."

"He?" asked Mr. Bentley from where he sat with his arm around his wife. "The child was a boy?"

Mrs. Bentley returned the laudanum. She shrugged off her husband's arm and stood, shakily.

"Mrs. Bentley," said the doctor, reaching for the woman, "you must retake your seat and give the laudanum a chance to do its work."

"No, Doctor. I must go to my baby." Still, she swayed on her feet. "Lindy needs me more than ever before. Now, if you please. Give me your hand, Alicia. Lindy should not be with strangers."

Alicia scrambled to her feet and followed her mother and the doctor into the passageway and into the next-door cabin.

Mr. Bentley remained behind, staring straight ahead and mumbling, "A boy . . . a boy . . . it was a boy."

Marion continued to sob, but Katie merely asked, "Does this mean we can no longer have the dance?"

Twenty-Three

The trip to Charles Town was halfway over before Alicia Bentley returned to the platform on the forward mast; the same day, Alexander took Susanna aside after she finished serving a round of tea and hot chocolate to the men sitting at the tables on the main deck. Today's debate was over the novel *Pamela, or Virtue Rewarded,* but since the debaters were all men, the course of the argument detoured into the virtues of another fine novel, *The History of Tom Jones, A Foundling,* whose main character, according to the story, became quite the ladies' man.

"Miss Chase," asked Alexander, "is there a reason you are no longer cooking for the captain?"

"The cook said that wasn't my responsibility."

"For a clever girl, you are being rather foolish."

Susanna didn't know what to say, so she said nothing.

"There are members of the staff who would appreciate your taking on the responsibility of cooking for the captain again."

"I'm quite sure the cook did not put my name forward."

"Miss Chase, please."

"What is it you want of me, Alexander?"

"A decent meal for the captain and his staff."

"Is that an order?"

"Do I have to make it one?"

Susanna looked off toward the horizon. A breeze came through but failed to disturb her dress, apron, or headscarf. "On occasion, the captain says words that are quite hurtful."

Alexander nodded, then gestured at the tables where the men enjoyed their literary discussion. "Despite what you may see, Susanna, this is no place for a lady."

"I know that, Alexander."

"Do you? Only a foolish person would ignore the possibilities of a friendship with James Stuart. He condescends to speak to everyone and is concerned with everyone's needs, whether they be lady or gentleman, officer or ordinary seaman. I doubt you could find a more condescending patron."

Susanna said nothing.

"So, you are to go directly to the captain's quarters and request to be taken off washing pots and pans."

"The captain knows I'm no scullery maid."

"Of course he does, but little of the jealousy harbored by the cook for your ability."

"Actually, the cook believes I will succumb to his charms just for the opportunity to stir another pot in his kitchen."

"And I can assure you the cook will tell the captain that not only is he jealous of your abilities but also has kept you thus occupied because of the number of young men who wish to spend time with you."

"The number of young men who . . . pardon?"

"You heard what I said, Miss Chase."

Susanna looked at the tables where the men debated the merit of novel reading. Several attractive young men sat there, but the attractive ones sometimes did not make very good sense.

Alexander saw her look. "You cannot dispute that there are several young men who find you agreeable."

"I believe that has more to do with the shortage of females on this vessel."

"As you will similarly observe in the colonies. And such a surplus of men has distracted many a young woman from her duty."

Susanna's eyes narrowed. "What are you trying to tell me, Alexander?"

"My wife, who lives in Charles Town, and someone I hope to introduce you to, says women are often foolish but never stupid."

"Meaning?"

"That your treatment of the captain, of late, has been rather foolish, but I expect that to change."

The situation did change, and by evening, Susanna was once again serving the captain a meal of her own preparation.

That same afternoon, Lucius hung around the galley until Susanna offered him a biscuit.

Lucius declined because he did not eat, only drank, and certainly nothing this girl could prepare.

"You certainly gave us a fright, Miss Chase, running

down the hallway with that piece of wood in your hand. Weren't you afraid you might fall and hurt yourself?"

Susanna looked up from the oven. Across the room, the cook glared at her, but it only took one look from Lucius to turn the fat man away.

"I don't know what you mean, Mr. Fallows."

"That wooden stake you had in your hand while running down the passageway to assist in the delivery of the Bentley baby. I'm truly sorry the baby was stillborn. I'm sure its parents were looking forward to their first child and the Bentleys to their first grandchild."

Red spots appeared on Susanna's cheeks, and not from the oven. "I forgot I had a stirring spoon in my hand when I left the galley. Well, I guess a wooden stirring spoon is a piece of wood."

Lucius laughed, and a bit too long to suit Susanna.

"Mr. Fallows, are you laughing at me?"

Lucius had to regain control before he could explain. It was so tense coexisting with these people while also keeping a rein on Gabriel and Portia's passions.

"No, no," said Fallows, waving off her concern. "One of my party said you were a danger to yourself and the other passengers."

"And I suppose you'll report me to the captain?"

"No. Why should I?"

Glancing at the cook, Susanna said, "Everyone else does."

Susanna returned to her biscuits and Lucius to his cabin. He didn't even dignify the concerns of the others by clarifying the purpose of the stirring spoon but turned in for the day. Paranoia ran deep in his people, so there was little he could do or say that would dissuade Gabriel, Portia, and Donato from their fear of this girl—who appeared to be a normal young woman just trying to get on in the world. Just a normal girl was his last thought as he pulled the bed securely over him.

In the next cabin, Gabriel continued to discuss the danger of Susanna Chase with Donato and Portia.

"This girl should be dispatched, Donato, whether Lucius has the nerve to do it or not." The singer put forth his argument while his sister watched his performance.

Portia knew Lucius had been disappointed when he'd asked what she'd learned of the girl taken aboard at Liverpool. Portia knew little. The girl was always cooking or working for Major Ladd's wife or gossiping with the Bentley girl. Truth was, Portia didn't care for Susanna, and the feeling was mutual. Lucius, being a man, never understood the instant dislike one woman could have for another.

"Why don't you dispatch this girl yourself," asked Donato of Gabriel, "if you feel so strongly about the danger from her?"

The singer gestured to Portia, who sat on the opposite bed. "If my sister can't get near her, do you think I, a celebrity, will have a chance? Why, the people crowd about me."

Donato had to agree. He wished he had a thimble full of the magic enjoyed by Gabriel that drew people to this singer.

Portia turned her charm on the smaller man. "Donato,

someone must do this for the sake of the group. For some reason Lucius's mind has been clouded by this girl, though I have no idea why. Still, you must agree that the longer Lucius takes to dispatch this girl, the more he puts the mission at risk."

"My dear," said Donato, taking her hand, "this is the first time I've heard you speak in favor of our trip to the New World."

"It's the first time I've felt our mission to be in jeopardy. Prior to this, I assumed Lucius was capable of protecting us, but now I see . . ." Portia looked away.

Donato squeezed her hand. "We could bring this girl over to the dark side, if that would make you more comfortable."

Donato felt the warmth of her smile when Portia returned her gaze to him. "That's what we were thinking, and with your experience as a pickpocket, such a task would make you just the man for this."

Thus, Donato spent the next few evenings shadowing Susanna Chase while the girl prepared dishes in the galley. When he found her alone before the big dance, he came up behind her and tried to sink his teeth into her neck.

Sick and tired of the cook's advances, Susanna swung back the stirring spoon with such savagery that the wooden handle shaft pierced Donato's silk shirt and plunged into his heart. Donato fell away, and when Susanna turned around, she was horrified to find the small man lying on his back, teeth snapping this way and that way.

In this manner, the cook found his assistant hovering

over Donato and begging the small man not to die. The cook's eyes widened in horror as Susanna pulled the spoon from Donato's chest.

The small man blinked and raised his head, eager for a second chance at the girl's throat. He opened his mouth, bared his teeth—only to swallow the gold cross swinging from Susanna's neck. Minutes later, Donato was dead and the dance was canceled.

Katie Bentley was not pleased.

Twenty-four

Stuart could not get to sleep with all the sobbing in the adjacent cabin. He had lain in his bed for the last hour, off and on falling asleep, only to be wakened again and again by the sobbing. He reached up and pulled back the curtain over the stern window and saw it was still light. He stuck his legs over the side of the trundle bed, pulled himself up, and dressed.

Stepping out of his cabin, Stuart summoned a cabin boy and gave him instructions on whom to fetch. The boy scampered off as Stuart tucked his shirt into his pants, and barefoot, stepped next door. His knock seemed to provoke the girl into another fit of weeping.

Kyrla cracked open the door. "What do you want, James?"

"I want the young lady to stop crying."

"Easier said than done. She just killed a man."

"But there's no reason for her to be concerned over the death of a man making untoward advances."

Kyrla glanced at the girl who sat on her bed, arms wrapped around her knees, rocking back and forth. Susanna saw Kyrla looking at her, whimpered, and turned away.

"She believes her reaction wasn't in proportion to the attack."

"What else could she do?"

"Nothing. That's what she's fretting about."

"Then have her fret at a lower volume."

"James, I cannot say that to someone who's suffering."

"Then consider this your last trip on the *Mary Stewart*."

Stuart turned to go, and Kyrla followed him, leaving open the cabin door. For a moment, the crying stopped, then started up again, well, more like sniveling. Lord, thought Stuart, he didn't have time for this.

Kyrla seized her brother's arm and turned him around. When Stuart looked at the hand on his arm, her hand fell away.

"What did you mean by that?" she asked.

"I mean, if you can't turn down the volume on this girl, then what good are you to me?"

"I can pilot this ship."

"I can always find another pilot."

"Not one as good as me."

"That's your opinion."

Across the deck, Martin Chase appeared topside, sweaty and agitated. The ship had sprung a leak, and although insignificant, sailors would have to go below and man the pump a half hour of each shift to stay ahead of the leak. Seeing Stuart's sleep had already been disturbed, he crossed the deck to the stern-side cabins.

"This is not right. You cannot leave me ashore."

"I can and will. This is my ship."

"I'll take it up with Mother."

"Yes, of course, whining instead of doing your job."

"My job? I do my job."

"But now, because you're a woman, you have an additional opportunity, one that sets you apart from everyone else, and you're squandering it."

Martin took Kyrla by the arm and steered her away. "If I've told you once, I've told you a thousand times, you're nothing more than an ordinary seaman aboard this ship, and no one's sister."

Stuart took this opportunity to return to the open cabin door and knock again. Behind him, the cabin boy appeared topside with Alicia Bentley dressed in black, including a bonnet.

"Miss Chase?" Stuart asked through the open door of the cabin on the starboard side.

"Yes?" whined the girl.

"You need some air. Take a turn or two around the deck with Miss Bentley."

"Miss Bentley is in mourning. Her nephew died."

"That's an order, Miss Chase."

He nodded to Alicia and headed for the center cabin, but before he ducked inside, he said, "You need to change from those clothes or remain below, Miss Bentley. They're not suitable for this heat."

"Aye, aye, sir." Alicia stepped inside Susanna's cabin and closed the door.

"You work for the captain now?"

"Oh, Susanna, don't be foolish."

"I'm tired of people calling me a fool. Somewhere in the Bible it's a sin to call someone that."

"Then stop acting like one and take a turn around the deck."

"You should be with your family. Your sister's baby died."

Alicia shook her head. "My place is wherever you are."

"What—what do you mean?"

"You and I are headed to a new world, a place where we shall, hopefully, meet our husbands and start families. But there are many aboard this ship that fail to understand how different the colonies are, and how different we and our families might become after living there. Susanna, don't be surprised if Donato is not the last man you'll kill to survive in this new world."

On their second turn around the deck, Kyrla tried to join them, but Alicia shook her head.

The Ladds strolled in the opposite direction, nodding and continuing down the deck. Then, dropping from the rigging, John Belle landed in front of them.

After the amenities had been exchanged, John said, "I was sorry to hear about your nephew. I was at the service, but I don't think you saw me."

"Don't concern yourself, Mr. Belle," said Alicia. "It wasn't meant to be."

"Yes, yes," he said, walking along, head down. "I heard it was a boy."

"Yes. A boy."

The three of them walked together, and John got around to telling Alicia that he missed their conversations on the foredeck platform.

"They were quite enjoyable, Miss Bentley." Then, very quickly, he added, "I meant no disrespect to your nephew."

"No offense taken."

Walking toward them, the Ladds took Susanna aside, leaving John and Alicia to stroll together, and shortly, Major Ladd found something to study over the side, perhaps another shark. Ladd had become quite fond of firing muskets at them; one or two he had even hit. Soon, he was discussing with a sailor the fact that sharks appeared to never stop moving.

Mrs. Ladd and Susanna walked on, the two women using the older woman's parasol as a shield against the sun, but nothing could stop members of the crew and other passenger from staring at Susanna.

Mrs. Ladd noticed this increased attention. "Miss Chase, since you've served more than one lady before coming into my service, I do not believe it presumptuous to say Donato was not the first young man to make untoward advances."

"No, ma'am, he was not."

"That point established I wish to warn you of more advances from that quarter *because* of your success in this incident."

Susanna tightened her grip on the older woman's arm. "My Lord, madam, what do you mean?"

"Young lady, do not blaspheme."

Susanna's hand came off Mrs. Ladd's arm and she crossed herself. "I'm sorry, ma'am. It's just that what you said was so unexpected."

"I understand, but remember, the more you push

them away, the more men press on you, and yours was a rather extreme push."

"I didn't mean to kill the man, you must believe me."

"Miss Chase, when you put the handle of a stirring spoon through the chest of someone, it had to have been a reaction to an extreme measure, though I do not care to hear the details."

"Still, I had no idea I would become such a temptation."

"Perhaps a more appropriate word would be 'target.'"

On their next trip around the deck, they passed Alicia Bentley and John Belle. John appeared to have said something to cause his companion to laugh, and Alicia's laughter followed them down the deck, floating on the breeze.

"As you can see, young women are meeting young men in circumstances other than the family parlor or the neighborhood church. It leaves a young woman open to all sorts of advances. And ruin."

"What am I to do, Mrs. Ladd?"

"Until you are safely in the bosom of the family to which you are indentured, find a man who will offer you his protection. A proper champion will make young men think twice about untoward advances, especially those young men who could later turn out to be far more troublesome than you could ever imagine."

Thus, the next time they circled the stern area, Susanna excused herself and knocked on James Stuart's door.

"Captain Stuart! Captain Stuart!"

"Yes?" groaned Stuart. "What is it this time?"

TWENTY-FIVE

"**I**'m uncomfortable with this new world you're describing."

Alicia and John sat on the forward platform sheltered by a canvas top made from a piece of old sail. Overhead, the sailor in the crow's nest stared down at them. As usual, they ignored him.

Alicia's head was covered by a bonnet; John's slough hat protected his face. Alicia wore her roughly cut dress fashioned into a sort of pants. She had gotten used to wearing the cut-up dress and had become quite happy in the company of John Belle. Still, there had been consequences. Her mother would not speak to her, and Katie and Lindy mocked her for falling in love with "the wooden man"—called that because of John Belle's extended periods of solitude.

To ward off Mrs. Bentley's incessant carping about Alicia's interest in John Belle, Mr. Bentley and Marion had begun borrowing books from the captain's bookshelf. Still, when her sister and her father began reading John Milton's *Paradise Lost,* this became another prickly issue for Mrs. Bentley to carp about. Everyone knew Milton had been a supporter of Cromwell and barely escaped the Restoration with his head.

"Why can't you read *Robinson Crusoe?*" demanded Mrs. Bentley, who read nothing and had learned little.

Still, after three weeks at sea, and though others in her family remained stuck in the life of country gentry, Alicia could tell she was changing, and she noted these changes in her diary.

John said she was becoming an American, and it mattered little where one came from or who one had been. Americans were all the same and fairly equal, because so many had so little. True, there were those quite rich enough to attempt to lord it over others, but most of the Englishmen who crossed the ocean had brought along few personal belongings—which is why Stuart and Company was growing rich from all the trinkets sold to both the Red Man and the colonists. Americans were becoming a people who wished to purchase this or that in an attempt to stand out from all others, and thereby became copies of each other.

"But how did the colonies develop a separate identity from the Mother Country? Aren't we all Englishmen?"

John said it was all the newspapers, journals, and books available in Charles Town, Philadelphia, Boston—as well as that new trading port of New York where a Philadelphia lawyer had successfully defended John Peter Zenger against the charge of libel. When the jury brought back a verdict of "not guilty," there had followed an explosion of information. Even Benjamin Franklin owned a newspaper in Charles Town, and all that information kept the colonists in touch with the Mother Country, yet made them think differently.

Alicia wondered if she dared ask if her diary might be published in this new world. But who could she ask? She dared not ask John. What would he think of a woman who harbored inclinations to write? Even Susanna, as bold and confident as she was, had been shocked to learn her friend harbored such a desire.

Alicia noticed the blue horizon had turned gray. Clouds had formed; dark shafts appeared to touch the sea's surface. A storm would be coming, and it would create a sharp contrast to the sameness of the ocean. Oddly enough, where Alicia was headed offered more sameness, a continent covered entirely by trees.

"Is the destruction of the forest absolutely necessary?"

John nodded, and when he did, he looked into her eyes with his own deep blue ones. His white skin had a sun-reddened tinge to it, but otherwise he bore no tan. This was not true for Alicia. Her arms and face were deeply tanned, and whenever she examined herself at night before she went to bed, the white of her stomach against her highly tanned arms was startling; certainly inappropriate for an English lady.

It saddened Alicia that she would never see Judith again, or Judith's children, but that was for the best. Lindy had disgraced the family with her pregnancy, and their landlord, a minister, had no alternative but to turn them out. Perhaps, over the years, the stain would fade, but her family would've always been looked down on, perhaps even sliding into poverty by the limited choices of men she and her sisters would have had to choose from.

"I'm sorry if I've upset you," said John.

"Oh, no, I was just thinking . . ."

"Of England."

"Yes."

"You'll soon forget all that. South Carolina is very different, and there's much to be done, so much that England will become but a distant memory."

Alicia pulled her legs up and wrapped her arms around them. "I know of Sherwood Forest, and I have visited the Major Oak where Robin Hood and his merry band of men lived. Sherwood Forest is so immense . . . it's hard to comprehend a whole continent covered with trees, and that we Englishmen shall be responsible for destroying all those trees."

Belle laughed. "Well, we could always become Frenchmen. The French leave the forest as they find it."

"As do you."

"I'm a trapper."

"And what do you do with all your money from trapping, John Belle?" she asked with a sly smile. "You are quite a shot with that bow of yours."

"In the forest I use a long gun."

"A long gun?"

"With rifling. It sends the bullet true to the target."

"Then you skin the creatures and sell their pelts?"

"Yes."

"As I asked before: What do you do with your money? Some of those pelts sell for quite a bit of money."

"I buy land in Spartan District."

"Where's that?"

"In the northern part of the colony."

And over a period of time, Alicia drew from her taciturn woodsman the following tale:

"Governor Johnson, the first royal governor, proposed, back in the thirties, that six townships be established in the Back Country. Most failed because Charles Town used those townships as buffers against the Indians, much like we use the colony of Georgia today. These days, new arrivals are German and Scots-Irish who travel the Great Wagon Road from Pennsylvania, down through Virginia and North Carolina. New immigrants are good for the Back Country since the French compete with us for the allegiance of the Cherokee.

"I spent much of my childhood in the woodlands along the Cooper River where Africans and Red Men were my tutors—in addition to the young man employed to teach me how to read and write and master Latin. From the newly arrived Africans, I learned potions and songs; from the Red Men, how to interpret the signs of the forest and my proficiency with the longbow.

"I admit I was a difficult child who would rather be at play in the woods, especially if that play included tracking animals. This, of course, would have all been for naught if I had not been a dead shot, a trait I inherited from my father, who was famous for his dueling skills with either a pistol or sword.

"At thirteen, I ran away from home and joined a wagon train of peddlers selling goods to the new arrivals in the Back Country. I personally favor the Germans myself. A Scots-Irish will fight at the most imagined slight or insult. And at the intersection of the road from

Charles Town and the Great Wagon Road, near the former Fredericksburg, I fell in with a party of hunters who wondered how accurate a boy my age could be with a long gun.

"Though my weapon was smooth bore, it was accurate enough to win a real beauty with rifling, and with this long gun from Pennsylvania I crossed the mountains, even once or twice joining a hunting party that included an excellent tracker by the name of Daniel Boone."

"But why in the world would you purchase land, John? I thought your heart belonged to the forest? You must've had more than one special friend over the mountains."

John looked away, in the direction of the approaching storm. "I might have other friends . . . special friends in other places."

"Oh, a girl in every forest?" Alicia laughed.

Still staring at the horizon, John said, "Perhaps one special one . . . on this ship."

Twenty-six

The following day, Lucius Fallows was called into James Stuart's cabin to discuss the attack by Donato on Susanna Chase. When Fallows arrived, he found the African posted at the door, the first mate and the major sitting where Lucius had once sat as a member of the court of inquiry judging Susanna Chase's virtue.

"What's this?" he asked, hurrying from the daylight turning to dusk in the shadows of an approaching storm. "The Spanish Inquisition?"

Stuart sat at the far end of the table and did not smile at Fallows' attempt at humor. No mallet lay on the table in front of Stuart, but he did have his Bible handy.

Before moving to the other side of the table, Lucius requested the Bible be removed. He said he would answer any questions plainly and honestly, as would any member of his troupe, but his people were nonbelievers and would not swear on a Bible.

"You're pagans?" asked the major.

"Or members of whatever denomination is passing through at the moment."

"What country is this?" asked the major.

"Transylvania. Part of the Hapsburg Empire. For this reason many of my fellow countrymen choose to live in the mountains among the gypsies. Very much like John Belle, who lives with other long-range hunters in the over-the-mountain settlements of North Carolina." Fallows did not smile when he added, "We would simply like to be left alone."

"As does everyone who sails for the New World," said Stuart. He took the Bible from the table and slid it into a drawer.

"I'm not so sure about that," said the major, watching the Bible go.

"Major, Mr. Fallows has promised to answer our questions truthfully and has admitted to not being a Christian. What else would you have me do? I certainly would not want to make Mr. Fallows place his hand on a Bible representing a religion he does not believe in. My mother was a Huguenot who fled France because of such persecution."

"Very well," grumbled the major. In his heart, he simply didn't trust actors.

"Catholics, Calvinists, Lutherans, Romans, Mongols, and Turks—they have all ruled my country, and always looted it. As some say: Transylvania sits at the crossroads of hell and suffers the world's sins."

"So," asked the major, "for one of your party to go stark raving mad . . ."

"Unexpected, yes. Startling, no." Lucius went to

stand on the other side of the table. "Now, gentlemen, what is it that you wish to know?"

"This is not an official court of inquiry," said Stuart. "If there are more serious charges to be brought, you will certainly hear of them, but we would like to know more about this fellow Donato."

"Very well. Donato joined our troupe before we left our homeland, and if anyone suffered from undernourishment when a child, Donato would be that child. He also had a high-pitched voice we valued because of the number of places Portia is not allowed to perform. And he was not self-conscious on the stage, which is what acting is all about.

"As for the attack on Miss Chase, none of the members of my group could've conceived that Donato would do such a thing. The only hint we had, looking back on this tragedy, would be that Donato did not like children. He would bully them. And kick dogs, cats, chickens, whatever was in his way."

"But you failed to warn us," accused Ladd.

"Warn you about what? That Donato was a bully? With his size, who would have believed me? And he bullied children, of which there are few on this ship."

The image of Billy flashed through Stuart's mind, and it must've shown on his face.

"I'm sorry, Captain. Did I say something to upset you?"

"No, no. But you're quite sure Donato had never attacked a woman before?"

Lucius shook his head. Attacking women was something his kind did on a regular basis, but certainly not in a manner anyone in this room would understand.

"I find that hard to believe," said Ladd.

"What can I say, Major? Captain Stuart and I worked out the details of the performances before my people came aboard, and since there was no objection to Portia performing while the ship was at sea, I could've easily left Donato behind if I'd thought he was a threat to the passengers."

Fallows looked around the table. "Everyone in this room is aware of the reputation of actors, and that is why, when I provided for this trip, I insisted on actors above reproach."

"That would be a trick," laughed Alexander from the door. "Actors above reproach."

Lucius opened his hands in a gesture of helplessness. "Everyone knows I have to tolerate Gabriel's high regard for himself and his sister's high-handed manner. You would think Portia would be able to make friends with anyone—she's certainly gracious enough, but Portia has been on the stage since she was a child and knows what the public thinks of actresses."

"And Oren?" asked Ladd.

"Acting requires a great deal of moving from one place to the next. Having Oren along makes life much simpler."

"And you, Mr. Fallows?" asked James Stuart.

"As I told you, Captain, I financed this trip from a gunpowder factory I built in central Europe." Fallows looked uneasy. "But I do harbor a secret."

All eyes focused on the actor.

He smiled sheepishly. "I'm rather taken with celebrities."

"One in particular, I would imagine."

Lucius smiled at Stuart. "Yes. That would be true."

"Meaning this woman who travels with you?" asked Alexander.

"Portia."

"Miss Portia is not a witch, is she?"

Everyone looked at the African.

"Members of the crew have inquired," said Alexander. "I, myself, come from an island known for its zombies. Witches, I don't believe in, but the undead, that's another matter."

Fallows studied the black man. "Mr. Alexander—"

"Just Alexander. My last name would give a clue to whom I once belonged, and I would rather die than be returned to that sugar plantation."

Lucius looked from one man to another sitting in judgment of him. "All of us are men, and as men, we realize that Miss Portia does not require witchcraft to bedevil any man."

In Gabriel and Portia's cabin, Lucius was not as reasonable. Brother and sister sat close together, holding hands. Oren was not there. After receiving permission from the captain, he was about to dispose of Donato's body.

"It would appear the captain held another court of inquiry," said Portia.

"It may as well have been," said Lucius, towering over them.

"Do you think you convinced them?"

"I don't know."

"What Donato did was nothing like my brother turning the transportees against the crew."

"Major Ladd is suspicious of everyone."

"I say we throw him over the side," said Gabriel.

"What if I throw you over the side? You're the one responsible for us falling under suspicion."

Gabriel shifted around on the bed. "I don't know what you're talking about."

"Please don't be that way," said Portia. "It would appear Donato took his own initiative, but we're the ones who must live with the consequences."

Lucius regarded the woman. "I wonder . . ."

"What are you insinuating?" asked Gabriel, looking up. "That my sister had something to do with this?"

"I hadn't until you mentioned it."

"Lucius, why would I encourage Donato to do such a thing?"

"Perhaps because you could not get close to this girl I was once concerned about."

"That you were *once* concerned about?" asked Portia.

"We are above these people," said Gabriel. "They should fear us and do our bidding, but you, Lucius, prefer that we remain below deck and slink about at night."

"If we do go topside, there's nothing but misfortune. This story will circulate, and I wonder if anyone will even be on deck for our appearance tonight."

Gabriel straightened. "They will come to hear me sing."

Lucius looked at him. "You really think Donato decided all by himself to bring the girl over?"

"Maybe," said Gabriel, again unable to meet Lucius' eyes.

"Portia, I've been observing this girl because you rarely leave this cabin—"

"You see how men look at me."

"Men have always looked at you in that manner, and if I won't turn you loose on them, you see little reason to leave this room."

"I—I have my tapestry," said Portia, gesturing at her workbag on the drop-down table.

"I act as though you are someone to be adored and treasured, but sailors are not so easily fooled."

"You are not to speak to my sister in that manner!"

"Your problem is Susanna Chase and the Bentley girl. Sailors look at those two and understand they must not stare or make untoward advances or someone will pluck out their eyes."

Gabriel was on his feet now. "Perhaps I should pluck out yours!"

Lucius paid him no mind. "Men know which women they may have their way with."

Gabriel slapped him.

Lucius looked at the brother and smiled. He did not raise his hand, nor did he raise his voice.

Portia shuddered. All Lucius said was true. Ever since she'd become a woman, men—young and old—had taken an excessive interest in her. At first, Portia thought it was because of her beauty, but it soon became clear, from observing other young men with their women, that many men thought she had been put on earth to please *them.* Watching young men court her friends, she'd been amused by their fumbling demeanor and lack of certainty, but when men approached her they seemed to know what they wanted, and on this ship were the worst of all men: sailors.

"It may have been vanity," concluded Lucius, "but I can now see there was little chance of my plan working on such a grand scale."

Gabriel returned to his seat beside his sister. "Good to see you coming to your senses. We can still seize control of the ship."

"The personnel failed, not the plan."

"What do you mean?" An edge returned to the singer's voice.

"There's nothing I can do to control you, Gabriel, so the next time something like this occurs, there will be consequences. I shall rip off your head and throw it over the side. A few knots from that location I will toss the rest of you into the ocean."

Portia came off the bed. "You cannot do this! You are not to threaten my brother so."

"My dear, I can do anything I wish. I am immortal."

Outside the cabin, an explosion rocked the ship. Lightning had struck the mainmast, knocking passengers and crew to the deck, some from the rigging. John Belle and Alicia Bentley were blown off the forward mast platform and into the ocean.

Below deck, and through a hole opened by the lightning, a splintered portion of the mast forced its way though the ceiling of the cabin, impaling Lucius Fallows.

Twenty-seven

Stuart and Martin Chase were in Stuart's cabin when the storm struck. Susanna was serving tea, and lying on the corner of the table was a pair of knitted gloves. Stuart didn't know what to make of the gloves but remembered to thank their maker. Perhaps he overdid it. A blush of surprise appeared on the girl's face.

"You are quite welcome, Captain. You walk the deck so late at night I thought you might find them useful." Her intention had been to bind this man to her for the duration of the trip, as Mrs. Ladd had recommended. Nothing more.

"Indeed, I shall. Thank you again." He rose from his chair and jammed the gloves into a rear pocket.

At the door, Susanna lifted the latch. "I have prepared a special lunch for you and your staff today, sir."

"Susanna, before you go . . ."

The girl turned from the door. Her hand slipped off the latch. "Yes, sir."

Martin watched all this with not a little curiosity. Handsome girls were always trying to catch the captain's eye, but in the past he always ignored their gaze.

"Please close the door," said Stuart.

Susanna did.

"I need to ask you a question."

Martin glanced at Stuart.

"Why, yes, sir. What may I do for you?" Perhaps the gloves had been a bit too much.

"The night the Bentley child was stillborn, when you ran down the passageway to assist in the delivery, did you see either Portia or Gabriel grappling with one of the passengers?"

The girl appeared perplexed. "Why, no, sir, I did not." She considered this. "I did see a passenger on the deck. I had to jump over him." Susanna thought for a moment, became aware of some of her hair being loose, and raised her hands to retie her scarf.

A sudden intake of breath by her cousin followed. Though the girl's dress covered her arms and had a high neckline, there was no mistaking the girl's figure for anything except that of the most winsome young woman on the ship.

Susanna saw her cousin staring at her and smiled. "By the time I received my instructions from the doctor, that person had left the passageway."

"Ill?"

"Could've been, but I don't remember any sign of sickness in the passageway."

There was a knock at the door.

It was Alicia Bentley. She stepped into the cabin and curtsied to the two men—who promptly got to their feet and nodded in her direction. She no longer wore her black dress and bonnet, but a simple dress.

"Sorry to intrude, Captain, but I'm to help Susanna make your cabin presentable for the ladies' tea club today." Volunteering was the only distraction she had until reaching Charles Town.

Martin grinned at her. "You're not spending the day aloft with John Belle?"

"I think not. There appears to be quite a storm approaching."

"And if there were not?"

"Martin," said the captain, "watch your tongue."

"I've—I've been forbidden to climb the rigging."

Martin turned on Stuart. "You did this, Captain?"

"Of course not. As far as I'm concerned, Miss Bentley and Miss Chase have the run of the ship, but are not to go below deck—beyond the passengers' cabins, that is—unless chaperoned."

"My mother forbade me," said Alicia, looking at the deck. Her mother had also discovered her diary and thrown it overboard.

"Miss Bentley," said the first mate, "I have no right to speak to you in this manner—"

"Then don't," cautioned Stuart.

"You are about to begin a new life in Carolina, and onboard an oceangoing vessel is just the place to learn the rules of life in the New World. The first rule is that the people of Carolina care little for form, or what you have been led to believe are the most important aspects of life: who your family is or your education. The people of Carolina care about what works, or what can be made to work. Or they will starve to death."

"Martin, do not frighten these girls."

But the girls didn't seem frightened, only quite interested in what the first mate had to say.

"Those who first came to America had to provide food and shelter for their families, sailing thousands of miles in some of the leakiest ships to arrive in the colonies completely responsible for themselves and their future. So my advice would be to reconsider the social mores of your previous life in light of what is to your advantage."

"Martin, keep a civil tongue in your head."

The first mate ignored his captain. "If you believe someone is a worthy ally, seek him out and cultivate—"

"Martin!" shouted Stuart, but he was barely heard over the sound of lightning cracking off in the distance and the resultant roll of thunder.

If Stuart had not been so involved in checking such an impertinent discussion between sexes, he would have realized the storm was quite nearby. Instead, he busied himself ushering Susanna and Alicia out of the cabin.

Shutting the door behind them, he turned to his first mate. "Martin, it's not the business of Stuart and Company to involve ourselves in the personal affairs of the passengers."

The first mate tried to object, but Stuart held up his hand. "If there had been an objection to the actress Portia performing on this ship because she is a woman, then Portia would not have performed. You should know by now we make very little money if our ship develops a reputation for impropriety. Families will not sail with us, and families, especially the wives, talk incessantly about whether they had a pleasant voyage or not. Letters are written, and cabins go empty."

"I only speak the truth, Captain. Neither of those girls is prepared for what she will find in America."

"Be that as it may, you may only speak to your cousin in this manner, not Miss Bentley."

"The Bentleys still believe they are in England."

"That is none of your concern. If I must forbid you speaking in such a manner to that young woman, I shall do it."

"Then do it, Captain, but until that time, I am my own man." And Martin left the cabin, leaving Stuart staring at the door.

Moments later, someone knocked.

"Come!"

Alexander stuck his head inside. "I have Miss Chase."

"Good. Bring her in."

The girl came back in, looking at Stuart at the far end of the table and at Alexander, leaning against the closed cabin door.

"What's this? Another inquiry into my virtue?"

"Miss Chase, don't be bold. It's not very becoming."

Stuart pulled out a chair and asked her to take a seat. Susanna did, but before he could question her, Alexander issued a warning.

"Storm coming in fast, Captain. I've alerted the lookouts, and Martin's gone below. I just hope the passengers have cleaned out their chamber pots. They may need them."

Stuart nodded his acknowledgment.

"If this is what I think it is," said Susanna, "you have nothing to worry about, Captain. I'm not about to take my cousin's advice."

Alexander looked quizzically at the captain.

Stuart sighed. "Martin's been relating tales of life in America to Miss Chase and Miss Bentley."

The African looked at the girl. "What'd he say?"

"Please, Alexander, this is none of our business."

Susanna could not pass up such an opportunity. The captain was so proper. She smiled when she said, "Martin said I should do as I please when I reach Charles Town."

Alexander grinned. "That has a nice ring to it. Right out of a romance, I would say."

Stuart tried to cut them off but didn't stand a chance.

Susanna raised her voice over the thunder. "You're the one who recommended the pants-dress so Alicia could climb the rigging. You, most of all, should understand."

"Alexander, is this true?"

"Oh, Captain, what do I know about ladies' fashion?"

Susanna just sat and smiled. She would see how the captain extricated himself from this.

Stuart let out a breath. Pretty girls on a ship always became a nuisance. They couldn't help themselves. "Miss Chase, this is what I would like to know: The night of your rescue, how did you escape from the window of that . . . house?"

"I jumped."

"Out a second-story window?"

"Mr. Fallows caught me."

"Fallows caught you?"

Susanna nodded. "He's quite strong."

"He had a ladder?" asked Alexander.

"Mr. Donato did." Susanna stopped and stared at the table. "Honestly, I—I didn't mean to hurt him."

"Miss Chase," said Stuart, "please do not let this upset you. You had no other choice."

Her head jerked up. "Violence is never a solution. I should've turned the other cheek." Tears ran down her cheeks. "I pray each night, but I feel my soul is consigned to hell."

"It was self-defense," said Stuart, rather lamely.

"I broke a commandment."

"No court in the land would hold you responsible."

"I hold myself accountable. God holds me accountable."

"Then find a way to redeem yourself," said Alexander.

They both looked at the black man.

Susanna wiped her tears away. "What—what do you mean?"

"Good works. Earn your way back into the grace of God."

Stuart could not believe what he was hearing. First, Martin giving social advice, and now Alexander preaching—

An explosion rocked the ship, knocking Alexander and Stuart to the floor of the cabin. They threw out their hands to catch themselves. Susanna shrieked and grabbed the table, laying her head and arms across it, trying to hold on as the world moved around her.

Had they been attacked?

It sounded like a twelve-pounder.

"Lightning strike," said Alexander, getting to his feet. "There will be burns, perhaps a fire or two."

Then the storm hit, rain pelting the ship so hard it sounded like marbles. The *Mary Stewart* shuddered under the impact and leaned with the blow. All three of them slid to the port side of the cabin and fought to regain their footing. Alexander used the latch on the door to return to his feet, but once he opened the cabin door, a gust of wind forced him back. As he watched, a sizeable piece of wood splintered off the mainmast and slid to the deck, piercing the main deck and bringing down one corner of the mainsail.

Twenty-eight

The deck was a mess, and people were hurting. Rain splattered Stuart, stinging like needles, and the wind tried to knock him off his feet. The lantern hanging from an overhead beam was missing and a metallic odor enveloped him as he struggled out the cabin door. In the darkness created by the clouds, he could barely make out passengers from crew—dead, unconscious, many calling for help. Quite a few were trapped under the rigging or the piece of mainmast sail brought down when the mainmast was struck by lightning. As Stuart moved toward the helm, someone bumped into him in the murky darkness of the downpour.

Katie Bentley, holding her arm. She'd suffered a compound fracture and the bone protruded through the skin.

"Please, help me."

Alexander was there, taking the girl. "This is not your job, James. Think of the whole ship, not just one person."

Susanna stood beside the black man, her mouth agape, head scarf soaked, and dress beginning to cling to her. She could not take her eyes off the sight of that bone.

Off in the cloudy darkness came the sound of the bosun piping all hands on deck. Sailors raced topside.

Stuart knelt down and felt the deck. As he did, he fished a string of leather from his pocket and banded his hair behind his head. The deck was wet but also warm, and for the first time he noticed a strip of wood burned away in a line leading to the cabin door behind him. That's why the lantern was missing. It had been blown to pieces when lightning had run down the mainmast, raced across the deck, and grounded itself in the metal lantern.

Was there fire below? Near the armory?

Thoroughly soaked, Stuart returned to his feet and pressed forward through the rain and wind. In the darkness, he could see those knocked to the deck, so others must have been blown overboard. He would have to do something about that, but not right now. The bosun was making his way toward the helm, but since he had been caught near the bow when the lightning struck, he was having trouble weaving his way through the spars, rigging, and the piece of the mainmast sail flapping madly on the main deck.

Kyrla raced past him, pulling on her stocking hat. She was headed for the helm, where the on-duty helmsman lay, the wheel at liberty and a member of the crew trying to regain control.

Stuart shouted at crew members when they appeared

topside. "Now listen up! You, you, you, and you, secure that wreckage! Put that piece of mainmast sail on the deck! The helm cannot see the bow and the ship is sailing blind. And one of you go below. You there—yes, you!"

The sailor raised a hand to shelter his eyes from the rain.

"Check for fire and report to me personally."

"Aye, aye, sir." He scampered off in the direction of the below-deck ladder.

Through a speaking trumpet came: "Hands 'bout ship! Hands 'bout ship!"

The bosun had paused mid-deck to issue an order from the tangle of sail, spars, and rigging. Blowing his whistle, he piped the crew to action. More sailors appeared topside, many skidding across the deck and slamming into the railing as the ship roiled in the heavy seas. Since the *Mary Stewart* sailed low in the water, the deck was awash with water, four or five inches, overwhelming the drains. When the wash reached the below-deck stairs, it poured into the passageway and, from there, into the hold. Bloodstains immediately disappeared from wherever they may have been.

"Man the pumps!" shouted the bosun. "Man the pumps!" Again the pipes shrilled.

Forward was a dangling menace of spars and rigging, but when Stuart looked astern he found the mizzenmast sail and the spanker intact. Facing the bow again, he noticed lightning had splintered the mainmast, and now he could see where the electrical charge had burned a hole through the deck, blackening the wood around the strike. The sky billowed clouds, thunder rolled, and lightning struck to the south, but not very far, once, twice, a third time. North of them appeared a shaft of light through the angry gray clouds of the storm.

Stuart saw his sister fighting with the helm, trying to bring the wheel under control. A member of the crew joined her but failed to set his feet properly, and the wheel flipped the sailor off. He flew across the deck and landed in a heap. He must've hit his head because he didn't move again.

Members of the crew struck by lightning gripped their heads and wandered or crawled along the deck, evidently blinded or burned so severely they could not stand the pain. Screaming and hollering, they stumbled and fumbled about, several running into the railing, and realizing where they were, threw themselves into the cool of the ocean. Their crewmates reached out for them, but taken by surprise by this odd behavior, the injured sailors were over the side and gone before anyone could grab them.

Stuart saw this. "Heave to! Heave to!"

The waves rose around them, spilling more water across the deck; the thunder became deafening, and the wind pressed into him. To steady himself, Stuart put a hand on the cracked mainmast and idly wondered if lightning could strike twice in the same place. With the ship rolling in the swells, Stuart finally grabbed a line running down the mainmast and held on tightly. Anything not tied down rolled or skidded across the deck: barrels, ropes, smoking pipes, members of the crew. A cannon broke free on the starboard side and slid in Stuart's direction.

"Loose cannon! Loose cannon!"

He sidestepped the weapon, and ended up facing astern—where he saw a yellow parasol in the rigging. He recognized the parasol as the one belonging to Katie Bentley.

The loose cannon slammed into the port-side railing, bounced off, and with the aid of the rolling ship, headed back across the deck. One of the sailors struck by lightning crawled across the deck and into the path of the oncoming cannon.

"Avast, there!" shouted Stuart, releasing his hold on the mainmast rope and reaching for the man's shoulder. "You there, hold up!"

The sailor shook off the hand and continued toward the stern—where the cannon hit him, carrying him across the deck and crushing him between the weapon and the railing. The sailor screamed, but was cut off quickly. Several sailors were on it, seizing the weapon, shoving it back into position, and making it fast. There was little they could do for the sailor.

Kyrla had the wheel under control.

"Heave to!" shouted Stuart. "Use the foresail and spanker!"

The bosun arrived and held onto the mainmast line with one hand, the speaking trumpet in the other.

Stuart shouted in the man's ear. "Reduce sails! All but the foresail and the spanker."

After glancing forward and aft, the bosun put out the word through the trumpet. That was followed by more whistling through his pipe.

Crew members raced to the stern, and those who did not slip on the roiling deck leaped into the rigging, climbed to the yards, and began hauling down the mizzenmast sail.

"Damage report, if you please!" shouted Stuart.

The bosun relayed this through the speaking trumpet.

Stuart saw Alexander with the Bentley girl and pointed north of their position. "I see light!"

Alexander saw the shaft of light breaking through and nodded. His feet were braced to stand into the wind. The girl with the broken arm was crying.

"When the storm's over," shouted Stuart, "I want two boats over the side, one port, one starboard."

"Aye, aye, Captain."

Alexander handed off Katie to Susanna. "Take her to the captain's cabin and tie off her arm to stop the bleeding. Use your scarf. When you have the bleeding stopped, cover her with a blanket, and once she passes out, leave her and attend to others."

"Leave her?" asked the girl, wide-eyed. In Susanna's world when people were sick or injured, there were more than enough relatives or servants to sit bedside, overnight or all day.

"She'll pass out from seeing her arm and be no further bother," finished Alexander.

Susanna saw the break where the blood oozed from the arm and her stomach turned over.

Alexander read the look. "Can you handle that, sailor?"

Susanna gritted her teeth. "Aye, aye, sir." She took Katie's good arm, and the two girls, hair and clothing soaked, staggered astern through the wind and rain.

"She shouldn't be on deck," shouted Stuart.

Alexander watched the girls struggle to the stern-side cabins. Katie fell, screamed, and had to be helped to her feet by Susanna.

"She'll do, James."

"No! Martin told me Susanna can't swim." He pointed to the north. "There!"

Again the African saw a shaft of light off in the distance. "Summer storm moving through fast!" shouted the African. "Short time and maximum damage."

"Then ready the boats!"

Alexander strode to the starboard-side jolly boat where several sailors gripped the railing, mesmerized by the wall of water breaking against the side of the ship. Once the water washed through, the black man issued his first command.

"Away boats! One each side."

The order was followed through the speaking trumpet by the bosun: "Away boats! One boat each side! Away boats!" Again more whistling.

"Away the boats?" shouted one of the younger crew making his first Atlantic crossing. "We're going down?" He turned to those beside him. "We're going down! Away all boats!"

Alexander picked up a piece of the mast and clubbed the man over the head. The hysterical sailor collapsed in a heap. Rain puddled around him.

Alexander threatened the others with the stick. "Away a boat! For the survivors!"

The men hopped to it, and Alexander peered through the grayness to the port side. The light to the north of them couldn't get here fast enough. On the port side, he could make out the crew fighting the wind and having a hard time swinging the boat out and away from the ship, but at least they were in action.

"Heave to!" shouted Stuart. "Drop the anchor!"

Stuart was at the helm now, and his sister had the wheel, after shoving away a sailor or two.

To one of the sailors shoved from the helm, Stuart said, "I said, drop anchor!"

The sailor stared at Stuart, then looked at Alexander, who had arrived amidships.

"What was the order, sailor?"

The sailor wiped the rain from his face. "Drop anchor."

"Then do it! The captain wants this ship slowed down."

When the stick of wood came up, the sailor raced toward the stern.

Again the bosun glanced at Alexander and then shouted through the speaking trumpet, "Drop anchor! Drop anchor!"

Another order from Stuart. "Bring her about!"

Cords stood out in Kyrla's neck as she gripped the wheel. "But—but I don't have her under control!"

"We're not leaving those people behind."

His sister glanced at him. "What people?"

"I don't know, but we're not leaving them behind."

"How do you know there are people out there?"

Stuart pointed at the mainmast, its sail flapping around on deck as several members of the crew tried to control it; the ones who could stand, that is. Occasionally, the rippling canvas got the best of them, and one of the crew would stumble or trip over someone on the deck, many of the prostrate sailors peppered with huge, wooden splinters throughout their bodies. Despite cries of agony and pleas for assistance, the sailors did not stop wrestling with the mainsail nor did they apologize.

"If there are injured people on deck," explained Stuart to his sister, "they're also in the water."

"That's their misfortune."

Her brother leaned into her face. "Remember who you're talking to, sailor, and bring this ship about or I'll find someone who will."

"But your father wouldn't—"

"Watch your tongue, girl." This from Alexander who had appeared out of the darkness. The African dropped the stick and grasped the wheel with his one hand. "All right! Let's bring this ship around."

Kyrla nodded and returned her attention to the wheel.

Alexander shouted to Stuart. "And that's why having relatives aboard is never a good idea."

"Or friends of the family! Steady as she goes!"

The sailor returned from below deck with the first of the damage reports. "No fire in the galley. The cook banked the fires when alerted a storm was on the horizon."

"Mid-deck cannons?" asked Stuart.

"No fire and cannons remain secure."

"Armory?"

"Lightning never got that far . . . powder's still dry."

"Water in the passageway?"

"Plenty! At least two or three inches."

Stuart clapped the sailor on the shoulder. "Then assist in lowering the anchor."

The ship had begun to turn, but it took all the strength of both Kyrla and Alexander. On both sides of the ship, jolly boats were being lowered away. Depending on the direction of the wind, the boats slammed into the side of the ship.

Martin Chase hustled over. Wiping water out of his face, he reported, "I have people below who are injured, but no further leaking in the ship's bottom. Where a seam threatens to part, I have men stuffing oakum. All passengers have been ordered to remain in their cabins. Cannons on the mid-deck all secured."

Overhearing this report, the bosun turned his speaking trumpet over to Stuart and disappeared below deck. After all, he was the officer in charge of hull maintenance.

Martin felt the ship making the turn. The rain stung his face when he looked into the wind. "What are you doing?"

"Bringing her about with the spanker and the foremast."

Martin raised a hand to shelter his eyes. Amidships, men fought to cut loose the sail from the splintered mainmast and rigging. The canvas fought back, knocking men to the deck. More men rushed topside and threw themselves into this chore.

"Can she take it?" asked Martin.

Stuart ignored the question. "I need lines over the side and one man on each side of the ship to watch those lines. People will want to come aboard."

Martin looked at Alexander.

"You need help throwing out lines, is that why you're looking at me? Remember, I've only got one good arm and it's occupied at this time."

Martin jerked a nod, raced to one side of the ship, and began to throw lines over the side. The first line wasn't secured and disappeared in the ship's wake after snaking over the railing. When one of the crew pointed this out, Martin held up tossing the next line and told himself to calm down. He'd served before the mast for over six years, enduring squalls and storms, but never experienced anything like this. Still, he did have the ability to calm himself.

"Line secured!" shouted a sailor.

And over the side the rope went, followed by a second line. Martin and a couple of crew members hustled to the other side, secured the lines, and threw them over the side.

The doctor reported to the helm, and Stuart told him a makeshift hospital had been set up in his cabin. The cook reported to the helm and was told to boil lots of water for tea.

"That is, when the ship rights itself. People coming out of the water will be cold and wet."

A sheet of water hit the cook in the face and he wiped it away. "Wetter than us?" He returned below deck.

Major Ladd and his wife were there, asking what they could do. Both were dressed in what could only be called foul-weather gear: hat and bonnet tied down with a string around their chins, coats buttoned up tight, and laced-up shoes. Stuart ordered Mrs. Ladd below to gather up the members of her tea club and to strip blankets off the cabin beds for the hospital. If someone would not yield their bedding, she was not to argue with them, just move on.

"I'll deal with them later."

Mrs. Ladd set off for the below-deck ladder, slipped in the wash, landed on her bottom, and slid across the deck until her feet jammed into the hatch. Stunned, she sat in three or four inches of water at the hatchway.

Her husband was there, assisting her to her feet. "Here we go, my dear!"

She shook him off. "I don't need your help, Edmund, but the ship does."

Ladd nodded and left his wife, who, instead of returning to her feet, crab-walked to the below-deck stairs. Before she reached the ladder, a member of the tea club stuck her head out of the hatch.

"We have people trapped in their cabins!"

"Good!" shouted Mrs. Ladd over the howl of the wind. "The fewer on deck, the less go over the side." When the woman made way, Mrs. Ladd climbed down the stairs to the passengers' cabins.

On his return trip to the helm, Major Ladd's feet went out from under him and he slid across the deck to slam into the side of the ship, just missing one of the cannons. Martin Chase was there, tossing the last of the lines over the side for those who may have been pitched into the ocean.

"Here you go, sir." Chase helped the officer to his feet.

Ladd grasped the railing, favoring a pained ankle. "I don't have the sea legs for this."

"I'm sure—"

"But I can swim."

Off came his boots, followed by his jacket, all stuffed between cannon and railing. Ladd had seen a woman waving and calling from the water. How the woman had gotten ahead of the ship, Ladd had no idea. But she might soon drown. Waves were at ten feet or more. He grasped the rigging, pulled himself up, and stepped on the railing. The pain in his ankle made him wince.

"What are you doing, sir?"

Ladd pointed at the woman. "I think that's Alicia Bentley."

"But, sir, we have boats for that."

The major looked to where the jolly boat bounced off the side of the *Mary Stewart* as it lowered away. "She may not have much time. It must be a struggle just to keep her head above water, especially with her clothing on."

Martin grabbed his leg. "No! Don't go without this!"

Martin had opened a chest. Now he pulled from it two thin oilskins. "Slip your jacket back on, button it up, and slide these oilskins underneath."

Ladd eased himself down to the deck in his stocking feet and dug out his jacket. The pain remained in his ankle. He had certainly broken something.

"What's this?" he asked.

"Cork—taken from a French vessel that went down off the coast of New Providence." Martin pulled the two sheets of oilskin apart. "One goes under your jacket in the front, one across your back. Wearing this, you cannot sink."

"Some sort of floating device." Ladd slipped into his jacket. "Never seen these on His Majesty's ships."

"And you won't—not as long as the navy press-gangs men into service."

"Ah," said the major as he buttoned up his jacket. "The press gang would go over the side and literally float away to freedom."

"That they would."

Ladd grasped the rigging, pulled himself up, and returned to the railing. He blinked and stared into the waves. He could not see the woman. She was gone!

Martin scanned the rising and falling waves. The woman was nowhere to be seen. "Stand down, Major. I must attend to others."

The ship was coming about, and Martin could see the sunlight breaking through. Though the waves remained high and the wind brisk, the storm was passing. Lightning cracked to the south of them and the wind dropped. Rigging had collapsed with the splitting of the mainmast, but that particular piece of canvas had been brought under control. The mizzenmast sails were being lowered in the hope the ship could be brought around, using the foresail near the bow along with the rear sail, or spanker, at the stern. Stuart was going back for those who may have been pitched overboard when the storm first hit.

Alexander strode up and down the deck, shouting at the members of the crew responsible for lowering away a jolly boat. He, too, ignored the cries of the injured as they pleaded with him from where they lay on the mid-deck. When a sailor refused to board a boat being lowered away on the port side, the African grabbed the sailor by the shirt and tossed him over the side. The sailor went in with a scream and a splash.

Alexander leaned over the side and yelled, "See how important those boats are now?"

Martin headed toward the helm and found Kyrla lashing the wheel into position so the wheel would cause the ship to circle.

"Your brother?" shouted Martin.

Kyrla pointed at the stern, then bent over to check on the helmsman who had been at the wheel when the ship had been struck by lightning. The sailor's hat was missing, his shirt in rags, and his skin covered with blisters. Not surprisingly, he was dead.

Martin saw Stuart directing the lowering of the mizzenmast sail. He hurried over, slipping and sliding across the deck. Stuart grabbed him as he slid by.

On his feet, Martin said, "Ladd wanted to go over the side for a woman he saw in the water."

Stuart didn't seem to understand.

"It could be Alicia Bentley." Martin scanned the deck. "Susanna?"

"In my cabin . . . assisting the surgeon."

"What's next, Captain?" Martin grinned at his friend.

"First, wipe that grin off your face until you can account for everyone, including Alicia Bentley and John Belle. Send a man below to report the status of the pumps, then start counting the passengers and crew."

Martin nodded, tapped a sailor on the shoulder, and they disappeared below deck.

To the cluster of sailors waiting for instructions, Stuart cupped his hands and said over the sound of the wind, "Start collecting the injured. There's a hospital set up in the stern-side cabins. Bring everyone there, including those injured in the crew's quarters."

There were several "ayes, ayes" and the men slipped and slid to their assignments, some of them headed below. A gust of wind threw rain in their faces but nothing compared to what they had previously endured.

Stuart studied the ocean. He could make out more than one body floating in the water. He held up two fingers to Alexander, who nodded from the port side. Both jolly boats were in the water now, and the ship had moved into the light that once had been to the north of them.

Stuart grabbed a couple of sailors as they went by. "Go to my cabin and find my glass. Post yourselves on the poop deck and direct the boats toward anyone found floating in the water. Use the signal flags if you need them. Find a trumpet and take it with you."

They nodded and headed for the middle cabin.

Stuart looked to the foremast. If John Belle had been on the top when the lightning struck, he'd be lucky if he'd been flung off into the water.

And what of Alicia Bentley, the girl encouraged to disobey her parents by Martin? Was she the woman Ladd had seen in the water? If she'd been on the top with John, it was her indeed.

Twenty-nine

The last thing Alicia remembered was talking with John on the foretop when the overcast sky lit up like one would imagine the Resurrection. A tremendous crack sounded like a million whips being snapped, and she had been flung off the ship. Sailing over the side, floating in the air, everything moved in slow motion, arms and legs extended; bonnet blown off; dress plastered against her body. She tingled all over, and every hair on her body stood straight up—all of which immediately ceased when she hit the water and plunged toward the ocean's bottom.

When she had left the captain's cabin, Alicia's heart soared. It was true what they said about America. One could begin anew there, and she would begin her new life with John Belle.

It would be difficult. Once they arrived in Charles Town, she would have to contend with John's family, and Alicia had no illusions about Catherine Belle, her future mother-in-law. The woman had been determined enough, even as a child, to travel the underground railroad to Switzerland and escape the mobs of Paris. And Catherine had brought along her younger sister, Nelie, the girl who would later become the mother of James Stuart.

James's father had been lost at sea during the hurricane of '28, and Alicia suspected the younger Stuart was trying to fill some rather large boots. His father had not only killed Blackbeard the Pirate but founded Stuart and Company, one of the largest shipping concerns in the American colonies. Interestingly, if she forsook John Belle for James Stuart, or even Phillippe Belle, as her mother wished she would do, she would possess more worldly goods than she would ever acquire as the wife of some obscure farmer in the upcountry of South Carolina.

And that was just what she wanted. Alicia wanted nothing more to do with her family. The break would be irrevocable. No one in Spartan District would ever know who she was, who her family had once been, or how they had been disgraced. And her family would never seek her out, much less ask for money, and they would certainly never make the trek from Charles Town into the backcountry of South Carolina.

Still, Alicia was under no illusions. A newly married couple cut off from the Belle largess, they would have no home to live in, no food to eat, no way to warm themselves against the approaching winter's cold. From a modest country house in Dorchester, she'd now learn to survive in a rough shelter made of branches and covered with dirt. Those she left behind would gossip about "poor

Alicia" living among the savages. And they *would* live among savages. John said no one knew who the Cherokee would side with in the next Anglo-French war.

All these images rushed through her mind as she mounted Jacob's ladder for the climb to the platform on the foremast. She was not wearing her restitched dress because her mother had thrown it overboard. Alicia paused long enough to see which way the wind blew. She wanted the wind at her back, plastering her dress against her legs and thoroughly covering her ankles.

And she desperately wanted to see John and tell him if he wanted her for his wife, he should speak with her father—without her mother around. Her mother had also forbidden her to climb this terrifying rope ladder. Of all her mother's complaints, the woman might've been correct about one thing.

Alicia reached the top and tried to step from the ladder to the platform, causing John to look up from rolling his kit.

"Alicia! What are you doing up here?"

She could not speak, not with the ladder swaying back and forth. She'd never really gotten over her fear of such heights. She strained, reaching out, trying to place one foot on the platform.

"Alicia, don't come up here."

She withdrew her foot and held on to the ladder. "Please help me, John. You know how anxious this makes me."

Swaying in a breeze that had sprung up, she couldn't help but look down. "Oh, John, please help me!"

"You need to return to the deck. There's a storm blowing in."

"No, no!"

"Alicia, return to the main deck and do it now!"

"John, I'm going to fall!"

"I've told you before, don't look down!" John reached over and steadied the ladder. "Alicia, return to your cabin. That last strike was very close."

"But the storm's off in the distance."

"If you can see lightning, you can be struck by lightning."

And evidently that's just what happened. Without warning, the mast exploded, and Alicia's hands jerked from the ladder. She sailed out over the side of the ship to land in the ocean.

The cold water revived her, and she struggled to reach the surface, coughing and gagging saltwater. To her surprise the water actually had salt in it!

Brushing wet clumps of hair from her face, she could see the ship, but a wall of water that hadn't seemed all that sizable from aboard ship washed over her and pulled her under.

Oh, Lord, help me!

Alicia fought her way to the surface once more, wiped the hair from her face again, and felt the splatter of rain.

It stung.

The wind howled at her, trying to force the waves over her head and draw her under. Once again, Alicia surfaced and watched in disbelief as half the mainmast steadied itself having split off from the other half.

Lightning shattered the darkness, and she saw the splintered mainmast teeter and sway.

Where was Katie? Had she been washed over the side, too?

But she had not been washed over the side! She had been blown over the side, and all at once she realized she could hear nothing. She was deaf. The wind blew, the ocean rose up around her, but she could hear none of that.

She could, however, feel the rain in her face and the power of the water rising around her. Another wave had her now, sending her up and bringing her down. Though Alicia knew how to swim, when she applied herself to that task, she could make no progress. And her clothing was so heavy . . . In this condition, it would be impossible to swim for the ship. The waves were huge, lifting her up like a rag doll and dropping her so quickly. She thought she might become ill.

Alicia stared at the *Mary Stewart.* The ship appeared to be coming about, the stern facing her. No one would ever see her from the stern.

Wasn't there supposed to be a rope trailing the ship? A rope attached to the stern in the event someone fell overboard?

A painter line?

The ship's stern faced her now.

Where was the painter line?

But that wasn't the problem. When she fought with the waves, her arms tired quickly, so, determined to conserve her strength, she concentrated instead on keeping her head above water and, from time to time, waving her hands over her head.

Then it struck her.

Where was John?

Unknown to Alicia, a dark form, barely on the surface, sliced through the waves and moved in her direction. And while she was thrashing about, trying to keep her head above water, the dark form rammed into her, dragging her under.

Thirty

Below deck, Mrs. Ladd took charge, ordering passengers into their cabins. Everyone was in the passageway, talking, some shouting for their children or trying to find their husbands. The passageway appeared to sway, and behind her, more water washed down the stairs, past the mid-level cannon arrays. There must be half a foot of water in the passageway. Where did it all go?

"What was that noise?" demanded Phillippe Belle, who had been headed for the above-deck ladder.

Mrs. Ladd put one hand against the bulkhead, took Phillippe by the arm, and turned him around, escorting him back down the passageway.

"Give us room," ordered Mrs. Ladd. "Return to your cabins."

Everyone's feet were soaked, and this was pointed out to her.

"The main deck is awash as well. That does not concern us. Lightning struck the mainmast; that's all."

The woman who had informed Mrs. Ladd of the trapped passengers below deck trailed along behind her as Mrs. Ladd calmly made her way down the passageway, pushing Phillippe Belle ahead of her. In a cabin, a woman screamed. She was ignored. Remaining on one's feet became the major concern.

At a cabin door, Phillippe put his hands on the bulkhead and looked around. "This isn't my cabin."

"Then which one is?"

Phillippe pointed at a cabin they had already passed, and Mrs. Ladd handed him off to the woman who had earlier come topside for her. "See that Mr. Belle remains in his cabin."

"But—but what if the ship sinks?" asked Phillippe as he was led away.

Several passengers looked in her direction or stuck their heads out nearby doors. "Is the ship going to sink?" asked more than one of them.

An older child burst into tears, and Mrs. Ladd recognized the child as Lindy Bentley, the girl who'd given birth to a stillborn boy. What was she doing outside her cabin in her condition?

Mrs. Ladd steadied her feet and raised her voice over the din. "I have an announcement to make."

When those in the passageway would not quiet themselves, she shouted, "People, hush!"

Eventually, the passageway became quiet, and in the quiet, someone muttered how rude that was of Mrs. Ladd.

"Well, what is it?" hollered Phillippe, who had reached his cabin behind her.

"Yes," asked another passenger. "What's happening?"

"What's going on?" asked another.

"This ship is not going to sink!" announced Mrs. Ladd.

"The ship's going to sink!" shouted a woman.

"What?"

"What was that?

"The ship—what?"

And the hubbub continued until Mrs. Ladd was forced to be rude once again. "Silence, please!"

Maybe she could've used her husband's assistance down here after all. Oren, Fallows' manservant, usually sat outside his master's door. She would welcome Oren's imposing size at this particular moment. Again, she steadied herself against the bulkhead and in a wash that threatened her foothold.

"This ship is not going to sink!"

"How do you know that?"

"If you'll just give me an opportunity to explain."

"Hey, let her speak!"

When the hallway became quiet again, Mrs. Ladd said, "The damage was to the mainmast. It was struck by lightning."

"I want to see!" shouted a boy, splashing away from his mother.

Mrs. Ladd caught the boy as he tried to slog past and returned the child to his mother. More noise until someone shouted the ultimate rudeness.

"Shut up, people!"

Everyone turned and found the shout came from Mr. Bentley.

"Please. Mrs. Ladd has the floor." And he led Lindy into her cabin. Where Alicia and Katie were, Mr. Bentley had no idea, but he had to begin counting somewhere, and here were Lindy, Marion, and his wife.

"You cannot go topside." Ladd braced herself against both sides of the passageway and ignored her wet feet. "The captain has ordered everyone to remain below."

"Easy for him to say. He's not below the waterline."

One man turned to another. "Have you noticed how low in the water this frigate rides?"

"Yes, yes, I know, and the captain is so young."

"The *Mary Stewart* is supposed to be fast, but if we're shipping so much water . . ."

"Everyone's to report to their cabin. It's much too dangerous topside."

"How much more dangerous?" demanded a woman. She pointed at the crack in the overhead bulkhead. "You see that? A hole's burned through the roof and water's leaking through. Why shouldn't we go upstairs?"

"Yes, why?"

"Why?"

Mrs. Ladd observed the crack where the water leaked through. "That I can explain."

"Then you'd better hurry if you don't want us to drown."

"Watch your tongue, sir, or you will be brought up on charges."

"Charges of what?"

"Brought up by whom?" asked his wife.

"Actually," explained Mrs. Ladd, repositioning her hand against the damp bulkhead as the corridor swayed under her, "the captain will bring you up on charges of mutiny on the high seas if you don't calm down and become more orderly."

"Mutiny?"

"Are you serious?"

"Unless you calm down and return to your cabins. The crack in the overhead deck is nothing more than where the lightning struck. There is no fire. There is no danger. There are no holes in this ship but the crack you see above you."

"There are people inside that cabin!" shouted the man occupying the cabin across the passageway. "Actors are in there!"

On the other side of the cabin door, Gabriel and Portia were gradually coming to their senses. A short period of panic had ensued once they realized Lucius could not have survived such a large shaft through his body. In addition to the tear in the overhead bulkhead, the deck at their feet had been smashed through when the separated piece of mainmast passed by Gabriel and Portia and wedged itself into the deck. Water began to drain from the floor and through the hole.

Portia put a hand on her brother's shoulder. Gabriel huddled against the cabin's bed, hands hiding his face. The swaying of the ship did not appear to bother either of them, but the body of Lucius was another matter.

"What—what happened?" he muttered. "What happened?"

"Lucius is dead."

A putrid smell filled the air.

Portia was not surprised. Lucius had been more than three hundred years old. Gabriel's eyes rolled back in his head when he recognized the odor. He went limp and collapsed on the bunk.

Portia slapped him. "Wake up, Gabriel! What's the use of being immortal if you can't become accustomed to the sight of people dying?"

Gabriel opened his eyes, saw the shaft through the cabin, and began to chant, "Lucius is dead, what shall we do? Lucius is dead, what shall we do?"

"Stop that, Gabriel, or do you want me to slap you again?"

He stopped chanting and looked at her. "What shall we do?"

"Complete our mission. Our kind is depending on us."

Gabriel nodded. "Complete the mission. Complete the mission. Complete . . ."

Portia slapped him again.

Gabriel jerked back. "Why do you keep hitting me? What did I ever do to you?"

"Oh, you mean besides bringing me over to the dark side?"

"Are you going to bring that up again? Being undead does have its advantages."

"Then perhaps you should demonstrate one or two of them, such as releasing us from this cabin."

The singer brushed off the water dripping from the overhead crack. He unfolded his legs and put his feet on deck, where they became instantly wet. He didn't like that, so he elevated himself. He stared at the piece of mainmast. Water oozed through the bulkhead around the splintered shaft and added to the puddle on the floor. Under the cabin door, more water seeped.

"What has happened here?" he asked.

Portia was not surprised. Ever since he'd been a child,

whenever difficulty arose, Gabriel simply went away, left for somewhere else. She had to be the responsible party, even after crossing over.

"Lucius was killed by a shaft that penetrated the ceiling and then penetrated him. Only we are left to complete the mission, and there is chaos in the passageway."

When she paused, Gabriel could hear this was so. A woman was trying to gain control of the crowd, but those in the passageway would not stop shouting.

"Fools!" shouted Gabriel at the door.

"Where are the sailors?" he asked Portia. "They should put down this riot." He brushed more water away. "I'm being soaked."

"The crew is topside. But that is not our problem."

"What *is* our problem? Does it have something to do with those people yammering in the passageway? If so, tell them to go away so I may return to bed. It is, after all, the middle of the day." He brushed off more water.

"That is not possible, my dear. Not only is this not our cabin and you cannot sleep in here, you are in charge of the mission, and the first thing you must do is bring some order to this ship or we shall never reach Charles Town."

"Oh, you mean the captain. Much too young to be in charge of a ship this size. I believe I have expressed my opinion on this issue before."

"And you were correct."

The handle rattled, but the door did not move.

Portia glanced at the door. "They'll never get that door open with that shaft against it."

From the other side of the door, a voice asked if they were all right. At the bottom of the cabin door, water oozed through, seeking the lowest level. From there, the water drained through the hole in the deck around the splintered shaft, then began dripping into the hold.

Now, someone was pounding on the door.

"Silly people," sneered Gabriel.

"Your people. Your subjects now that Lucius is dead."

More thumping could be heard on the other side of the door, people hollering loud enough to raise the undead.

"Portia, I insist you make them go away. I need my rest."

"Not the best idea," said his sister.

"Lucius is dead, and even those in the passageway are familiar with death. It comes to all of them unless they have the good sense to come over."

"Dear brother, it would be best if they do not enter this cabin until we have a chance to prepare the room, and to do that we must locate Oren, if he is still aboard."

"Why would he not be? He serves me now."

"If he were topside when the storm struck, he may have been washed over the side."

Gabriel glanced at the pull-out drawers under both beds, its contents sure to be too damp to sleep in. "What do you suggest?"

Portia did have a suggestion, and moments later, a fine mist appeared in the cabin, then dissipated through cracks in the bulkhead. When the mist disappeared, Lucius' cabin was empty.

Thirty-one

Topside, both jolly boats had been lowered away, and without most sails and the anchor dragging, the ship had practically come to a standstill, if you did not consider how the waves still roiled the vessel. Moments before, two people had been hauled aboard, a passenger and a member of the crew.

Stuart stood on the poop deck, above the stern cabins, a spyglass to his eye. He peered into the wake of the ship, thought he saw someone back there, and ordered one of the jolly boats to pick up whoever it was.

The sailor blew his whistle and called to the jolly boat through the speaking trumpet. The oarsmen dug into the water, and the boat cut across the ship's wake. If someone were back there, he'd be struggling to simply keep his head above water. The sailor was handed the glass and told to remain there until properly relieved.

"And the crow's nest?" Stuart asked before leaving the poop deck.

The sailor shook his head. "Lightning got him."

In one last look, Stuart scanned the waves. Where was John Belle? Both he and Alicia Bentley were among the missing.

The storm lay south of them; the ship and everything topside and below deck were soaking wet. In the bright sunlight, the halved mainmast was a strange thing to see, creating a nearly matching pair, one mast section standing taller than the other after being split off. Rigging, spars, and sails cluttered the deck, and the crew worked to remove the debris from where it covered the dead and injured. Rigging was being cut away from spars.

The Presbyterian minister was on his knees anointing the sick, and the doctor, accompanied by Susanna and assisted by sailors with litters, was going from one body to the next, culling the injured from the dead. Once an injured party was found, he was put on a stretcher and carried to one of the stern-side cabins.

As Stuart passed the helm, Kyrla called to him, asking how long before they would be able to get underway.

"Not until we've accounted for everyone."

"Sooner or later . . ." she began, but saw Alexander staring at her. She shut off her complaint.

"I'm going below," said Alexander. "The deck is yet to be made safe, and I don't want passengers venturing topside." He clapped Stuart on the shoulder. "You did well, James. Your father would've been proud."

Stuart inclined his head toward his sister. "They still don't believe in me. The bosun remained at the helm throughout the storm. His place was below deck checking the hull."

"I'll speak to him about that."

"If you do, he'll never come around."

"Then perhaps it's time for me to find work in one of the warehouses."

Susanna stopped on one of her return trips to the stern-side cabins with a stretcher. Shoulders slumped and dress covered with blood, smears of blood ran across her forehead where she'd wiped the back of her hand. She was missing her scarf; her hair and clothing soaked.

"Alicia Bentley and John Belle?" she asked.

Stuart only shook his head.

"Her—her sister passed out, just like Alexander said she would. She's lying on the deck in your cabin."

"You need to go below and tell Katie's parents she's safe. We don't need Mrs. Bentley topside."

Susanna nodded as if in a daze.

Stuart took the girl's hand. "Let me see that marvelous smile of yours, Miss Chase. Whoever may or may not be alive, you're still with us, and that's a gift from God."

She smiled, warming to this hard man. "A gift to whom, sir?"

In the passageway, Phillippe Belle pounded on the door of Lucius Fallows' cabin, but no one answered. "Portia! Miss Portia!"

"What's this?" asked Alexander, evaluating the crack in the overhead bulkhead.

A weary Susanna came down the stairs behind him, turned the corner, and sloshed in their direction.

Mrs. Ladd speculated that a piece of the mainmast had crashed through the overhead bulkhead and into

Fallows' cabin, preventing anyone from being able to open the door.

"Thank you, Mrs. Ladd. Now, if you would, report to the hospital cabins."

Mrs. Ladd left, taking her tea-club friend with her. In the hospital, she would find the major with a broken ankle and some very strange protective inserts front and aft, inside his jacket.

"Ladies and gentlemen," boomed Alexander, "you need to return to your cabins for a count."

"But I'm missing my wife."

"Yes," said Mr. Bentley, "and we are missing two daughters."

"Katie Bentley is in the hospital on the main deck with a broken arm."

Mrs. Bentley pushed her way down the passageway. "I must go to her." She sloshed passed him toward the above-deck stairs.

A baby cried and would not hush. Alexander ordered the baby's mother to close the door of her cabin.

"We can't open this one," said Phillippe, thumping on the door to draw Lucius Fallows' attention. "The actors are trapped inside."

"Do you know for sure they were below deck when the storm hit?" asked Alexander.

Everyone looked at everyone else.

The cabin door behind them opened with a screech, and Portia stepped out. She was followed by her brother.

"What's this?" asked Gabriel, surveying the crowd up and down the passageway.

Passengers gaped. Babies even stopped their crying.

"My dear Portia," said Phillippe Belle, "you are alive."

"We were trapped in our cabin," said Gabriel. "I only now was able to free the door."

The singer returned to the door and tugged on the latch. The door barely moved and would not completely close. It squeaked horribly when it did. Children squealed and covered their ears.

"Something tightened the jamb," said Gabriel, pulling on the door. It was no use. The door could not be forced closed.

A passenger gestured at Lucius' door where the bulkhead had buckled. "Here's your problem, and your fellow actor's problem. We can't get him out of there."

Gabriel went to the door and tried the latch. The latch moved, but the door would not open.

He shook it. "Lucius!"

No answer from inside the cabin.

Water dripped on Gabriel. "What's this?" He stepped back and looked up.

Alexander explained what had caused the leak.

"Lightning?" asked Gabriel. "I thought you were firing cannons to settle the seas."

"You fire cannons to make bodies surface, not to drive off a storm."

"Oh. Well, I'm not familiar with the customs of the sea."

Oren climbed up the ladder from the hold and sloshed down the passageway to the gathering.

Gabriel explained that Lucius was trapped inside. "Funny," added Gabriel, "he's not making very much noise."

"My master is dead. I found his remains in the hold."

Gabriel turned ashen, which was quite a trick for someone as pale as him. "You don't say."

Portia brought a handkerchief to her mouth. "No, no, no! Not Lucius." She took her brother's arm. "Lucius cannot be dead. No, no, this is not possible. He was our leader and our provider."

"I'm sorry, miss, but it is so." To Gabriel, Oren said, "With your permission, my lord, I shall take care of the remains and return for further instructions."

Gabriel clapped the burly man on the shoulder. "Take as much time as you need, Oren."

The burly man looked at the singer quizzically, then sloshed along the passageway and disappeared down the ladder.

"This cannot be happening," said Portia, "not after Donato's death."

"*That* was self-defense," said Alexander.

At the mention of Donato's name, Susanna turned away and moved in the direction of the above-deck ladder.

Gabriel watched Susanna go. "Yes, yes, I'm sure it was."

James Stuart paced back and forth where the jolly boat had been lowered on the starboard side of the ship. Something caught his eye. He stopped and stared. Two sodden forms could be seen being brought back from certain death. Or one.

A woman sat with a sailor's jacket over her shoulders and huddled over a form in the bottom of the boat. Alicia

Bentley. According to the count given him by Martin, they were the only two still missing, Lucius Fallows having been accounted for only moments ago.

Stuart leaned over the railing to call out, "Who do you have aboard?"

The helmsman leaned forward and asked the woman huddled over the body.

The sailor shouted, "Alicia Bentley and . . . John Belle; I'm told he is—or was."

The woman burst into tears. With the stiff breeze, the sound of grief drifted to those along the railing. Drawn by the noise, Mrs. Bentley came out of the hospital and joined those at the railing.

"Have you tried to revive him?" called out Stuart.

"Captain, he was with us when we hauled him aboard, but now . . ."

Stuart had heard enough. He went over to where the boat had been lowered, pulled on the gloves that Susanna had knitted for him, and stepped up on the railing. He grabbed one of the ropes that lowered the jolly boat. From there, he slid down the rope to where his feet landed on the pulley.

When he saw oars-up on the jolly boat, he shouted, "Avast there! Bring that boat over and bring her now!"

They did, and Stuart leapt into the bow and stepped over seats to reach for the man lying amidships.

"Oh, Captain Stuart, John's dead. John's dead."

"He's not dead until I say he's dead."

John lay with his head against the port side of the jolly boat. His skin was pale, but that wasn't significant for a Belle of Charleston. John wasn't breathing. Now that was significant.

To an oarsman, he said, "Give me a hand here!"

The oarsman only stared, so the jolly boat's helmsman stepped between two oarsmen, bent down, and grabbed Belle by the arm. Between the helmsman and Stuart, they got John up and lay him over the side of the boat.

"What are you doing?" demanded Alicia, seeing the man she loved roughly handled.

John lay on his stomach, his head almost in the water. When a wave rolled past, water lapped against Belle's long, black hair.

"No, no! Please don't do that!"

Stuart straddled Belle, pushing down on his back, trying to force the water out, and he continued to work on his friend until he fell back, spent. The helmsman stared at his captain.

"Well?" demanded Stuart from where he lay.

The helmsman took his turn but gave up quickly. "Captain, with all due respect, I think all the water's out of him. It's his heart that's give out."

"Then turn him over!" roared Stuart. He scrambled to his knees and grabbed his cousin.

Belle was turned over, face up, and at the sight of her beloved's head lolling side to side, Alicia burst into fresh tears.

"Oh, John! John!"

"Shut up, woman! I'm trying to work here."

Stuart thumped on Belle's chest.

After a moment, the helmsman asked, "Begging your pardon, Captain, but what are you doing?"

"You believe his heart has stopped. I'm trying to make it work again." Stuart thumped Belle on the chest again. "It certainly can't hurt."

"But—but why would it start again?"

"I don't know that it will, but it's a pump, and pumps have to be primed. I'm trying to prime the pump."

Alexander peered over the railing. "Avast there!"

Stuart didn't answer so the helmsman had to inform the African of the captain's attempts to revive Belle.

"Check his tongue."

Stuart stopped thumping Belle's chest.

"See that he hasn't swallowed his tongue."

"Oh, Lord," moaned Stuart, "I'd forgotten about that."

He and the helmsman looked at each other.

The helmsman shook his head. "Not me, Captain."

Stuart bent over his cousin, opened his jaw, felt around inside, and pried out Belle's tongue.

"Now throw him over the side," shouted Alexander. "On his stomach."

The helmsman looked up. "We've already tried that."

But Stuart was hauling Belle up the side of the jolly boat. "Give me a hand here," he ordered.

The helmsman did, and they laid Belle across the side of the boat once again.

"Push on his back!" shouted Alexander. "Even if you have to crack his ribs."

"Oh, no," screamed Alicia. "No, no, don't hurt him."

"He's already dead, ma'am," explained the helmsman as Stuart began to push on Belle's back.

Stuart pushed and pushed until he thought he heard a cough.

He stopped. "What?"

"He coughed!" screamed Alicia. "He coughed!" And she swooned, landing in the arms of one of the oarsmen.

Stuart returned to his work, and John bucked and coughed and put his hands on the sides of the boat. He tried to rise up but didn't have the strength.

"Enough!" More coughing, then, "Stop! Please . . . have mercy!"

"Straighten him up!" shouted Alexander.

Both the captain and the helmsman grabbed Belle by an arm and stood him upright. That did not last long, as John was not finished retching. Eventually, Belle stopped spitting and hacking. Moments later, he waved them off and slid onto a seat.

When Belle saw Alicia in the oarsman's arms, his face dropped. "I didn't get her to the line? There was so much water in my face, I couldn't see her. I couldn't even call out."

"Oh, you saved her, sir," said the helmsman, grinning. "That's where we found the two of you—being pulled through the water on the painter."

Belle coughed again. "Then—then what's wrong with her?"

"Nothing a little water won't cure." Stuart leaned over the side of the jolly boat, scooped up a handful of saltwater, and threw it in Alicia's face.

Alicia blinked, opened her eyes, and saw John sitting there, right as rain. She swooned again.

From the railing, Mrs. Bentley called to them. "One of you young gentlemen is going to have to marry my daughter the way you're treating her with such familiarity."

Thirty-two

Since the ship was only five or six days out of Charles Town, it was determined that lines and leather straps would be applied or tightened around the splintered mast, maintaining it upright until the *Mary Stewart* could reach her home port. Still, though the ship had been secured, there remained a sense of urgency. The storm had left many of the passengers unnerved, some dead; only enough potatoes and boiled cabbage for a few meals left in stores. Included with the remains of Lucius Fallows were six others, two adult passengers and three crew members, and one child, recovered by the insistent James Stuart.

"Captain," said his first mate, "we need to add more canvas. Privateers always lurk around ports of call."

"The *Mary Stewart* has always been able to outdistance anyone."

"Begging your pardon, sir, but the *Mary Stewart* isn't the ship she used to be."

All six bodies were wrapped in sailcloth; words were

read over the dead before they were dumped overboard, causing a member of the crew to remark that they had spent a day and a half locating these remains, only to dump them over the side again.

The sailor was upbraided by a fellow mate. "What's this? You're willing to go to Davy Jones' locker without some words being spoken over you?"

"Now that you put it that way . . ."

The funeral was held at dusk, so Gabriel, Portia, and Oren turned out in their finest. Because of the number of religious references, crosses, and bibles in evidence, they chose to remain on the poop deck.

Gabriel whispered into his sister's ear. "If Lucius could only see this . . . this blaspheme."

"Well," said his sister, looking into the evening sky, "I'm sure *he's* watching and *he does* consider this blaspheme."

Once John Belle recovered, he was put to work pumping, then mucking out the hold. No more solitary days on the top for John Belle, or Alicia Bentley, though they were newly engaged—over the strenuous objections of both Mrs. Bentley and Phillippe Belle.

"Mother will never accept this woman into our family," he said.

"She doesn't have to," countered John. "Other than Alicia's wishing to be married in St. Philip's, we're at Mother's disposal after the service, whether that be for several minutes, several days, or several weeks at Cooper Hill."

"There'd be a better chance for the girl to be accepted if her family brought a present to the union, but the Bentleys are penniless."

"And how do you know that?" asked his brother, John.

"Because everyone in that family can't help relating their family history. My Lord, Jacques, don't you realize the baby stillborn to Lindy Bentley was a bastard?"

"Phillippe, I'm sure you heard none of this from Alicia."

"Why does it matter from whom I heard it? It's all true, and furthermore, it's a disgrace."

"All I can say is that if you wish to inherit Cooper Hill, you'd best remember who inherited our late father's skill at dueling."

Phillippe drew himself up. "You wouldn't dare! What would Mother think?"

"Little more of me than she thinks now."

The ship's doctor set Katie's arm, bandaged it, and she rested below, but her sister, Lindy, had fully recovered from her miscarriage, and despite wearing black, strolled the deck with a parasol asking sailors what this instrument did and why they were doing that. And each night, Gabriel and Portia serenaded the passengers and crew, but the repair work went on, many times to the sounds of hymns sung from where sailors toiled on deck or in the rigging. And when sailors sang "Jesus, Lover of My Soul," they placed special emphasis on: "Till the storm of life is past . . ."

The deck had been cleared, water pumped from the bilge, and spars, sails, and rigging repaired. Flocks of gulls appeared, which meant they were approaching land, and the first thing James Stuart vowed to do when he reached Charles Town was to pitch Susanna into the harbor and make her learn to swim.

"You should never have attempted this voyage without the ability to swim, Miss Chase."

Looking at him from under her eyelashes, she asked, "Why, Captain, why should I ever learn how to swim? In a few days, you will safely deliver me to Charles Town, and if I understand correctly, there, I will be put in a horse-drawn, two-wheeled riding chair to Cooper Hill where I'm indentured."

"Actually, Miss Chase, you're indentured to Stuart and Company. The Chase family didn't have the pounds to pay for both your indentureship *and* a trip to Charles Town. And I am not about to have you subjected to Phillippe Belle at Cooper Hill."

Susanna stared at him long enough for Stuart to face her.

"Is there anything you don't lie about, Captain? You lied about why you kicked Jenkins off the ship, you lied to the major about why your ship could not leave Liverpool, you even lied about why I came to be onboard this ship. I don't mind lying for a good cause, but I never know when you're telling the truth. Why did you lie to me about my indentureship?"

"We didn't know your character, Miss Chase, or how you would perform at sea. We have four examples of young women on this ship in the Bentley family, and Alicia Bentley appears to be the only one with any sand. How were we to know what you were made of? You might've been another silly girl the crew would prefer remain in her cabin for the duration of the trip."

"You could've taken me at my word."

"Miss Chase, sailors must prove themselves. That's the world I come from and the one in which I live."

"And I'm willing to chance you were relieved when Major and Mrs. Ladd came aboard so I would not be underfoot."

' To this Stuart said nothing.

"Say what you may, but I think I acquitted myself quite well while aboard this ship."

"You certainly have. I'm very proud to have made your acquaintance, Miss Chase."

"Acquaintance? Shall I be permitted to meet your family when we dock in Charles Town?"

"Yes, of course. Why should you not?"

"Because I'm a mere scullery maid, and probably indentured in your kitchen. I doubt I'll see much of you once you've unloaded the cargo destined for Charles Town, after which you shall be on your way again."

"Such are my obligations."

"Your obligations are to your children, sir."

"I've told you that my mother cares for my children."

"Your children need a mother, and lacking that, a father."

"Miss Chase, I am not prepared to be lectured by—"

"Some scullery maid."

"I have never referred to you in those terms."

"No, sir, your inference is quite enough."

"Miss Chase, I try to avoid any appearance of familiarity."

"And now I understand why you lied about my indentureship, as you believed you could keep me at a distance."

Stuart frowned. "And why should I wish to keep you at a distance?"

"For the same reason you've always kept women at a distance. You're afraid one of them might tempt you to desert the *Mary Stewart* before you've measured up to your father."

"My father? What does my father have to do with this?"

"You used your father's broadsword to rescue me from that . . . that house, and you brought the *Mary Stewart* through that storm. Your obligation to your father has been fully discharged, and now you must discharge your responsibility to your children."

"Miss Chase, you speak out of turn."

"I speak as someone who knows what it's like to lose family. Each time you depart Charles Town, you break not only your children's hearts, but your mother's."

"Miss Chase, I do declare if it doesn't sound like you're applying for an opening other than scullery maid in my house."

From the crow's nest: "Deck! Ship ahoy!"

It was a French privateer off the starboard bow and it was closing fast.

Thirty-Three

"South by southwest!" yelled Stuart.

"South by southwest!" shouted Martin to the helm.

The wheel turned, the whistle piped men to their stations, and extra canvas was laid on. The colors were run up, joining the Stuart and Company flag visible on the stern.

"He's angling to cut us off," shouted Martin, a glass at his eye.

"Can he do that, Captain?" asked Susanna.

"You should go below, Miss Chase."

"No, sir. I wish to see, and I promise I shall not fall overboard."

"It's not overboard that I'm worried about."

Stuart placed his glass on the French ship. It would be close—which meant the *Mary Stewart* would not make it. The privateer had cannons that could reach them at such a short distance.

To Martin, he yelled, "Clear for action! Run out the

cannons starboard side and send sharpshooters to the top!"

Martin repeated the order, and the cannon crews came topside. With them, Alexander reported for duty, and the guns were run out by their excited crew. Overhead, men with muskets hustled up the rigging. There was a moderate breeze and a smooth sea, both of which favored the privateer.

"I'm running southwest by west," said Stuart to those grouped at the helm, "then hard northwest to cut across the Frenchmen's stern. When Kyrla makes the turn, run out the cannons on the port side, and we'll give the frogs a good spanking as we cross their stern. That ought to take the steam out of them."

But turning across the Frenchmen's stern put too much pressure on the mainmast canvas. The leather straps parted, one of the spars snapped, and the sail split down the middle.

Stuart shot an angry look at the bosun.

The French vessel reached the *Mary Stewart* later that afternoon, and a longboat was lowered over the side from the *Madras.*

"*Madras?*" asked Martin. "What the devil kind of name is that?"

Major Ladd explained. "It's the name of one of the cities in India controlled by the British East India Company, and lately captured by the French East India Company." Because of his broken ankle, Ladd made his way around deck on a pair of wooden crutches, his wife always accompanying him.

Stuart stared at the privateer. The *Mary Stewart* had

never been stopped before. She had always been much too weatherly. An excellent sea bird.

Susanna joined him at the railing. "You all right, James?"

He didn't appear to notice the use of his Christian name. "I was an ordinary seaman when last stopped by the French. They kept the cargo and ransomed the crew and the ship. Stuart and Company paid the ransom, and while I was held in France, I saw a new type of frigate developed for the French navy. Though she had a mid-level deck for her guns, all the *Medee's* guns were carried on the main deck. And because of her long hull and low upperworks—two reasons we shipped so much water during the storm—the *Medee* could fire all her cannons in rough water, making her a formidable opponent. But what I took note of was her speed in the open sea. Her sailing times were beyond belief for a frigate."

"You were allowed onboard?"

"My family has relatives in France, on my mother's side, and they handled the ransom demands. One of those relatives is a member of the French navy, and he could not resist demonstrating how fast the *Medee* was in open water."

"So you had the *Mary Stewart* built in the image of the *Medee* once you returned to Charles Town?"

"Only after a great deal of wrangling with Martin's father, my mother, and Alexander. The *Mary Stewart* was built in Boston where they build the best ships in the world because of their insistence on using live oaks. The *Mary Stewart* could outrun any French ship, even with the loads she carries, but not today."

Others had joined them at the railing and heard the last of what Stuart had said.

"We are at war with France?" asked Alicia.

"No, Miss Bentley," said Major Ladd. "It's a conflict between the British East India Company and the French *Compagnie des Indes.*"

"But if you died during a conflict halfway around the world, it would still make you dead, is that not correct?"

"Alicia, please."

"I'm sorry, John. I just don't understand all these wars. What does it prove to be at war all the time?"

"Yes, Miss Bentley," said the major. "You most certainly would be dead if you died in a commercial war." Again, he looked at Stuart. "But the captain will see that does not happen, won't you, sir?"

Stuart studied the longboat approaching under a white flag. "Alexander?"

"Sir?"

"Go below and explain our predicament to Gabriel and his sister. Inform him that we shall need their assistance tonight. If he won't come topside in the sun, we can still use their talents after dusk." The African turned to go. "And dust off the cannons on the mid-level deck."

Alicia gasped. "We are to fight?"

"No, Miss Bentley, but we must play the game."

"What game is that?"

"Surrender."

The cook reported to the helm.

"Take Miss Chase to the galley," said Stuart. "We shall expect your best effort for our guests tonight."

"We are expecting guests for dinner?" asked Susanna.

He ignored her question and spoke to the doctor, who had also reported to the helm.

"Take Miss Bentley and prepare my cabin—"

"And ours," interrupted Mrs. Ladd.

"Yes," said Stuart, glancing at the woman. "Prepare all three cabins in the stern for hospital duty."

"But I thought we are to surrender," said Alicia, becoming more anxious. Ever since the storm, she'd had a case of the nerves.

Stuart looked where children jumped rope or played marbles, a few of the older ones having noticed the French ship and lined up at the railing. "Yes. That does appear the most prudent course of action."

Alicia turned to John. "But I don't understand."

The longboat was close enough to hail them. In English.

Martin looked to his captain.

"Throw a ladder over the side and invite the Frenchies aboard."

Martin used a speaking trumpet to inform the French sailors that they were welcome aboard.

"Pipe the men to their posts."

The whistle blew, and men came thundering up the ladders from below and took up positions at the railing with their arms.

Seeing this, Alicia said, "John, please don't let them fight. Make them surrender."

John Belle said nothing, only watched the longboat draw abreast of their ship.

"I'm going to send the children below," said Alicia.

"Thank you, Miss Bentley."

When Alicia hurried off to round up the children, Stuart said, "Miss Chase, I asked you to report to the galley."

"I would rather remain with you, James."

With the use of the captain's Christian name, everyone stared at her.

"Susanna, you cannot swim. For that reason, you must take your place in the galley below. In any naval battle there is a chance people shall be knocked overboard, and it would be unlikely that I could come to your rescue."

"You could be a distraction, cousin," added Martin.

Susanna smiled. "Now that has a pleasant sound to it." And she left to report to the galley.

"John, go below and move everyone in the starboard-side cabins to the port-side cabins. Pack them in there, if you must."

"Aye, aye, Captain."

"Major, you'd best remove that red coat."

On his crutches, Ladd drew himself up. "Sir, an English officer does not cut and run."

"There are women and children aboard this ship, sir, and I shall turn you over to the frogs myself if you don't show a bit of discretion."

"Why you young whippersnapper, I wear this uniform with pride."

"I'm sure you do, sir, and we civilians would not like to lose you. We may not be at war with France today but come the morrow, who knows?"

Ladd looked over the side at the longboat bearing eight oarsmen, two per thwart. At the longboat's stern stood the helmsman, and in the bow, a French officer held a pole with a white flag. For this reason, it took little encouragement from Mrs. Ladd to prevail on her husband to return to their cabin.

"Martin, post someone at the Ladds' cabin door."

"Aye, aye, sir."

Following the ladder over the side from the *Mary Stewart* came a rope flung upward from the longboat. A sailor at the railing caught it and made the French line fast. Soon, a young man dressed in blue stood on deck. He was followed by a sailor carrying a musket. Most French sailors dressed in blue, but this young man wore no insignia. He and Stuart bowed to each other.

"Mr. Fourier, at your service, sir." The smartly dressed sailor spoke English with a French accent.

"And what can we do for you today, sir?"

The Frenchman looked about, taking in the crew with their weapons. "You could have your men put away their weapons. I travel under a flag of truce."

Stuart nodded to his first mate.

Martin Chase shouted: "Stack arms!"

All the men leaned their muskets and swords against the railing and stepped away. Several men climbed down from the rigging, leaping to the deck. They, too, stacked arms. A knife plunged from the rigging and bit into the deck in front of the Frenchman. The young Frenchman did not move but watched the knife vibrate in the wood. His companion's musket followed the movement of the last sailor from the rigging.

"Sorry about that, mate," said the sailor, landing on the deck.

He picked up his knife and sheathed it, then bowed

and stepped back. The Frenchman with the musket lowered his weapon.

"Captain, please have your cannon crews stand down."

Stuart ordered the crews away from their cannons.

Fourier studied the damage to the mainmast and its sail. "Your ship appears to have run into some rough seas. Perhaps you need our men to assist in refitting your ship."

"We are doing quite well with our repairs, and five days from now we shall arrive in Charles Town. You came aboard my ship for what purpose, Fourier?"

"Sir, as you know, our countries are at war."

"Since you've lately returned from India, you may not be informed that England and France are at peace in the Atlantic."

"Then where is the British officer who stood on this deck?"

"What British officer?"

"The red coat we saw through our glasses."

"Oh, that red coat." Stuart unbuttoned his jacket, revealing a red shirt.

"That was you, sir?"

"Indeed. We are a commercial vessel."

"And forbidden to conduct business with France, if I understand your laws correctly."

"Am I given to understand that you stopped my ship so we could conduct business in international waters?"

"Actually, my captain wishes to examine the contents of your ship to make sure you are not carrying armaments or English soldiers to your colonies in

America. Those items, or soldiers, shall be confiscated, along with anyone who cares to return to France."

"I doubt we have any of those aboard, though there may be one or two Huguenots."

"Huguenots are considered enemies of the state, sir, and you will be so kind as to point them out to me."

"Sir, I will do no such thing. It is a point of honor."

"Then your ship shall be seized as a hostile vessel."

"If so, sir," said Stuart, jerking his thumb toward the railing, "then how will you and your men return to the *Madras?*"

"Sir," said Fourier, shaking his white flag, "this is a flag of truce."

The French guard raised his musket once again.

"Tell your man to get that weapon out of my face."

Fourier glanced at his aide and nodded.

Stuart pointed at the flag flying from the mast. The Union Jack had been lowered. In its place flew a white flag. "As you can see, the *Mary Stewart* has already surrendered."

"Then I shall conduct my inspection."

"And I shall accompany you. Bosun!"

Reluctantly, the bosun reported to his captain.

"You have the keys?"

"To every cabin on this ship, sir."

"We shan't need to inspect the passengers' cabins, but—"

"Captain Stuart, if you please, I shall make that decision."

"Very well, Fourier, but try not to do anything silly while aboard my ship."

Stuart ordered the bosun below deck. The Frenchman followed Stuart, along with the French guard with the musket. At mid-level, they found another set of cannons ready to fire.

"Sir," protested Fourier, "this is a flag of truce you are violating."

Behind the guard, a sock filled with sand appeared and the French guard crumpled to the deck. The unconscious man was relieved of his musket and laid flat. The bosun now held the musket.

"As you said, Fourier, you are to inventory the contents of my hold and report to your captain that there is nothing of interest onboard my ship."

Martin Chase took the flag of truce. "I shall keep this while you are below, sir."

"You—you will not be able to get away with this."

"Fourier, you and your captain have secret codes to relate what is actually happening on this ship, such as signaling you have been taken hostage, but please don't do anything silly in the next couple of minutes."

"You cannot do this! You are violating a flag of truce."

"Please, sir, concentrate on the matter at hand. The flag of Stuart and Company flies from our mast. You could have turned a blind eye to this ship, but you chose to take advantage of our disability. Now, you shall suffer the consequences."

Stuart gestured to the cannons where a group of sailors stood, one with a torch to touch off the fuses. The sailor with the torch was a one-armed black man. Fourier's head spun around as though on a stick. On the starboard side of the mid-deck, two arrays of cannons pointed at gun ports that appeared to be closed.

Alexander handed off the torch to Stuart, then bent down and tapped a gun port.

"Papier-mâché." Alexander grinned, still bending near the gun ports. "No one on your ship will see a cannon barrel until it's fired."

When the African stepped back and straightened up, Stuart returned the torch and said to Fourier, "Listen closely. We have moved our passengers from the starboard to the port side of the ship. In a few seconds, we are going to touch off all six cannons on this side, which are focused on the *Madras's* waterline. We believe, though your ship is on alert, that we shall get off the first shots, and seconds after we suffer *your* return fire, your ship will begin sinking. Meanwhile, the survivors on the *Mary Stewart* raise her sails and the ship drifts away, leaving the crew of your ship to determine whether they should fire on us again or away all boats."

"You'll never get away with this."

"Cannons returned," shouted Martin from the main deck.

Fourier glanced up the ladder.

"This means," added Stuart, "that your captain believes that you have made me withdraw our cannons from their firing ports. Now, we appear to be even less of a threat to the *Madras.*"

Stuart clapped the Frenchman on the shoulder. "You have had great success today, Mr. Fourier. We have surrendered, our cannons are spiked, and you have found the treasure we carry."

"Treasure? What treasure?"

"Let us go below and see."

With the aid of a second torch, Stuart led the Frenchman into the hold and over to a door with a huge lock. Taking a key from the bosun, Stuart unlocked the door and pulled it open. Inside sat a single chest, and the Frenchman's mouth fell open as the lid was raised by the bosun, revealing gold and silver coins aplenty. Stunned, Fournier put out his hand to maintain his balance. He used the corner of the trunk to stand.

"Think your captain would care to see this?" asked Stuart.

"Yes, yes," said the Frenchman, dipping his hands into the coins, "but he will wish to have it transferred to the *Madras* for inspection."

Stuart laughed. "Sorry, it's your task to induce your captain to board *my* ship." He stepped over and hollered up the ladder. "What's the status of the *Madras?*"

"Their crew is ready to throw out hooks and grapple us as we are almost close enough."

Stuart returned his attention to the Frenchman. "Fourier, make up your mind. For once you have grappled our ship it will make no sense to your captain, or your crew, to release us, and we shall be forced to sink your ship with all hands."

"What is it you wish me to do?"

"Convince your captain to board the *Mary Stewart* for dinner and a night of entertainment. You've just returned from long duty in the Indian Ocean. Wouldn't you prefer a dance or two with a winsome young lady on this ship?"

Fourier was at a loss for words.

"And once you return to your ship, I do not care to

see the *Madras* drift away, or come any closer, but to remain"—Stuart looked at Martin Chase, who had stuck his head into the hold—"how many meters?"

"I suggest fifty meters, Captain."

Fourier stared at the open chest of gold and silver coin. "I appreciate the inducement, Captain Stuart, but I do not think that is possible."

Stuart scooped up a handful of coins and thrust them at Fourier. The Frenchman tried to hold as many as he could, but many of them fell to the deck and rolled away into the darkness.

"Think, Fourier, think! What has your captain to fear from us? And look at what he has to gain!"

Less than a half hour later, a second boarding party came aboard with the captain of the *Madras,* who had to see the situation with his own eyes. French grappling parties were kept ready to leap to the deck of the *Mary Stewart* from the *Madras*, or swing aboard from the rigging; sharpshooters, too. All were told to stand down until their captain was through with his inspection.

Fourier ushered his captain below deck where the cannon arrays pointed at the *Madras's* waterline, and finally into the hold with the chest of gold and silver coins.

Stuart flashed an evil smile. "I think it's a good idea not to grapple the *Mary Stewart*. Some of your crew might board us and discover all this gold and silver, and you know how excitable Frenchmen become."

The captain, whose name was Chevalier, asked the same question as Fourier: "I assume I am your hostage? What is it you wish of me, sir?"

Stuart clapped the Frenchman on the shoulder. "Sup with us tonight, sir, enjoy our entertainment, and over dessert we shall discuss the terms of your surrender."

Thirty-Four

Oddly, the last song performed by Gabriel and Portia for the two Frenchmen was sung from a jolly boat that hung over the port side away from the French privateer. When Gabriel and his sister took their bows, the jolly boat rocked back and forth, and the crew members who were musicians broke out their instruments and began to play. The brother-and-sister act did not leave the boat but watched as lanterns were lit and mounted on poles fore and aft of the jolly boat.

On the opposite side of the ship, Susanna made the Frenchmen in the longboat comfortable, even going so far as to pass down to the oarsmen sufficient food and drink, including a good French wine. Still, the sailors were not allowed to come aboard, and very soon grousing was heard from those remaining in the longboat.

"Why don't you dismiss those sailors?" suggested Stuart from the table. "It's going to be a very, very long night."

Chevalier rose to do so, but on the way to the railing was intercepted by Susanna.

"By your leave, Captain," said Susanna, nodding to Stuart.

Stuart returned the nod, Susanna curtsied, and the Frenchman bowed. Susanna could not help noticing that it was true what they said: Frenchmen really did know how to bow.

"You, too, *mademoiselle,* have a demand for me?"

"Sir, I wondered if your cook might furnish the recipe for mayonnaise. I have heard so many good things about mayonnaise, but I have never tasted it."

The Frenchman bowed again. "I am your servant."

"Thank you, sir." Susanna performed a full-blown curtsy.

The breeze carried their conversation to the table to be overheard by Stuart, Fourier, and Martin Chase.

"Well," said Martin, "that certainly ought to break the tension."

Which was not in our favor, thought Stuart. Women! What would they think of next?

Susanna thanked her captain with another deep curtsy.

Stuart nodded. "Don't get carried away, Miss Chase."

Chevalier issued orders to the helmsman of the longboat and returned to Stuart who reviewed the Frenchman's options.

"Let's say you're able to alert your ship, and your sailors come to free you; that is, if your men can successfully reach the *Mary Stewart* before my cannon arrays are discharged. I, myself, would come from the port side and hope the noise on the main deck would screen such an operation."

Susanna leaned over the table to light the lantern, but Stuart waved her off. When she looked around the main deck she realized no lanterns had been lit on the *Mary Stewart,* but she could see the lights of the *Madras*—and a pair of red and white lanterns on the jolly boat being lowered away out of sight of the *Madras.* At the helm of the jolly boat stood Gabriel, and Susanna watched as Gabriel struck a pose, one hand in his jacket as the boat was lowered away.

Where were Gabriel and Portia headed?

"Unfortunately," continued Stuart, after a sip of that good French wine, "my guards expect such an attack, but even if your men should seize control of our ship, it will be several moments before they secure the mid-deck area and the cannons. By then, your ship will have received two holes at the waterline, perhaps even more.

"Then there's the option of the full attack, which your men will not execute unless they're sure they are acting under your orders. Again our cannons shall fire, and though we shall take your initial blows, our women and children are on the port side of the ship."

Stuart smiled. "Of course, in the event of a full attack, your crew knows they may inadvertently hit you and Mr. Fourier."

Through a speaking trumpet on the *Madras,* a voice interrupted Stuart's narration. It was Chevalier's second-in-command, who had taken note of the returning longboat. The officer spoke in French and wished to know if he should bring more sailors over to the *Mary Stewart.*

Chevalier looked at Stuart.

"By all means. I have room enough for all in my brig." He toasted Chevalier. "Confusion to the French!"

Chevalier got to his feet; his aide did also, and they walked over to the railing. Behind them, on the far side of the deck, the musicians ceased their playing, packed their instruments, and disappeared below deck.

A short discussion ensued between the two Frenchmen at the railing; then Chevalier used the speaking trumpet furnished by the *Mary Stewart's* bosun to hail his second-in-command on the *Madras*. Chevalier told his officer to remain where he was, and once the night's entertainment was over, he and Fourier would return to the *Madras*.

Chevalier paused, then continued in French. "And the mayonnaise?"

"Sir?" came the reply.

"The recipe for mayonnaise—do you have it?" By this time, the two men had switched to French.

"Er—sir . . ."

Martin sat up and laughed. "The frogs thought it was a code!" He translated for those who did not speak French.

Everyone around the table laughed with the exception of Susanna and James Stuart. Stuart glowered at the young woman. He was losing control of the situation.

"Shut up!" shouted Stuart. He was on his feet now, and Susanna on her way to the galley. Fast.

"Please allow Captain Chevalier to conduct business with his ship in dignity."

The laughter was reduced to the occasional chuckle, and Stuart stood behind his chair, steaming.

When the recipe came over the horn in French, Martin Chase jotted it down and rushed off to the galley. Chevalier returned to his seat, but Stuart had a much more difficult time reseating himself.

"Sir," said Stuart, thinking fast, "I wish to apologize for that imposition on your honor."

For the first time, Chevalier smiled. "Think nothing of it, Captain Stuart. My mother believed men were put on earth to serve women."

The *Mary Stewart* sailors within hearing distance stared, openmouthed. It was the most preposterous thing they had ever heard.

"Actually," said Stuart, continuing to stall, "if everything goes according to plan, there won't be anyone with a feeling of resentment on either side."

"That would be quite a trick, *mon capitaine.*"

"In any case, you will not secure the gold and silver coins in our hold no matter what your decision."

"Perhaps," said Chevalier, smiling again, "the chest of gold and silver coin is not what it appears."

The Frenchman was challenging his authority, and if there was anything Stuart understood at age four and twenty was a challenge to his authority.

He removed the chain with the key from around his neck and tossed it on the table. "You are welcome to go below. You've already taken enough bites out of those coins to break a tooth."

The captain motioned to Fourier. "Take the key into the hold and report back what you find, after you have stuck your hand all the way to the bottom of the chest and bitten a couple of the coins from that level. Thrust your hand all the way to the bottom, you hear me?"

"Yes, sir."

Fourier turned to go and found Stuart holding his arm.

"But what are you risking, *mon captain?*" asked Stuart of Chevalier. "Isn't this some sort of wager?"

"There is nothing to wager."

"Still," said Stuart, releasing Fourier's arm, "let's make this interesting. If the chest is filled with counterfeit coins, then Mr. Fourier returns topside and says so, but if the chest is full of coins on which Mr. Fourier has broken a tooth or two, your aide forfeits his life."

Susanna had returned topside with a big smile and the freshly mixed mayonnaise. When she heard the terms of the wager, she dropped her bowl and it shattered on the deck.

"Sorry, sorry," she said, quickly wiping away the spill.

"But," argued Chevalier, "there is no wager."

"Indeed there is not, and you are just as safe calling my bluff as you were when you held the power of life and death over the women and children on this ship. Alexander!"

Before the black man could report, everyone on the main deck heard Gabriel break into song off the *Mary Stewart's* stern.

"Jolly boat at one hundred yards," called the bosun as Alexander came up from below deck.

Stuart explained the wager once he had taken his seat. "Alexander, this Frenchman wishes to go below and check the hold. Would you accompany him?"

"Aye, aye, Captain. It will be my pleasure."

"Before you go, would you tell these Frenchies who sold you into slavery?"

"A rival tribe in Africa."

"And who operated the slaver bringing you to America?"

"Frenchmen."

"And whose plantation were you sold to?"

"Frenchmen."

"And each time you escaped and were recaptured, whose hand held the whip that punished you?"

"Frenchmen."

"So, would you hesitate to slit the throat of any Frenchman?"

"No, sir, I would not." Alexander drew his knife from his sheath. "My only disappointment is that Captain Chevalier isn't going below to call your bluff."

The captain arched an eyebrow. "Is this supposed to frighten me, Captain Stuart?"

"No, sir, but I'll bet we have Mr. Fourier's attention."

Chevalier got to his feet, pulled down his tunic at the beltline with both hands, and held out a hand. "Give me the key, Fourier. I shall inspect the chest."

His subordinate clutched the key. "No, sir, it is my responsibility." And the young man went below with Alexander.

"Jolly boat line at two hundred yards," called out the bosun. Gabriel and Portia's voices were now much more difficult to hear, and because night had fallen, the deck area was in total darkness.

Mr. Fourier did not return, but Alexander did, wiping blood from his knife blade. Instantly, Chevalier was on his feet.

"Captain Stuart, I will have to ask for satisfaction."

"Very well, sir," said Stuart, looking up at him from the other side of the table, "but since I have the choice of weapons, I must ask: Have you ever handled a broadsword?"

Thirty-five

Portia and Gabriel had blood all over them when their jolly boat finally returned to the *Mary Stewart* and they were brought topside. Phillippe Belle's legs weakened at the presence of two elegantly dressed people covered in so much blood, especially after almost losing Jacques, his brother, in the storm. He slid to the deck and sat there next to the railing. Off in the distance, shouts and screams issued from the *Madras.*

Stuart and Martin lifted Portia and Gabriel from the boat. The brother and sister had spent the last hour singing arias from operettas, quoting works of Shakespeare, and bickering over political articles in the newspapers current when the *Mary Stewart* had departed from England. What the outburst on the *Madras* was all about, no one on the *Mary Stewart* knew, nor would they understand if they had been told.

"Our cabins, please . . ." This from Portia.

Gabriel was unconscious.

"The surgeon should examine you," said Martin Chase.

A call for the doctor went out.

"No," said Portia, waving off the suggestion. "We shall be fine if we have time to rest."

Martin was having none of that. He had grown quite fond of Portia. Her problem, as Martin saw it, was being too much the lady. He was sure her refinement accounted for her remaining in her cabin where she would not have to hear comments about women appearing on stage.

"Miss Portia, you must be attended to."

"Please, please, can you not do as a lady requests?"

"But the blood—"

"Mr. Chase, with the first pull of the rope to return us to the *Mary Stewart*, my brother slipped and fell on his face. He was spurting blood when I turned him over and stanched the flow. Please allow Oren to take us below so we may rest and gather our strength." She cleared her throat, which appeared to be cracking. "My throat is so very sore."

With this, Martin acquiesced, and Oren was allowed to pick up Gabriel and take him below. Portia, however, was taken below by Martin Chase. She felt so light in his arms.

To show his heart was in the right place, the first mate called over his shoulder, "Find out who pulled so hard on that rope. From the look of this, he deserves ten lashes!"

Stuart moved to the helm and whispered to his sister, "Hard to larboard and run with the wind!"

The redheaded woman nodded and turned the wheel. Hand signals were used and orders whispered so men went into the rigging and sails unfurled silently. Soon, the *Mary Stewart* had resumed her voyage to Charles Town.

"Have you no shame?" asked the Frenchman. "Not only have you kidnapped me, but you have done so under a flag of truce."

"You threatened my ship and all those on it."

"That is a risk anyone takes when they put to sea."

"Spoken like a man whose life's work is to rob and steal, not to mention to kill civilians."

"As did your father. The name James Stuart is well known on the Spanish Main. Many a Frenchman and Spaniard died at the hand of your father and of those pirates who sailed with him."

"My father was a pirate during an age of piracy. I am a commercial trader. You have attacked Stuart and Company and expect to suffer no consequences? You, sir, shall suffer the ultimate humiliation, and you'd best hope our countries soon go to war, or you'll never command another ship."

He turned to Alexander. "Take the Frenchman below and have him properly secured. I will not have him committing suicide before he discharges his responsibilities in our duel once we dock in Charles Town."

Thirty-six

When Nelie Stuart came downstairs from her quarters over Belle Mercantile on East Bay Street in Charles Town, she found her sister, Catherine Belle, in the office at the rear of the store. Though women were not allowed to own or run businesses, Catherine could not get Belle Mercantile out of her system. This was where the family fortune had been rebuilt after she and her sister, as mere children, escaped from Paris with banknotes sewn into the hems of their dresses. Upon the death of Catherine's husband, Denis Belle, the store was bequeathed to Nelie's son. Both sisters were widows, Nelie having married James Stuart, Senior, and with Catherine's marriage to the sisters' cousin, Denis, and the birth of her two sons, Jacques and Phillippe, the Belle name survived in America.

During the preceding hundred years, France became more passionately Catholic as Great Britain vacillated between Catholicism and Protestantism before becoming the strongest voice for Protestantism in the known world. And though Charles Town was recognized as the most liberal colony in the New World when it came to religion, very few Catholics lived in Carolina. Instead, the Huguenot influence had grown to rival that of the official church, the Anglican Church.

Huguenots dominated the commercial district along the Cooper River, and in that district a Scot and former pirate, such as James Stuart, had been sorely outnumbered by the multitudes of Huguenots who continued to arrive from Europe. In Charles Town, these Calvinists multiplied despite the pestilence and disease that cut into their numbers each sickly season.

Catherine looked up from her paperwork at the noise of the children preceding her sister into the office. In contrast to the Belle sisters with their pale skin, blue eyes, and raven hair going grey, Nelie's twin grandchildren were brown-haired and brown-eyed, scrawny, and tanned. They raced into the room and clamored for attention from their Great-Aunt Catherine. This was not to be, as Catherine Belle was not only a miser with her money, she was also miserly with her love and her attention.

"Now, now, children, I'm sure after such a fine dinner you'd prefer to play in the street."

"Actually," said her sister, "they would prefer some attention from their Great-Aunt Catherine."

Catherine gestured at the desk littered with papers, legal documents, invoices, and receipts, some of which the twins already had in their grasp. The clerk, a skinny bird in a black suit, stepped back so he would not be blamed for the impending disaster, or called upon to discipline a child.

"Please stop that, children," said Catherine. "I have work that must be done."

Nelie laughed and separated the children from the paperwork. "That will not work, sister dear. You've been in Charles Town almost a week waiting for the *Mary Stewart*, and the children are onto your game."

"As you know, I play no games."

"More's the pity. As I've pointed out in the past, when you come to Charles Town, you must make time for James's children. They are your relations, too."

"James should find a wife and not allow these two Red Indians to run wild."

"I cannot believe you have forgotten that James had a wife."

Catherine glanced at the clerk in the corner of the small office. "He should find another. These children need a mother, and someone who will not spoil them as you do."

Seeing the look of dismay on her sister's face, Catherine hastily added, "Why don't you come to Cooper Hill? As long as they stay out of my flowerbeds, they may have the run of the place."

"It's not Cooper Hill they wish to see, dear sister. They already have the run of Charles Town harbor, a much more fascinating locale than anything along the Cooper, so if they traveled to the countryside, it would be to see you."

"You, yourself," said Catherine, picking up her pen again, "have not been there for several weeks. The second floor is in a dry state. Soon I shall be able to sleep in the master bedroom and sit on the veranda and take my morning tea."

"If I'm able to slip away when James returns, I shall, but you know how he employs the *Mary Stewart*. I'm sure he'll unload tonight and sail by morning."

With her two grandchildren trying to get at their great-aunt, Nelie said, "I'll leave you to your work while I take these two out and throw them in the harbor!"

The twins shrieked in mock terror and anticipation, and clung to their grandmother, laughing as they made their way through the store to the front entrance on East Bay.

Catherine shook her head, then checked herself when she remembered the clerk standing in the corner. "You know I'm correct about raising children. Spare the rod and you spoil the child."

"Madam, you are always correct."

"And, you, Jacob Huger, are wise to remember that."

Aboard the *Mary Stewart,* Stuart stood at the helm, watching the horizon as Kyrla sailed the ship. Like her father, Kyrla had no peer when it came to sailing, with the exception of her brother, James Stuart. Phillippe Belle stood next to Alicia Bentley, and on the far side of Alicia stood John Belle and Susanna Chase. Beside Phillippe stood Mrs. Bentley and two of her three girls, Katie's arm in a sling; behind them were Mr. Bentley and the bookish Marion, whose choice of books for the day was *The Admiralty Manual of Seamanship.*

Mrs. Bentley had not given up on Phillippe Belle as the future husband of one of her girls. Alicia might not care if hers was an inopportune marriage, but a good mother would hover over her other three girls and give them her good advice.

"I can't wait to announce your engagement," said Phillippe. "Mother will be so surprised."

"I thought your mother was on her deathbed," said Alicia.

"Oh, no," said Phillippe, smiling, "no one believed that."

"I did," said Alicia, looking at John.

"Well, you see—" started John.

"My time for studying law at the Middle Temple had ended, Miss Bentley," cut in Phillippe, "but I so enjoyed England someone had to be sent over to fetch me or I might've remained there the rest of my life, and I do have the responsibilities of the eldest son."

"Thankfully they did." Alicia glanced at John. "I think."

"You're always welcome at Cooper Hill," said Phillippe. "There's no reason for you and John to immediately journey into the upcountry. Fall is coming on and there will be endless balls."

"Oh, balls!" squealed Katie and Lindy. "We do so much love balls!"

"Yes," said Mrs. Bentley, "an amiable way of meeting new acquaintances. I, for one, am looking forward to meeting Lady Catherine."

"Yes, Mrs. Bentley," said John with a straight face, "I do believe you and my mother shall get along famously."

Alexander had gone below and now brought Captain Chevalier and his aide, Mr. Fourier, topside.

"You're alive!" exclaimed the women.

Susanna and Alicia stared at the man they believed had been murdered by Alexander. Many a conversation had taken place between the two as to what a horrible man James Stuart was. In this, Susanna was torn, while Alicia had failed to gain her fiancé's support.

John Belle had said, "You are no longer in England, my dear, and things are done differently on the high seas."

Alicia had puffed up. "I believe this calls into question our engagement, sir."

"Very well," John had responded, "you and I shall end our engagement once you next put your feet on dry land."

This had made absolutely no sense to Alicia—until the French captain and his aide were brought topside, just about the time the *Mary Stewart* reached the Charles Town Bar. From there the sweepers would bring the ship into dock, and out of the gun ports appeared a series of long paddles, dipping into the water in synchronized motion.

Once the ship safely passed the Bar, Susanna confronted James Stuart. Her hands went to her hips, and with great energy, she said, "You, sir, remain the biggest liar a woman could ever know. You knew all along these men were still alive, but you allowed us to believe Mr. Fourier had been murdered."

Alicia gave the African a hard look. Alexander paid her no mind.

"I appreciate not being murdered, Captain Stuart," said Fourier with an exaggerated bow.

"You had an advantage, Mr. Fourier," said Stuart. "I expected you to make sure your captain did not commit suicide."

Chevalier's eyes narrowed. "This is why I was in chains and could hardly move?"

Stuart nodded.

Chevalier surveyed Charles Town Harbor with its buildings hugging the Cooper River and a new, brick wall going up across the Neck. "I can still do away with myself once I am ashore. Unless my country goes to war, I have no future in France."

"I will not apologize for what I have done, sir. My obligation was to the men, women, and children of the *Mary Stewart.*"

"One special woman, I would think."

The Frenchman doffed his hat, and if possible, Susanna turned red under her tan. Her hands slipped from her hips.

Stuart bowed as graciously as any Frenchman. "Susanna, it was all misdirection. I simply did what was expected of me and what my opponents found in me to be most agreeable."

Chevalier had to agree, but he only nodded.

"South Carolina is a good place to start a new life, and during our dinner a few nights ago, I learned neither of you men is married nor has any children. You shall miss nothing in France."

Chevalier laughed. "Evidently, sir, you have never seen Paris. I think, Mr. Fourier, the Englishman is offering us employment."

Stuart nodded. "You may sign on with any Stuart and Company ship sailing the American coastline, but not the Spanish Main."

"So we are not tempted to jump ship? I have observed your life-saving devices with the cork, and might do so."

Stuart only shrugged.

Fourier, who had been ashore for no more than a few days at any time since joining Chevalier as a cabin boy, said, "It is something to consider, Captain."

The young man gestured at the peninsula with the huge homes going up on Oyster Point. The sun dropped quickly on the far side of the Ashley and darkness was immediately upon them. Still, one could discern the prosperity of the peninsula by the great number of lanterns being lit.

"Charlestonians appear to know what they are doing, sir."

"You would desert our country, Mr. Fourier?"

"Sir, I have stood beside you man and boy for over eleven years, and I believe, until France and England are at war again, that I may be a bit tired of sea life, especially our last trip around Cape Horn where we lost some very good men."

"There is considerable money in the banks of Paris— all in your name. You will forgo that, Mr. Fourier?"

"I have heard there are excellent opportunities in America."

"More than one can imagine," said John Belle. "But, like France, it all depends on who one knows."

At this, Susanna's head came up and she saw Alexander smiling at her.

Stuart handed his diary to Alicia. "Miss Bentley, I thought my diary might be useful to you in reconstructing your own diary lost during the storm."

Looking at the girl's mother, Stuart added, "You realize, of course, Mrs. Bentley, that such a diary is property of Stuart and Company and not one particular individual."

Steve Brown

Mrs. Bentley only stared at him. It was left to her husband to remark, "I'm sure she does, Captain Stuart."

"There is one question I still have," said Chevalier. "I wish to know if the chest of gold and silver coins was full, all the way to the bottom."

Stuart shook his head.

"It's even worse," said Martin.

Alexander's laughter boomed across the deck. "Only the removal shelf had decent coin. The rest was counterfeit coins collected over the years by Stuart and Company."

"But I don't understand," said Fourier. "Why would anyone carry such a temptation aboard his ship?"

"Mr. Fourier," said Alexander, "that tray of gold and silver coin, the chest where Captain Stuart scooped up coins and thrust them into your pockets, that was the crew's pay, and at sea, it was safe from anyone—"

"Anyone but a thief," said Chevalier, nodding.

"Yes, sir," agreed Alexander.

"I suppose we deserved that."

"Then you and Mr. Fourier will consider my proposition?" asked Stuart. "A good seaman is an asset to any company."

"And if our countries go to war?"

"As they most certainly will," said Stuart with a long sigh. "I will put you ashore on one of the French islands on the Main."

"That, sir, is certainly worth considering."

Martin cleared his throat—all Susanna needed to hear.

"Yes, Martin, what is it you wish to lie about this time?"

"Cousin, I have never lied to you." Martin glanced at Stuart and Alexander. "Although, I may have participated in a diversion or two."

"Then what is it?"

"It's like this: My mother's name is Susannah, and I thought you might like to change your name before going ashore so there'll be no confusion as to who you are and who my mother is when the two of you are referred to in conversation."

Susanna glanced at James Stuart, who only smiled.

"And what name did you have in mind, Cousin?"

"How does Susan Chase sound to you?"

Susanna crossed the deck to James Stuart and took his hands in hers. "Actually, I'd had another name in mind."

On the poop deck, Gabriel and Portia surveyed the evening sky as the stars came out over Charles Town Harbor.

"Well," said Portia, "we are here, brother, the very first of our kind to reach the New World."

"Yes, yes," said Gabriel, watching torches being lit and Charlestonians rushing to the dock to meet the *Mary Stewart*. "And it would appear that there is much work to do."

One of those in the crowd was Billy, the cabin boy, and he waved enthusiastically to his lord and master.

"Oh, how nice of you, Gabriel. You sent the boy ahead once we passed the Charles Town Bar."

"Yes," said her brother, "and never has there been a more eager disciple."

About the Author

One of South Carolina's most versatile writers, Steve Brown is the author of *The Charleston Ripper,* a novel of suspense set in modern-day Charleston; *The Belles of Charleston*, a historical novel set in 1856; and *Carolina Girls,* a portrait of what it was like to vacation on the Carolina beaches in the sixties and the seventies. You can reach Steve at www.chicksprings.com.

Carolina Girls

They were Carolina Girls, the best in the world, and they came together in the mid-Sixties on Pawleys Island, where life began to mold them into the women they would later become. Each summer they would return to Pawleys to renew their friendship. The Carolinas in the turbulent Sixties, a time as different from the antebellum South as the Sixties were different from the modern South of today.

The Belles of Charleston

Set in Charleston during the years leading up to the War Between the States, *The Belles of Charleston* is a coming-of-age story about two sets of cousins: one set indentical twin boys, one set indentical twin girls. One male cousin attends West Point, the other the Citadel, and of the two twin sisters, one sister can do "sums" in her head, consequently, she cannot be a true Southern belle.

The Pirate and The Belle

When the pirates came for the girl, they snatched the wrong one, so any protests made by the young woman were ignored. Not until the following morning, when the pirate ship had long sailed from Charles Town, did the pirates discover their error. Now it became a matter of what to do with the girl, and it did not help the young woman's predicament that she'd been screaming all night to be returned to her family in Charles Town. Blackbeard was not known to be a patient man.